I0683144

Mel

(CALTER CREEK 3)

LizAnn Carson

Mel (Calter Creek 3)

© 2015 Elizabeth Carson

All rights reserved. No part of this book may be reproduced, stored, or used in any manner whatsoever without the express written permission of the publisher except for the use of brief quotations in a book review.

ISBN: 978-0-9949036-2-4

Cover photos used under license from:
Shutterstock.com, Deposit Photos, Elizabeth Carson
"Mel" font: Stalemate, ©2012 by Jim Lyles for Astigmatic

Thank You

To Sylvia and Beth, my critique partners. I feel so much more confident about this book, thanks to your wise and thoughtful advice.

1

It had been one of those weeks.

On a misty Saturday morning in May, walking through downtown Calter Creek, Ohio, Mel Chesterton knew she needed a serious attitude adjustment. Too much these days challenged her predominantly sunny disposition.

Mostly it was minor stuff, but even the minor stuff knocked her off kilter. Take the mustard stain on her white blazer, courtesy of a barbecue fundraiser at Sinclair Imports, where she was executive assistant to the president, Amanda McKinnon. She'd fumed all afternoon.

More serious was the shouting match with Amanda a day or so later. Mel loved her job, and they had a great working relationship, bordering on friendship. But at three months Amanda could be in a bear of a mood, giving the lie to that maternity glow stuff. Mel wasn't worried about her job or anything like that, and peace had been restored, but the fact of the confrontation had shaken her.

She waited at a stoplight and sighed, shifting the bag of books she'd brought with her from one hand to the other. Day-to-day events weren't to blame, and she knew it. There'd been a lack in Mel's life lately, as if her world didn't have the same bright shine as before. Mundane, that was the word for it. At thirty-five, she'd expected to have the man, house, kids, and dog by now. Instead she had a singular lack of excitement, a one-bedroom apartment with white walls, which she abhorred, and no prospects for the man-and-kids situation to change any time soon.

1

Not much she could do about the rest of it, but she could use this Saturday morning expedition to renew her generally positive outlook on life. First she'd call in at Morrison's, Calter Creek's go-to source of books both new and secondhand, and spend a cheerful half hour picking out a book or two.

Second, and most important, she'd visit the downtown branch of the Dublin and Central Ohio Bank. She needed to know how much mortgage they'd approve, based on their assessment of her salary and savings. It was high time she escaped her neutral rental apartment and bought a place of her own, where she'd paint the walls whatever glorious, glowing colors she chose. She couldn't stand the thought of living with off-white for the rest of her life.

First things first, though. She needed a book or she'd never survive the weekend.

Calter Creek, situated half an hour southwest of Columbus, sported the quaint architecture and hanging flower baskets typical of a smallish, prosperous town, but none of that caught Mel's eye this morning. Because while waiting for the light to turn green she had plenty of time to see the brown paper covering the windows of her favorite bookstore.

She stormed across the street before the light had fully changed. A small sign in pencil had been taped haphazardly on the ancient wooden door. *Under new ownership. Reopening after a while.* The writing was angular and the letters oddly formed, as if taken from a book of arcane magic spells. Someone was moving around inside; she'd seen shifting light in the upstairs windows.

Enough was enough. She ignored the sign and started pounding. Repeatedly, until whoever had the nerve to close the store gave up and opened the door.

"Ah," said the man in the doorframe. He studied her for a beat or two. "Titian, with a net of diamonds. Luscious."

Since there was no possible response, Mel simply gaped at him, as if caught in a hypnotic web. *Tishun? What was that?*

He looked stunned as he reached out and touched her mop of curly red hair, which, thanks to the weather, had attained new heights of frizzy. His hand barely grazed the wild halo before he pulled away. Normally she backed off when someone invaded her personal space, but this time she didn't move.

She guessed he'd be tall, if he didn't slouch, and he wasn't in the least prepossessing. Glasses in old fashioned granny frames perched on his straight nose, though he studied her over the top of them. An otherworldly glint danced in his mild, light blue eyes, as if they didn't miss much, but might not see what everyone else did. His eyebrows and shaggy hair were the shade of gray her mother visited a salon to duplicate. The gray messed up her sense of his age, but he wasn't ancient, she figured between thirty and fifty.

He wore a string of mixed jewel-tone glass beads on his left wrist, where ordinary men wore important-looking wristwatches with dials. An oversized sweatshirt that once had been navy swamped his torso, and black slacks that should have hit the trash a decade ago led to equally worn out sneakers.

However decrepit his wardrobe, he himself was immaculate, clean shaven, clean hands. He reminded her of a mildly daft scholar who caught flies to put them outside instead of swatting them.

The word he'd used tickled her mind. Tishun... Was he saying 'titian'? Wasn't that a hair color? One that turned up in historical romances? She'd read the word but had never heard it spoken, and suspected it had nothing to do with her own hair, which, as far as she was concerned, was miles from romantic.

They simultaneously snapped out of whatever trance they'd fallen into, and the world got back on its axis. She started breathing again. Whatever tishun meant, it didn't fit her, she'd bet on it. "No, it's more carrot."

"True. And the bane of your existence—the word, but perhaps also the reality? Might as well put a poetic spin on it, don't you agree? Especially on *such* a gray day. Please, come in." He stepped aside and gestured toward the interior of the store.

"That's not such a good idea." Mel experienced a flutter of unease. Going into a closed and deserted store with a strange man, even in Calter Creek, which had to be among the safest communities on the planet, wouldn't rank as one of her cleverer

3

ideas. She hadn't considered what she'd do if the person upstairs answered her pounding.

But the anger that had driven her to assault his door had been supplanted by curiosity. Mel couldn't pinpoint where the appeal came from. It wasn't a sexual-chemistry, girl-places-quivering reaction. More a magician thing? She'd always wanted to meet an honest-to-goodness magician.

He got it, suddenly. "I'm sorry, I get carried away. You're right to be cautious, but I promise I'm harmless—although I can't say the same for the piles of books all over the floor. Tripped yesterday and gave myself a whopper of a bruise on my shin."

A whiff of home baking drifted from somewhere inside.

Mel caught the aroma and abruptly decided to ignore everything she'd read and heard about the dangers of strange men in isolated places. She stepped into the once familiar store, now cast into an orange murkiness by the brown paper on the windows.

He gave her a delighted smile and no time to reconsider. "I'm afraid we have to hurry. Mind your step, the lighting..." He gestured at the room. "It's approaching 'Abandon all hope, ye who enter here'." He rubbed the bruised shin, then hurried toward the wide staircase bisecting the space. "It's better higher up, but there is a need to rush."

He left her stranded amid stacks of ancient books that appeared almost threatening in the strange half-light. Mel thought of Gothic novels.

At least she'd gotten into the place, which, as near as she could tell, was unchanged from the last time she'd called in, three weeks ago. Was there a chance she could buy a paperback or two from this peculiar man? She stood still for a moment, assessing the situation, then closed the door, dumped her bag of books, sent a quick text to Julie so someone would know where she was—she wasn't a total idiot—and followed him. Her radar would alert her if anything felt off, and the vibes weren't threatening at all.

Besides, whatever was baking smelled like heaven.

The building must be a hundred years old. The wood floor sagged under the weight of the massive, overburdened bookshelves. She'd long admired the elegant flight of stairs, with its worn treads and elaborate banisters, that rose from the middle of the room parallel to the front wall. In the past, a decidedly inelegant do-not-enter sign had always closed it off. With no sign in evidence, she climbed up.

He had disappeared by the time she reached the second floor, which proved to be a gigantic, mostly empty room with a few books and bookshelves strewn around. An area against the back wall to the right of the stairs had been walled in. The natural light from the towering, unpapered windows was a relief. She reckoned the wide-open space spanned not only Morrison Books but also the adjacent stores.

"In here." His voice came from a door in the wall.

In for a penny.

Besides, whatever he was cooking precluded bad things happening, didn't it? She poked her head through the doorway.

He stood at the stove in a bright, if dilapidated, country-style kitchen. "Made it in time." He stirred around the contents of a baking sheet. "Darker than usual, but still tasty. Try."

He held out the sheet to her. Homemade granola. She nibbled, nodded, and grinned. "Way better than the stuff from the store." Clearly her radar was working just fine.

"Please, sit," he said over his shoulder. He pulled a serving dish off a shelf, coming close to spilling the granola out of the pan. He talked as he scraped the cereal into the dish. "You know, some old wisdom is valid. A healthy breakfast— well, never mind. You're a coffee drinker, I expect? But tea is being served this morning, so I hope you're flexible." He abandoned the granola and produced tea from one cabinet, a teapot from another. "One day I'll be sensible and store these two together, since they're obviously meant to be mated. Not yet, however."

Grateful to be anchored on the other side of the table, Mel said, "I've never had tea in the morning. Coffee's sort of an office ritual."

In the midst of the whirlwind, the man commanding the kitchen had put a kettle on to boil. He removed it from the heat, poured water into the teapot, swirled pot and water around, then poured the water out and measured the tea.

5

Measured. Loose tea. For Mel, loose tea was a novelty, not a staple. When he'd suggested tea, she'd automatically assumed he meant iced.

"However, in the absence of coffee, I hope you'll join me." He saluted her with the teapot, which appeared to be from an old-fashioned line of fine china.

Surely no one trusted this frenetic man with antiques?

"Next time you drop by, I won't leave you bereft. I have a French press around somewhere."

"You're expecting a next time?"

"Oh, yes. Aren't you?"

Mel shrugged off her jacket and slid onto a rickety chair at the battered wooden table. She took stock. Through a door behind her she glimpsed a living room as shabby as the kitchen. An apartment, then. Based on the boxes and miscellaneous articles lying on most flat surfaces, her host, while at home, hadn't fully moved in. Or was he the sort who never completely unpacked? She couldn't decide whether he lacked focus entirely or was able to focus on fifteen things at once.

He elaborated. "When people share a breakfast it's a fair bet there'll be a next time. Lunches and dinners mean anything or nothing, but breakfast? Maybe it's because of the extra effort to get out of bed for it."

He added boiling water to the teapot, then set a digital timer and sat across from her, placing the granola dish between them. He bounced up again immediately, coming back with his hands full of bowls, cups and saucers — mismatched — and cutlery. "Purists say four minutes for this tea, but I prefer two and a half. A bitter principle begins to develop. Best to nip it in the bud, so to speak." He looked pleased, as if he'd made a joke, but if so Mel didn't get it. She drew her brows together, puzzled.

"Tea buds? Best part of the tea plant? Harvested — nipped?" He sighed. "Well, you can't say I didn't try."

"Sorry. I almost never drink hot tea, and then it's in bags."

"A sin. They virtually powder the leaves, no subtlety, and the tea goes stale. With practice you'll recognize the difference."

Anchored at the table, she studied this strange man who held her weekend reading fate in his hands. He was ageless. Was it the hair? The haircut, or lack thereof? Or the glasses, with their refugee-from-the-seventies frames?

His gray cowlick flopped onto a high forehead. His mobile mouth seemed poised to speak, or maybe eat. Whichever, she didn't expect that mouth to be still for long.

At first she'd taken him to be slight, but as he moved around the kitchen she realized he was no weakling. Not ripped, but not a wimp, either. He was tall, but not abnormally so, about six feet, which was still a good eight inches taller than Mel.

By now he'd pulled containers from an ancient white refrigerator. "I regret the berries are, as they say, previously frozen. May's not the best time for fruit. Help yourself. I prefer almond milk, but I can offer yogurt."

He enthusiastically spooned granola into his bowl. She wondered if he ever decelerated and wished he'd sit back down.

"Thanks. The almond milk is fine." She accepted the granola dish, which was quality china, although it didn't match the teapot, and took a spoonful. "But you don't have to feed me, I mean, I had..."

"A piece of toast and a glass of juice? Pfft."

Was he peering in her second floor windows?

"How do I classify that? A lucky guess?"

"Intuition? Experience?" He pulled the tab on the new carton of almond milk. "Take more. We have a lot to do this morning."

"Like what?" She added another spoonful to her bowl before topping it with berries and almond milk, then tasted. *Bliss.* "I don't even know what your name is."

"Umh." He'd followed her with berries, almond milk, and tasting. He held up a finger, chewed, and swallowed. "Names are symbolic, don't you agree? A name reflects who you are, or imposes a societal expectation. Now, if I'd been burdened with a name like Clint or Lance or Butch, I'd find it difficult to live up to it. All very masculine, but do real people have that kind of name? Not in my experience. Or maybe in

7

Texas? I might aspire to extreme masculinity—no, I confess I don't. Book binding and minor home repairs have more appeal than roping and branding and such. I'd need calluses."

He opened his hands for her inspection, turning them palm up, palm down. Trim nails, businesslike, no calluses. "A pianist's hands, my mother says." He stopped and took a breath, which she didn't believe he'd done up to now.

She seized the moment. "So, do you play piano?"

"Only to the extent that the parents signed my brother and me up for lessons at a tender age. When we showed not a thimbleful of talent, they allowed us to make our own choices. Huff went on to guitar, and I chose Renaissance recorder. But to return to the subject at hand. What would you expect my name to be? Translating your impressions into the symbol that is a name."

One of the containers he'd shuffled to the table held honey. Before she could reply, he frowned at the jar and murmured, "And another spoon, yes." He bounded onto his feet again and dove into a drawer, from which, after rummaging, he produced a dented and tarnished silver tablespoon.

Finally, he sat, took a breath, and picked up his spoon, as if he just might stay put.

Mel didn't answer immediately. The combined force of this man's monologue, the breakfast, and his assumption she'd be helping him today needed time to be absorbed. She occupied herself with a bite of the exceptionally tasty granola. Then, fortified with a deep breath, she plunged in. "Did the Pied Piper have a name?"

He leaned back and laughed. "From what I've read, no, he's a legend, and a creepy one at that—although the fate of the children is a mystery. Did he lead them off to paradise? But the poor parents... I've heard a theory that the story might refer to the Children's Crusade. Bad piece of business, not a suitable breakfast topic."

The timer rang.

All that in two and a half minutes?

He poured the tea, marmalade orange, into their cups. The sort of cups she associated with great-grandmothers.

Slightly breathless, Mel was catching up. "I never knew this was up here. Is it a whole apartment?"

"It is, and if the rain ever stops I'll show you the view. The sundeck looks out over half of Calter Creek, quite lovely, or it will be with repairs. I bought this place because of the second floor. It's not difficult to find bookstores for sale these days, alas."

Alas?

"I combed the Midwest before finding this one. It has amazing potential. The staircase, the massive upstairs room. The hidden elevator. There actually is a hidden elevator," he assured her.

"But then," he continued without pause, "we need to reflect on the matter of 'pied'. I doubt I qualify. All of a piece, as they say in England."

Mel remembered her manners and swallowed her bite of granola before she spoke. "I guess I don't know what 'pied' means."

"And you're willing to ask. I always ask, which can be tedious for others, but I love learning new things. We'll share our combined knowledge."

"Yes, well..."

She remembered 'titian' with a twinge of embarrassment and resolved to look it up when she got home.

"Pied means many colored, variegated. Much though I'd like to be variegated, I'm not sure... but could it depend on what scale we're using? My poor parents might argue that my mind is multifaceted. They've had a lifetime of frustration, poor dears, trying to lure me to alight on one thing and stay with it. Possibly my definition of 'one thing' is different from theirs?"

If she'd believed she'd caught up to him, she'd been totally, completely deluded. "How do you do that?"

"Do what?"

"Move around that way. Hit three or four topics in the same sentence. That should qualify as pied."

"Possibly, taken in a narrow context. Problem is, I do it constantly, so overall it might be considered one thing. I was never skilled at essay writing. Lack of focus, the teachers informed my parents. I'm afraid it caused more grief for them than it did for me."

He rambled on. "Sugar for your tea—besides being a poison, I'm out, but we do have the honey. There *will* be milk, once the grocery and I find mutually satisfying hours. Would you care for honey? I'm told it transforms the nature of the tea experience. The same for almond milk." He tapped the quart carton, which, like the honey jar, was seriously outclassed alongside the china serving bowl and teapot, the great-grandmotherly cups.

"All right. I mean, thank you, but I'm no closer to learning your name." Nor did she want to be, Mel realized. He'd drawn her into his words, his game, and she wasn't in any giant rush for enlightenment.

"Try a guess." Those large hands cradled his teacup as he sipped.

Yes, perfectly safe to entrust the fine china to him.

"Okay, a name to suit you." She idly stirred honey into her tea. "Francis, maybe, or Robin."

"Less he-man-ish, yes. Not that Francis was any slouch—the saint, I mean. Led a harsh life, even if of his own making. Those early saints tended to live rough and die gruesomely. Different times, of course."

"Of course."

"And Robin—a songbird of the thrush family and no friend of earthworms. Or Robin Hood? Television's diluted the old legend. It must have been dreadful, with tents made of skins and freezing in the winter. They were probably smelly, too. We have to hope it was endemic, or Marian would have rejected him outright. You're picking gentler sounding names, or gentler associations. Am I correct?"

"Ye-e-s." Mel drew the word out while she absorbed a few new ideas about Robin Hood and considered the *why* of her selections.

"And right you are. My name is Adrian, which is so un-mystical. It means a place in northern Italy, where I've not been, so far. Not terribly creative of my parents, but in terms of sound, the predominance of vowels, I believe it's appropriate. Although I've also come across the meaning black, or dark—do you suppose the Adriatic is dark? Now, for you, a name like Boadicea, a true warrior's name—but no, it wouldn't suit, would it? A warrior you may be, but there's too much music in your soul."

Mel stopped with her honey-laced tea halfway to her lips. "What? Forgive me, but you don't know me well enough to say that. Were you expecting someone else?"

He grinned. "And behind that question you're thinking, is this guy for real?"

It was possibly the first hint of normality she'd experienced from him since stepping into the bookstore.

"No, I'd never... that would be rude. You're... a little unusual?"

"Or a lot. I'm afraid I'm totally for real, although occasionally those who know me doubt it. I do possess a conventional side, trust me. Sometimes it's dominant, but those aren't the happiest times in my life. But to answer your question, no, I wasn't expecting anyone else. I wish I'd known I was expecting you. I'm not always so disheveled."

"If you're cleaning up the store... it's sort of grubby down there."

"Exactly. I'm glad you understand. You'll have me wrapped around your little finger by the time we whip this place into shape, I've no doubt at all. It's the lure of that music in your soul."

He dove into his cereal. Mel followed suit, hoping to ground herself against the tide of Adrian's enthusiasm, which stood a reasonable chance of pulling her under. Like a riptide, or the rapture that came when a mermaid kissed you—but that was men, wasn't it? How did he do it?

But Mel wasn't faint of heart. It was past time for her to snap out of the spell he'd woven and speak up. Boadicea-like, she girded her loins and let exasperation tinge her voice. "Just to clarify, *we're* not getting this place in shape. I'm here for something to read. When I saw the papered-over windows—"

"Oh, the mad came through loud and clear when you tried to batter the door down, believe me. Since it's a day for new experiences, possibly I should try this." He'd drunk half his tea, but he added a generous spoon of the honey. "As for the book part, the pharmacy carries romances and such, and the library has all manner of things. No, my dear, you're here for another reason, and the most likely one, besides sharing my breakfast, is to participate in the rejuvenation of the bookstore. But now, we must turn to your name."

"Mel." She didn't have the mental energy for the guessing exercise again.

"Mel. Melissa? Bees and honey, most appropriate. Wait." Adrian rose and disappeared through the door behind her, emerging a minute later with a large and ancient-looking book.

A tome. This is what they mean by a tome.

"Dusty, I fear." He rested it gingerly on the table and shuttled the granola, berries, teapot, honey, and almond milk to safety on the counter. "This will tell us. It's positively loaded with what we might call archaic lore—herbs, remedies, how to predict the weather or pickle a calf's foot, and names and their meanings. I found it a day or two ago on the shelves downstairs. I could spend a lifetime rummaging in old books. In fact, I am, I guess. Let's see." He sat across from her and began to flip through the pages. "M... Mel..."

"The book's upside down."

"To me. To you it's indubitably right side up." He glanced up. His grin was lopsided. It was sort of endearing.

"It was part of my misspent youth. Once I worked out that letters are symbols, and groups of letters are symbols of concepts, I resolved to find out if there was any intrinsic meaning to the symbols themselves. I was twelve and bored, so I figured if I learned to read upside down, the inner meanings of the symbols would be forced to show themselves."

Adrian continued to search for Melissa while Mel stared at Adrian.

"Ah, yes, here it is. A honeybee, also a nymph who had dealings with Zeus. Dangerous, messing around with those gods. But bees and honey, that's a satisfying image."

At last she could contribute. "*Melissa officinalis*, too. Lemon balm. It's a medicinal herb that calms you, gently. Works pretty well for PMS." She realized what she'd said and pinched her eyes closed, muttering, "Dunce."

"A terrible affliction, I hear. But although it's sad, I do not believe your name is Melissa."

At least he hadn't given her a treatise on PMS, or worse, inquired about her own experience of it.

"No, it's Melanie. I never use the whole thing. I've been Mel most of my life."

"That might change." He didn't elaborate, but found the citation in the book and read. "Melanie. Black, dark. Interesting that we both were given names with dark connotations. But while I might have my black moments, it's not you at all. I'm not surprised you choose not to use it. Although we should consider Melanie Wilkes. Full of light, a counterpoint to Scarlett, but complex."

"She was? I never saw much depth."

"To get through the Civil War with her integrity intact, well aware her husband was in love with her close friend, and love the friend anyway? A lot was going on, but none of it dark. Now Mel... On its own it's a bald man, hardly the case with you, my dear, your hair is luminescent. I can't wait to see it in sunlight. Melvin has to do with swords and chieftains. That could be you, but really, this time historical meaning carries little weight. Much though I like Melanie for its sound, I'll call you Mel. Besides it being your preference, you are truly a creature of light, not dark."

Mel gathered her wits together—those he'd left intact. "I'd better go. Thank you for breakfast."

Some of the animation drained out of Adrian's face. He slumped. She worried she'd hurt him.

Talk about irrational.

He closed the book gently, so the dust stayed trapped. She could hear regret in his voice. "I'm sorry. I do tend to

13

overwhelm. There's so much inside…" He paused, waving his hands aimlessly. "And it wants out so badly. As soon as I have a captive audience, I crack open and out it pours. Please don't go yet. At least take a few minutes to look around. We face a big job ahead, renovating, but the potential—"

She wanted to get a few things straight before she left, if that was even possible. "You keep saying 'we'. I'm not involved in the bookstore."

"You are." This time he stated it as a quiet fact, not as an enthusiastic sledgehammer. "So let's see what we've got."

Did he hear her at all? Could this be some kind of elaborate scam? "I don't have any money," she said. "I'm not investing."

His eyes widened, as if shocked she could imagine such a thing. "No, of course not. It's energetic, not financial. Can't you sense the bond between this space and you?"

Before she knew what was happening, he'd squared the book on the corner of the table and placed their bowls and teacups in the sink. The couple of sips of tea she'd taken had been—okay. No bitter principle.

"We can start up here, although I don't expect you to discuss the interior design of the apartment with me yet." His magnified eyes twinkled at her. "A bit too intimate for first acquaintance. Another day, perhaps. And downstairs is overwhelming."

He took off into the vast, nearly empty space outside the apartment, leaving her no choice but to gather up her rain jacket and follow.

"Now this excites me. It's like undiscovered territory. The wiring's solid, thank heaven. Imagine the heartbreak if the electricity shorted out and the whole building went up in smoke before we brought out its full potential. What could we put up here, Mel?"

In this bizarre morning, and with this unusual man, it seemed the most natural thing in the world to ask, "Do you catch flies and release them instead of swatting them?"

"Certainly. Don't you?" His smile returned. "We're on a shared wavelength."

Shared wavelength? Why should she be surprised?

Mel couldn't figure out what he wanted from her. Or why she suddenly felt guilty about flies. "Do you think I should?"

"Put yourself in the fly's place. To them you're a great goddess with the power of life and death. Are you willing to be the kind of goddess who'd squash you? Or maybe it's a Zen thing. Or an aversion to squished flies on my walls." He shrugged, then rambled on. "Now, I see a coffee bar in the corner — we'll have easy chairs scattered around, that's a given, and I suppose we'll need to stock electronics. Did you know you can't do the reading-upside-down thing on one of those tablets? I tried, and it flipped."

"Some people at work have tablets. I think there's a setting."

"I'll let you find it for me one day, and we'll force the text to behave. Now, we might want the coffee bar on the ground floor, for easy access, but marketing strategy suggests we propel the customers further in, so they're forced to pass more of our merchandise. I wonder if that actually works. The idea is to sell books, I suppose, but it isn't very welcoming to coerce people just so they can get their coffee."

"Selling's what a store's for, though, whether it's books or coffee. You can't renovate Morrison Books and make it into a modern bookstore without worrying about sales."

"Not my favorite subject, it's true. My family assures me it's absolute folly to run a bookstore for the fun of it. I wonder if I'm not constantly trying to prove myself to them. Do you suppose we ever believe we've proven ourselves to our parents? Possibly... my brother has, I think."

"All my mother wants me to prove is that I can make her a grandmother. She's proud enough of me, or at least she says she is."

"I don't doubt it. I expect I'd like her." Adrian propped himself against a wall, studying the room. "As of when the store closed, the walk-in business was marginally self-sustaining. Up here... as you can see, it spans two stores to the west, as well as Morrison Books. And it's ours, an empty canvas to create what we want."

Mel wondered again how old he was.

"Samuel Morrison did a brisk mail order and internet business, it turns out. He must have spent his life in the stacks downstairs, given the lack of a written inventory. Impossible to tell what's there, which means we can't risk bringing in the bulldozers. There are treasures buried in those rotting books, but we'll have to dig them out one book at a time." He rubbed his hands together, and she could have sworn she caught an excited spark in his eyes. The thought seemed to energize him.

The thought left her limp. She'd always headed straight for the new books section near the windows, or the 'lightly used' paperbacks, and never paid much attention to the endless shelves of secondhand books. "You're kidding, yes? There can't be anything valuable in that mess."

"Oh, they're in there. Finding them will be like excavating a ruin, exposing a long-lost golden temple to the light of day." He laughed. "Mel, if you could see your face. We'll have fun, even if you don't believe me yet. It's not all Franco-Prussian War — though that does seem to be a popular subject."

"I'm just here for weekend reading, remember?" Mel headed for the stairs.

He followed her. "You're here for much more, but your purpose hasn't revealed itself to you yet. But I promise, no Franco-Prussians."

In the dim orange light at the foot of the stairs, she turned to face him and they collided. Her hand inadvertently landed on the dilapidated sweatshirt over his chest. He felt solid enough. Not a figment of her imagination, then. His hand covered hers for support while she regained her balance. She peered into the gloom. "What'll happen to the new book section?"

"We'll return what we can. The stock will be out of date by the time we reopen."

"How about a sidewalk sale one weekend? To introduce your store to the neighborhood."

"It might work." His face lit up. "Yes, a sidewalk sale. You're better at marketing than I, that's evident. Oh — you can help now by taking some books away with you. That was your original impetus this morning."

The morning that was nearly over.

She looked toward the old checkout counter. "The cash register's gone."

"But you surely don't expect to pay. Energetically the books are already yours." He found a switch and turned on the downstairs lights, reducing the dimness by a few levels. "No new romances have come in for a couple of months, but see what you can find."

They stood eyeball to eyeball, except for the eight-inch difference in their heights. He wasn't that old. The gray hair was deceptive. "How do you know I like romances?"

He smiled at her. He smiled a lot, this Adrian. "Besides your being a romantic at heart, you arrived with a bag full of books. I noticed a few of the titles. What I believe is, you don't want grim, and you don't want boring. You want to be uplifted and happy. Go on and look, I'll be right back." He gave her a gentle shove toward the front of the store, then disappeared into the dusty secondhand shelves.

Mel had shrugged into her jacket and chosen a couple of best-sellers and a handful of romances when he turned up again, his clothing grubbier than before. "For you." He handed her a book. "Romantic, yes, but thought-provoking, too. Try her."

She turned it over, trying not to dislodge the dust along the upper edge. "Emily Dickenson. We read her in school." Not that she remembered what she'd read; English lit hadn't been an attention grabber back then.

"The trick to reading poetry is not to overdo it. One a day, unless you get hooked. I recollect in my college years lying under a tree with a young woman as delightful as you, at least in my memory. I had the idea we should sip wine and I'd read her some poet or other, in the original German. Needless to say, I saw little of her thereafter."

"I bet," Mel said under her breath.

He caught her comment. "I won't do the same to you, I promise. Now, you need to be elsewhere, so I won't detain you any longer. Tomorrow? Or next weekend? We have so much to discuss." His eyes shot question marks at her.

"Next Saturday?" She spoke hesitantly, unable to imagine saying no, while her logical angel wondered what on earth she was doing.

His entire face smiled. He positively radiated happiness. "Excellent. Come early. I'll create an imaginative breakfast, and then we'll brainstorm floor space and layout, books, coffee shop."

He walked her to the door, his hand grazing her coat. *Pianist hands.* What was it about this man? Definitely a magician.

Stepping into the light of day was like stepping out of a fairy tale. As she stood on the sidewalk and looked up and down Main Street, she felt disconnected and unexpectedly wished she hadn't been in such a hurry to leave the bookstore.

Mel abandoned her plan to visit the DCO bank. Post-Adrian there wasn't enough time before they closed at noon, so she sighed and resigned herself to sacrificing her Monday lunch hour for a visit to the bank.

2

Monday morning, Mel settled at her desk, anticipating the day ahead. For her, catching up on the news, the happenings in her co-workers' lives, ranked equal with her work in importance. As Amanda's executive assistant, she carried a fair load of responsibility. As social central at SI, she celebrated new babies, gushed over vacation pictures, provided a supportive shoulder, and wasn't above kicking a little butt when someone needed it. She was trusted and popular, and she responded with competence and affection. Her job suited her to a T, and a guy at work had once called her sunshine personified.

She made an appointment with the Dublin and Central Ohio Bank and arrived with two minutes to spare, leaving Amanda holed up with the latest financial reports. Her feet had sent dance-step messages to her brain as she passed the papered-over bookstore. She thought fleetingly about Adrian poking through the books, or baking something sensational up in that homey kitchen of his.

But her mind wasn't on the bookstore. It was on the DCO Bank.

The prim woman at DCO's reception counter sounded a note of apology. "Our usual loan officer left early with a bout of spring flu, so you'll be meeting with Mr. Pope, the branch manager. I hope that's all right with you?"

"Sure. I just need some information."

The woman glanced across the lobby. "Here he is now. Mr. Pope, Ms. Chesterton." Introductions perfunctorily made, the receptionist returned to her computer.

Mel turned from the information counter to the man before her. A man—

Holy crow.

She belatedly remembered to close her mouth.

This was no man. This was a god.

Blond. Surfer blond. Ripped, she could tell from the way he moved, the way his suit shifted over his—she nearly gulped—his *body* as he held out a hand to her. His eyes were the blue of summer skies and bluebirds. He wasn't overly tall, which meant he didn't tower over her, a plus in Mel's estimation.

He grasped her hand. "Ms. Chesterton? Welcome to DCO. I understand you've come in to inquire about a mortgage?"

Had she? For a moment she forgot why she was standing in the DCO lobby.

But nothing fazed Mel for long, not even the most gorgeous man she'd ever seen in person, so she pulled herself together. "Yes." She pretended to be calm and businesslike. "I've decided it's time for me to invest in a home of my own. I want to know what I can afford."

He held out a business card. "Let's go back to my office, shall we? I'm confident we can offer you something that will work for your circumstances."

Oh, I'm sure you could offer plenty that would work.

No ring. She checked that detail as he guided her into his office and installed her in a chair.

Mr. Ryan Pope—she learned his first name from the business card—filled the office with pleasant, bank-managerial talk. Even her lust-besotted brain couldn't confuse his professional courtesy with genuine interest. He asked some questions and pulled some papers from his printer. She trained her eyes on his printouts, followed his points with at least half of her mind, and self-created herself as a mature, intelligent woman.

Rather than a quivering ninny.

She'd find the information from her meeting in the reports the printer spewed out, thank heaven. She'd go over them later, once her brain had anchored firmly back inside her cranium.

Twenty minutes later, clutching an envelope and remembering his incredible eyes as he'd once again grasped her hand in his, Mel found herself on the sidewalk outside the bank. She congratulated herself on pulling off the meeting without hyperventilating. Her next stop was the real estate office across the street, where she intended to corner Julie Peters, supposedly her closest friend. Except Julie had *not* shared about the DCO bank manager.

"You never told me about Ryan Pope," she burst out the moment she turned the corner into Julie's cubicle.

"Huh?" Julie frowned at her while she sorted this out. "Oh, over at the bank. He's been around for six months or so. You bank at DCO. Haven't you run into him before?"

"How can I keep track of drop-dead gorgeous branch managers with ATMs everywhere? Jules, he's the hottest man in town, and you don't *tell* me about him?" Mel sank into Julie's client chair. Another idea found its way into her overheated head. "He's married?"

Julie tossed her dark mane out of her eyes. "Single. But I go for lunch with some of the gals at the bank, and they say he's strictly hands-off, so I didn't extrapolate to a horny friend."

"He gave me a major hot flash, right in the lobby. He probably thinks I'm a cretin."

Julie laughed. "He'd never think that. Give yourself more credit."

"And you're not interested?" Girlfriends' honor; if Julie saw him first...

"Nah. I met him when he first turned up in town. I wasn't the lucky one who got to show him houses, but from what Suzanne told me, he's polite, distant, not very interesting. And not on the prowl. Unlike you."

"Not interesting? I don't believe it."

"Telling you what I've heard. How'd it go? Do I start showing you starter homes?" Julie flapped a hand in Mel's face. "The meeting? Mel, are you in there?"

21

Mel popped back to the present. "My mind's fried into mush." She shoved the envelope across the desk.

Julie flipped through the reports. "Hmm." She looked up. "It won't be spectacular, but there's a decent selection on the market right now. Says here he'll expedite a pre-approval on a mortgage."

"That's good, right?" By now Mel's heart was back in step with her body, and her girl parts were behaving again, but her brain hadn't got the message yet.

"Control, woman. Drooling is not attractive. A house is probably out of reach, but go home tonight and think about whether you want a townhome or a condo. Pluses and minuses, I'll give you some brochures. Call if you have questions." Julie tapped the report back into the envelope and handed it to Mel. "Heard from the mysterious bookseller?"

Saturday afternoon, shopping for spring wardrobe additions, Mel had given her friend a full rundown on her unusual morning.

"No." She flipped her hand dismissively. "We didn't even make it to last names. I'm not likely to hear from him. That was weird."

"Which was weird? Adrian No-Last-Name or Ryan Pope?"

"Either. Both. What happened to boring? My life could do with better pacing. I don't need two encounters in three days. I'm exhausted. It's not fair."

"You're overdue for excitement, but don't get your hopes up about Mister Bank-Manager Pope. Word is, there's nothing doing."

But the word was wrong, because that evening she received a phone call from Ryan Pope. And ten minutes later she'd arranged to see him Friday night for dinner and who-knows-what.

Not that he said or implied who-knows-what. But what else are you going to do after a meal? Calter Creek wasn't exactly a hotbed of nightspots, and Ryan Pope didn't look like a club type person anyway. He looked like a bank manager… but in a *good* way.

A very good way.

On the other hand, maybe he'd take her to Columbus. There were clubs in Columbus. He might know of a romantic, intimate one where you could listen to jazz and order cognac and gaze into each other's eyes…

Mel gave herself a shake and opened one of the romance novels she'd taken from the bookstore. But she had to deal with some serious palpitations first. At the moment, her own life was far too intriguing to allow her to lose herself in fiction.

3

Mel's closet held four types of clothes. Work, which was mainly pantsuits; dress-up, mostly light and frothy; fun, for kick-back casual; and grubby, which could range from beaten-up shorts for touch football, to paint-spattered for refinishing the little table and chairs in her kitchen. What her closet didn't have was black or any shade of drab. For Mel it was rich colors, all the way.

She was unsure which category would be best for her date with Ryan. Her fluttery self suggested an out-on-the-town outfit with cleavage, while her met-him-in-a-bank logical self dictated one of her dressier work suits.

She had a whole workweek to stew. She stewed.

In the end, she chose a favorite, a burnt orange pantsuit with a silky green camisole. Not flirty, but dressy enough for Columbus, only a little too formal should he be planning on Joe's Café, the local hamburger joint. She wouldn't have minded showing off her legs, but none of the clubbing outfits felt quite right for a date with a banker. She stuck green barrettes in her hair to tamp it down, checked her face—subtle; however bright her clothes, she used little makeup—and considered herself ready for a night to remember.

Ryan was right on time, and Mel, in a rare state of nervous excitement, buzzed him up to her second floor apartment. He took the stairs, she could hear his feet from her open door, and then there he was.

The single most gorgeous man who'd ever stood in her doorway was standing there now, smiling at her.

"Good evening, Melanie. Are you ready?"

"Yep," she said cheerfully. "Soon as I get my shoes on I'm good to go." She shifted away from the door to let him step in.

"This is nice." He wandered toward the living room window.

Mel looked up from where she balanced on one foot while she adjusted the first strappy green sandal. "You reckon? It's a basic one bedroom rental. Adequate, but nothing to write home about. Tell me what catches you."

"It's clean and uncluttered. And the view's not bad." Mel's apartment faced south over a scattering of suburbs and cornfields.

"True, I suppose." She worked her foot into the other sandal. "But it's not me. There's not much personality here. The sofa maybe."

Ryan looked dubiously at the burgundy sofa, which sported a bright cerulean and green throw and a pile of cushions in primary colors. "I guess I see your point. You prefer bright things?"

"Definitely. And I'm ready." She got the dressier of her two lightweight coats out of the closet and looked over to where he stood near her window. Their eyes met and locked.

Locking eyes wasn't her idea, it just happened. But it drew the two of them toward each other like opposite poles on magnets. Before she knew it he was in front of her and had his hands resting on her upper arms.

"You look very nice tonight."

"Thank you," she said a little breathlessly.

And he kissed her.

It was barely a peck, which was just as well, given they'd been on their first date for under five minutes, but Mel's stomach nosedived before it bounced and ricocheted around in her chest. Which was inconvenient, since the underused female places further down were twitching, too.

"Thank you. It's not my intention to rush things, but it felt right."

It sure did.

She handed him the coat, and he held it for her while she put it on. "Shall we go?"

25

"Let's." He waited while she locked up. "Elevator or stairs?"

"From the second floor? I haven't been in the elevator since I moved my furniture in."

"Here's the thing," he said as they walked to his car, which he'd parked in front of the building. "When I know what I want, I'm not hesitant about going for it. Something happened between us Monday morning. Attraction, but more than that. It was like... fate."

Mel smiled at him but didn't speak. At that moment she didn't have any idea what she could say without being corny or implying more than she was ready to. But she sure did enjoy that little hint of a kiss.

Ryan drove a shiny black sedan. "Nice," she said. Every guy liked to have his ride complimented.

"Freshly washed in your honor." He held the passenger door for her, then circled the car and settled in behind the wheel.

"Where are we going?" He'd picked her up at seven o'clock, so there was still an hour or more of daylight left. She took advantage of it to study the interior of the car—a Ford, she learned—and without conscious thought reached over to the radio.

"For our first time together, the Madison Inn's dining room. It's the best Calter Creek has to offer other than the Country Club, upscale but not pretentious. What are you doing?"

"Pushing buttons," Mel answered. She landed on a song she liked. "Here we go."

Ryan's eyes flicked from the radio, to the road, to her, to the road. His expression was guarded. "You're a fan of country and western?"

"Almost any music, actually." She was drumming along with her fingers on her coat-covered thighs.

"I'm glad you're eclectic, but I have to admit, country's not my preference. You must prefer some genres over others."

"I don't understand jazz, but I can get into Beethoven."

26

"Beethoven's promising, since I'd like to propose a compromise." He pressed the first pre-set button, and they were back where they'd been when she'd turned the radio on, a classical station, probably NPR.

"My family always had the rule that the driver gets to choose, so I guess that's you." It wasn't only the radio's buttons she'd been pushing. Mel had the uneasy sense that her willingness to listen to anything had been used against her. "It does mean that I get to drive occasionally, so I can have my pick," she said, brightening up. Might as well rope him into a next time.

Ryan laughed. "I'm old fashioned. I tend to believe the man should do the driving."

"Don't count on that."

Mel asked herself in the silence that followed if she'd just heard a warning bell. No, she decided. Much too soon for warning bells. She was an independent woman, making her own decisions about how to live her life. He'd see, as they got to know each other; there wouldn't be a dominant force in this relationship.

"You've been to the Madison Inn before, I assume?"

She nodded. "Not to the dining room in years though. The café, sometimes. Mostly it's out of my social stratum."

"Hmm."

It didn't take long to get anywhere in Calter Creek. Ryan maneuvered into a parking place in the lot. The Madison Inn might be the best in town, but it wasn't anywhere near valet parking status. In the same way that he'd formally opened the door for her earlier, he gave her a hand exiting his car. Walking to the entrance, he asked, "What do you see as your social stratum, Melanie?"

She grinned. "The one where people don't call you Melanie, for starters. No one does. I'm Mel, most of my life."

He shook his head. "I'll be the different person, then. To me, you're Melanie. Always will be."

"I don't actually like my full name very much."

They were in the lobby by then, waiting for the elevator to the sixth floor restaurant.

27

"Give it a chance. Once you get used to hearing it from me, you may change your mind. It's a lovely name."

The elevator delivered them, and the hostess showed them to their table, one with a view over the east side of Calter Creek. In the distance to the left she could make out what must be the site of Landmark Center, where construction had only just started. She and Julie were itching for the new mall to open.

The waiter came to take their before-dinner drinks order. Ryan named a Merlot, and not the house red. Either the man knew his wine or he was trying to impress. Then he looked at her. "Perhaps you'd prefer to start with something else?"

"I've been looking forward to a dirty martini."

Ryan nodded to the waiter, who gathered the wine lists and disappeared. "We'll finish the bottle with dinner. You'll like it. It's one of the nicest reds I've come across."

Mel made a mental note to order a red wine meal. "About my name—did you know Melanie means dark or black? It doesn't suit me."

He took her hand across the table. "I don't get why anyone cares about the meanings of names. It's irrelevant in this day and age. A name's a name. I believe that using your full, proper name rather than a nickname gives you gravity. It says that you're not a kid anymore. I mean, Jimmy Carter? How could you take him seriously? Trust me." He squeezed her fingers, then let go. "Let's have a look at the menu. I missed lunch and I'm getting desperate."

Adrian's beaten-up old book wouldn't carry any weight with Ryan. Did that matter? To be in his position he had to be pragmatic. Instead of perusing the menu, she studied him. "I'm curious. What happens in the life of a bank manager that you miss lunch?"

"The menu, Melanie, or I'll faint on you. I'll tell you while we wait for our meals."

At least he didn't try ordering for you. Feeling vaguely reprimanded, Mel scanned the menu and picked out a salad and a salmon dish. Ryan signaled the waiter and ordered her selections, soup and a largish steak for himself.

"I'm sorry about that," he said when the waiter had left. "It was rude to hurry you, but it's a blood sugar thing. I've noticed before that if I let mine plummet, I'm a real grouch. I guess I should have had a snack before I picked you up."

"I get that. Maybe you should keep energy bars or something at work to tide you over."

"A wise suggestion. I did manage some crackers and cheese earlier, but the effect's long since worn off.

"So, about today," he continued. "To start with, there was a staff problem that had to be sorted out. It's never pleasant to deal with that kind of situation—I'm sure you understand I can't give you any details. Then someone misplaced the key to the safety deposit boxes. Nonstop meetings this afternoon, some of the brass from head office were in town. The usual, but it's a nuisance when it all happens at once."

Ryan chatted on about the intricacies of branch management. He warmed up as he talked, drawing her deeper into his daily life at the bank. He spun a good story. You could almost imagine that a bank manager's world was exciting, to hear him tell it.

Mel listened, sipping her martini and occasionally adding a comment. She wasn't competent to ask in-depth questions, but she could get a profile of what his work involved.

Part way through dinner—which lived up to billing—he asked about her work. From her mortgage discussion he knew that her title wasn't exactly elevated; executive assistant was still an assistant, the kind of nebulous title that could mean anything. But he didn't understand how involved she was in the day-to-day running of Sinclair Imports, how much authority Amanda delegated to her. So she touched on the wide variety of her responsibilities and the close working relationship she had with her boss.

Ryan said, "It seems to me that she might consider promoting you, if you really do all you say. Doesn't she recognize your value?"

"That sounds harsh, Ryan. And yes, she does. Amanda's usually the easiest person in the world to work with, and I get full credit for what I do. Promotion's come up a few times, but the bottom line is, I don't want it. I enjoy what I do. I have just the right amount of responsibility, the right level of authority, and I don't have to be anybody's boss. It lets me be friends with everyone at SI without staff problems like you had today." That summed up her work life. She was precisely where she wanted to be.

"You are well paid, for your position." Ryan took a bite of steak.

His words felt off to her. She thought it over while she chewed and swallowed, then said, "Forgive me, but mentioning my salary's kind of creepy. I mean, we've only just met."

He looked up from his meal, surprised. "But I have your financial profile, from Monday. I never want to pretend, Melanie. I want to be able to say what's true, right up front. Honesty, that's so important. Don't you agree?"

"Yes, of course." Mel thought it over. Who didn't want openness and honesty in a relationship? She'd never been one to play games, herself. But she had an equal right to identify something that felt creepy to her, and say so, just as honestly.

She let it go. Their meeting Monday left them both in an awkward position where her net worth was concerned. They chatted for the rest of the meal, touching on movies—they agreed on avoiding shoot-'em-ups and soppy sit-coms; books— Ryan preferred biographies, Mel sought out quality romances; food—he was meat and potatoes, she had vegetarian leanings. But he ate vegetables and she ate meat and differences added spice to a relationship, right? So she listened attentively, told him about herself, and when the plates had been cleared she concluded that the dinner had gone well.

As they walked to his car through a mild May night, he took her hand "Come back to my place, Melanie? I'm not ready for this evening to be over yet."

The words she wanted to hear. "I'd like that."

Ryan owned a townhome in the eastern end of the city — the same complex that Amanda had lived in before her marriage, Mel realized. His place had vanilla walls, taupe furnishings. Her fingers itched to add the cerulean and green throw to the mix.

"Could I offer you a glass of port? It's an excellent label. I personally don't think this vintage is as good as the previous one, but it's still exceptional."

Mel settled on the sofa. She'd started shaking her head half way through the vintage presentation. "Thanks, but no." She smiled up at him—what was it about smiling up at a guy? It made her feel feminine. Desirable. Go figure. "We drank a whole bottle of wine, and I've passed my limit. Could I have a glass of water?"

"It's good that you recognize your limits." Ryan headed for the kitchen. He re-emerged with a lovely crystal tumbler of water and a matching stemmed glass holding a dark red liquid. Mel had never had port before, but it *looked* good.

"Wow," she said. "Elegant."

"Nice things matter."

Mel accepted the glass, sipped, and set it on the coffee table. He instantly picked it up again, put his own glass down, then opened a drawer in the table and extracted a couple of coasters.

"Sorry. There wasn't a mat, so I didn't know…"

"You'll know next time. It's a matter of taking care of things."

"I'm guessing you don't put this crystal in the dishwasher."

"Never." Ryan settled on the sofa beside her.

"What'll happen when little Ryan Junior gets his hands on one of these and it gets broken?"

His face went solemn. "Ryan Junior will learn. Children are teachable, and he'll understand very early what's out of bounds."

Mel looked around and concluded that most of the room was likely to be out of bounds. But they'd have a big rumpus room where the family would spend most of its time and the kids could make a mess. Save the living room for entertaining and breakables.

He placed the port glass on its coaster. "So here we are," he said.

31

"Here we are." There was a pause that just avoided being uncomfortable before he spoke again. "It's been a good evening. We have a future, Melanie. We'll make a good team. Don't you agree? I'm very much looking forward to seeing where it goes. Getting to know you better."

He was close; Mel's brain missed a circuit or two before she organized a reply. "So far, yes, I agree. We both have a lot to learn about each other, though."

He reached for his glass. There was a pause as he savored the gorgeous ruby liquid.

"My life's straightforward," he told her. "I believe we share fundamentals. We're successful in our spheres. We both want to invest in a home. I suspect we have common goals where partners and children are concerned."

"There could be a few speed bumps." She thought about the ones that had tripped her up this evening.

"We work through them. We're adults. However, that isn't entirely what I meant when I said I'd like us to get to know each other better." Ryan placed his port glass back on the coffee table. "This is more what I had in mind."

What he meant was what she'd been hoping for all evening long. He pulled her against him, and this time it wasn't a peck. Mel's heart thudded as she allowed him to encourage her mouth to open for him. After an indeterminate time, during which they both lost their suit jackets, the buttons on his shirt came undone, and she learned that his chest was well muscled and lightly dusted with coarse blond hair, Mel pulled together the shreds of her willpower and moved away. "Before this goes any further..." This was their first date, after all.

Ryan's incredible eyes met hers. He took a breath. In fact, he took several; she could see his chest rising and falling. When his breathing normalized he said, "Will you stay?"

She shook her head. "It's too soon. You'd better take me home, Ryan." She pulled away from his hands and located her camisole, which had landed on the back of the sofa.

He sighed. "You're right. The sort of woman you marry, you don't take to your bed when you've only known her a few hours. I hope you believe that I do respect you, Melanie." He stood, fastening his buttons, then reached for her hand and pulled her up.

Marry?

Mel swallowed. How had they gone from first date to marriage? "Thank you," she said. "It's been a lovely evening." Lame, she thought. But he'd stunned her vocabulary right out of her head.

"It has." He helped her with her suit jacket and coat and escorted her — that was the only word for it — to the car.

"Could I see you next weekend?" he asked at the door to her apartment. "Friday night?"

"I'm going to a concert at the high school on Thursday. Some of my co-workers' kids are in it. Want to come?"

He shook his head. "I think I'll pass this time. But Friday?"

Early days, Mel.

"Sure. Let me know what we'll be doing. I'll have wardrobe decisions to make."

"I'll call you."

He gathered her up and gave her one last, more-than-friends kiss, then he left her at her open door watching him as he headed for the stairs.

Mel went into her apartment, locked the door, and leaned against it.

It had been an evening for the record books. This gorgeous, successful man had focused his full attention on her. He'd been a gentleman, and Mel appreciated that. She'd had enough, over the years, of fighting men off. He'd treated her as if she was special. He was hot, and for sure he knew what he was doing with his mouth, his hands...

She gave a happy little shiver.

But something niggled at her. Everything about him, from his career to the mats on his coffee table, from the way he actually liked her apartment to the way he seemed to expect her to fall in with his plans, was well controlled, ordered to his specifications. And those specifications were so restrained, so *colorless*. Would it be possible to make a comfortable place in Ryan's life?

Well, he'd loosen up. Everyone was uptight on a first date. It was sort of sweet that he'd been even a teeny bit nervous. It meant she was special, not just another Friday night date.

Mel paused to type their next date into her phone before she headed for the shower.

Yeah. As if you'd forget.

The next morning Mel presented herself at the door to the bookstore. Adrian must have been downstairs, because she'd barely knocked before he had the door open. "Mel. You came."

He cleaned up well, she noted. Checked shirt, slacks that hadn't been around since the dinosaur age. Something different that she couldn't quite figure out.

"You promised breakfast." She grinned. "After the granola, I figured it'd be worth a trip into town at the crack of dawn."

The crack of dawn was nearly nine o'clock, but on a Saturday, and after Ryan—well, Mel might comfortably have stayed in bed for another hour or two, daydreaming about exploring hands, a clever mouth...

She snapped back to reality, which had more to do with the orange light in the bookstore and the promise of food than a nebulous future with a blond bank manager. Hopeful aromas drifted her way.

He returned her grin. "I aim to please. Come on in." He led the way to the stairs. "I've been wondering why it is that we prefer the eggs of chickens. Because they're the easiest to mass-produce, I suppose. I'm not sure I've ever had any other type of egg, but I believe grouse eggs were considered a luxury once. Do you know?"

"I've seen grouse eggs in novels. And ostrich eggs, but only as decorations."

"We could feed an army with one of those. I've made bacon. Your choice how I fix the eggs."

Half way up the stairs he stopped. "My grandmother would not be happy. You should precede me. The gentleman leads on the way down, so he can catch the fair maiden should she trip. What's your opinion of conventions like that?" He gestured for her to go first.

"I never heard that one. If I fell going down the stairs we'd both go flying. But I like it when a man opens the door." She paused at the entrance to the apartment and looked around. Not a box in sight. He'd unpacked and moved in.

"It feeds the myth of frail womanhood, I suppose. I'd try valiantly, of course, but I suspect you're right about going flying. Now for those eggs." He headed to the stove, rubbing his hands together.

The place smelled heavenly. Bacon did it for her, every time.

"I could whip up a hollandaise for eggs Benedict," he said, "but I'd prefer something simpler. We can save the Benedict thing for lunch one day. Too much richness first thing in the morning."

Especially after a martini and all that wine last night. Mel's stomach wasn't exactly rebelling, but it did feel like a day when simpler would be better.

"Can you do poached? I haven't had a poached egg in ages." In fact, it had been months since Mel had eaten any type of egg for breakfast, figuring it wasn't worth the extra work and washing up.

"I can. Hang on." Bread went into the toaster, water into the frying pan. "I realized after you left last Saturday that there are a million things you don't know about me, or I about you. Perhaps we should exchange basics? My last name is Forsythe, my age is forty-one. My hair was gray by the time I turned twenty-six. It was an ordinary brown before that, in case you're wondering. There are photos somewhere, probably at my parents' house. Your turn."

"Chesterton, thirty-five. Do you want me to see to the toast?"

"Wonderful. Two pieces for me, please." The first round of toast popped up. Mel found butter conveniently next to the toaster. "I have plates in the oven, we can stack the toast there. Are you a native?"

"Since my teens. My sister lives here with her husband and my nieces. The folks moved to Florida."

"Philadelphia for me. Doesn't that have a magnificent ring to it? All those F's. The Philadelphia Forsythes." He laughed.

Mel laughed with him. An at-home feeling swept over her, and she relaxed. "Are you rich and famous?"

She was joking, but she caught a shadow flickering across his face before he answered. "My family's done well enough. They think I'm nuts, of course."

"You mention them a lot."

He shrugged. "I have great parents, all things considered." He eyed the simmering water. "Just right. One egg or two? Two for me."

"Two. This is great, Adrian. I haven't had a cooked breakfast since Christmas with my sister."

"Then we'll make a habit of it." He deftly slid the eggs into the simmering water and set a timer while Mel buttered the second round of toast and put the slices in the oven.

The food cooked and plated, they sat across from each other at the table. "That was a delightful experience," he said. "We work well together in a kitchen, which doesn't always happen. It's like a ballet, moving in sync with each other. I had a housemate in college, once she was in the kitchen we all just stayed out. No matter what you wanted to do, she was in the way. She had other uses, I suppose," he mused. "A fiend for vacuuming, which I'm afraid I'm not. I guess once you have a store you have to vacuum."

"Broom? I'd rather sweep than vacuum."

"That's because there's probably some witch in you. I'm pretty sure that's the case, in fact. Eat."

Mel cut into her first egg and watched the yolk sink into the toast. Perfect. Just the way she liked it. Before the bite made it to her mouth she surveyed the table. He'd put a cheerful oilcloth with a pattern of cherries and trellises over the battered wood. There was a bowl of fruit salad and a dish of jelly — grape? She hadn't had grape jelly since she was a kid. He'd found the French press and made coffee. Excellent coffee.

36

As was the egg. She could have moaned. Possibly she did.

And that reminded her of Ryan.

"Your face is pink. I make good eggs, but I doubt they're truly orgasmic."

Mel barely got her bite swallowed before her laugh burst out. "You might be surprised. This is wonderful, Adrian."

"My pleasure to see you so at home and—oh, dear. An adjective for a person who's enjoying something a lot. Orgasmic wasn't my best effort."

Mel turned it over in her mind. "Stronger than content. Blissful?"

"Sated? Satisfied?"

"Fulfilled?"

"Closer."

"Sorry, gotta eat." Mel could have crammed the bacon and egg into her mouth, except that Adrian ate with tidy precision. Manners clearly were a big deal in his family, so she conformed and slowed herself down.

A few bites later she said, "I suppose you made the jelly, too? It seems like something you'd do."

"This? Yes, last year. Draining juice through cheesecloth and such. My first time, and very likely my last."

"I made soap once."

"So did I. It was only a partial success. It's possible I don't have the patience or accuracy to pull off a chemical reaction. Not a scientist."

"More a big picture man?"

He scrunched up his face as if he had to think about it. Adrian didn't seem as odd as he had the day they met. It suddenly hit her what was different about him today. The glasses. The wire-rim granny glasses were gone, and conventional, businesslike frames sat on his nose.

"I suppose this store qualifies as a big concept. I don't really know what I'm doing here, but between us we can figure it out. Perhaps it means we have a better chance to be unique, not derivative."

37

She picked up a crispy slice of bacon, but paused before taking a bite of it. "Why are you doing this, Adrian? You don't strike me as a businessman. These days I doubt that a love of books is enough reason to open a store."

"You're partially right." He frowned at his plate. "I have a solid background in business, and didn't enjoy it. What matters to me is the books. This store's going to rely at least as much on the second-hand and rare book trade, so I'm itching to dive into the mess downstairs, but cleaning out the second floor and making this place livable had priority. The first floor... you've been in and out for years, I suppose, so you know. For anyone but me, it'd be horrendous."

"Fifty years' accumulation of grime," Mel agreed. She helped herself to grape jelly and spread it on her second piece of toast.

"Not worth tackling cleanup until we've been through the books, though. We'd kick the dust back up again."

"I won't be any help there. I don't know anything about old books."

"I'll coach. You can handle first screening, perhaps. If a book's worm eaten..."

"Yecch."

"True, but not uncommon. If it's in appalling condition, unless it's a rare first edition, out it goes. Most of what's there, in all likelihood. Online and mail inquiries come in daily, so I'm confident good stuff's in there. But there's no consistent order, so it's like a mad treasure hunt. We'll work together, don't worry. I hope you don't mind getting grubby."

"You should see me after a game of touch football." Mel downed her last bite. "Let me help with dishes."

"Nope. You're still my guest. Another week or two, and you'll be washing dishes, but not yet." Adrian filled the sink while she ferried plates and cups to the counter, then he grabbed a pad and pencil and they went out into the second floor space.

"About that coffee bar..."

"Definitely upstairs."

His face lit up. "You've been thinking about it."

Mel paced through the empty space. "Once these windows are cleaned, it could have a kind of old fashioned ambience, especially with the staircase..."

"Keep going. Tell me about the staircase." Adrian was propped against the back wall, poised over his pad.

"Well, it's so elegant. You could picture the debutantes of the family descending in their gowns, going to the ball. If it could be refinished... I'm not sure it's even safe now, the way the risers are so uneven."

"Generations of feet. Romantic image, but you're right about the safety."

By now Mel was standing at the top of the stairs, looking down to the first floor. When Adrian joined her, she glanced at his pad; at the bottom of the page he'd written 'refinish stairs' and drawn two dark lines underneath.

His handwriting was upright and angular. She speculated on whether he'd had a career writing mysterious formulae in esoteric books of magic. The bookstore was getting to her.

"So they'd come up. I see broad-brimmed hats." He expanded her vision. "And there at the top they'd find this coffee place. Elegant? Casual? Elaborate on 'old fashioned', please. Did I tell you about the mystery elevator?"

"Only that it exists. I had no idea."

"I haven't dared use it, but it's there, tucked around the corner behind the stairs, near the washroom. Which is just plain awful." He jotted down 'elevator service', then 'gut the washroom'. "It's the kind that has a gate—the elevator, not the washroom. We might have to hire someone wearing white gloves to operate it."

She snickered. "These days it's self-serve or nothing. But I don't see the upstairs as ultra-modern. Downstairs has plate glass windows, but up here? Since it's an old building, and with these gorgeous windows, you should play on that. Make it feel like the kind of timeless place people have been coming to for years. How about mismatched tables and chairs, mismatched dishes and cutlery? Like out of Granny's attic."

He raised an eyebrow, a bemused look on his face.

"Like your kitchen. Granola in that fancy dish, but nothing matched, not the cups or the cutlery or anything. Your chairs don't match either."

"You're observant. And you extrapolate. I like that." He led the way back into the room, to the wall of giant windows.

Mel looked out, watching the traffic on Main Street. "But we'd risk it looking like family hand-me-downs a kid took to college."

He smiled. A big smile. "You said 'we'."

Mel tried to backtrack. "I meant 'you'. It's just that since we're both talking—"

"You're still fighting it. You're destined to have a hand in this. Doomed, if you prefer."

"It's your place, Adrian. Not mine."

"Ours. You think I'm living in a dream world?"

"Delusional?"

"Unrealistic?"

"Deranged? No, sorry. That's mean."

"Wouldn't be the first time I was accused of being deranged. But not where you're concerned. I like the mismatched theme, but my guess is we'll be forced to use sturdy and white for plates and things. But if we scour the second-hand stores and garage sales… that could be fun."

"Here's another idea. We go for Victorian. Aspidistras."

"That word always makes me think of spittoons. I suppose because it reminds me of 'expectorate'. Initial vowel, second syllable beginning in a 'p'. None of those, please."

She laughed. "Gross. Everything matching, but furnished over-the-top. So we're sort of making fun of the period, even while we're using it as a theme."

"Another good idea. But your thoughts are on the feminine. The earliest coffee houses were masculine places where they sat around and smoked and talked politics. Lots of disputes."

"A way to get out of the house? Maybe their wives threw them out. So that leads us to a male refuge—but without the smoke, please."

"Besides that smoking's against code, it wouldn't be good for the books." Adrian started pacing in front of one of the windows, his eyes more on the room than on her. She had the feeling he saw something she didn't, the room as it one day would be.

"You need to do field work," she said. "The downtown Coffee Shack's only three blocks away. See what the gender balance is. Consider how it's decorated and how you could do better. The Coffee Shacks all look alike, but they've started to add some touches to make them less institutional. Certainly not feminine."

He stood still and gave her a pained look. "Do I have to?"

"I think you do."

Adrian sighed. "Mel, you have far more of a marketing mind than I do. I'll grab a coffee next week. Unless you'd like to go right now?"

She shook her head. "You've filled me up with breakfast and coffee. Anyway, is Saturday going to be your target market? Or will it be the people who work and shop downtown on weekdays?"

"So much to figure out, isn't there? Thank heaven for lists. My mind isn't linear, so without a list I'm doomed. Do you mind map?" He brandished his pencil. "And speaking of mind maps—I don't quite see what the connection is, but I'm confident there is one—perhaps you understand cloud storage? I believe one of those might let us share ideas."

"I'll look into it, if you like."

"Please. Then you can show me the mysterious setting on a tablet that keeps the text where you want it to be."

"Adrian, do you actually have a tablet?"

"Yes, although it seems strange. They make good readers for electronic books."

Mel turned on her strongest incredulous stare. "You can't convince me you read e-books."

"At times, yes. It's handy to get into the library system when you don't have any other access, like around midnight. Do you know that one, by the way? 'Round Midnight'? It's a jazz standard."

41

"Don't think so."

"Wonderful. Something else to explore together. Or it's a good way to read a book you know you won't want to keep."

Mel made the mental jump from jazz back to e-books. "I'm surprised."

"We have to decide if we need to stock electronics, e-readers and such. I wonder if there's a way to sell e-books?"

"Maybe on the website?"

"We'll have a website? Yes, I suppose we must."

"The real question is whether you want to sell them. Plus a learning curve."

"True. Might be biting off too much. But we've made one decision. We put the coffee shop in that corner. Décor to be decided." He chuckled. "For the rest of it—move second-hand up here?"

"We'd have to find a way to contain the dust." Mel had slipped into 'we' mode again, but let it go.

"Point well taken."

They'd drifted over to the corner of the future coffee bar and stood underneath the big window. Mel estimated the ceiling at fifteen feet or more, and the windows towered almost that high while going to within three feet of the floor. An arch of multi-hued stained glass topped each of the five enormous windows, giving the place an otherworldly glow when the sun came in, as it was this morning. "It's a beautiful space, Adrian."

"It crossed my mind that if we can't make a go of a bookstore, we could rent the space as a dance studio. I love the image of little girls practicing plies in their tutus with these rainbows dancing around them."

"Here's another concept. Heavy on art. Degas prints and such."

"Old pairs of ballet shoes hanging on the walls with pink ribbon?"

"Street scenes. Old Calter Creek photographs. A bicycle with a woven basket."

"Dresses from the eighteen hundreds. A box radio."

"You're a romantic."

"Yes," he agreed. "That, I assuredly am. Come on, let's have a look downstairs."

But downstairs defeated them. She stood next to Adrian at the foot of the stairs and stared at the rickety, over-laden shelves of books, the uneven flooring. They both sagged.

"It's the effect of the paper on the windows," he said. "I was assured that it was necessary, so that when the great day comes everyone will gasp in amazement. But until we're closer, we need to get rid of it."

Mel grinned at him, the idea catching her imagination. "I'd love to get rid of it."

His face held pure mischief. "Let's do it."

They split up at the door, Adrian going left and Mel going right. Mel whooped as she ripped the horrible paper from the windows. Sheets of the stuff fell on top of her, got trampled underfoot. She heard Adrian across the room, having as much fun as she was; he laughed out loud. "This is why I put the stuff up," he called to her from underneath one of the giant sheets. "So we could tear it back down. I wouldn't miss this for the world."

They met again by the door. "Folding the paper for recycling won't be half as much fun," he said with regret.

"Is there a place to store it? You'll want paper back up before the opening. I think your advisors were right about that."

"Not this paper, though. Plain white. I can't endure that orange glow again—although it did do magnificent things to your hair. Not that your hair needed it." As on the day she'd first turned up at the door, his hand lightly brushed the edges of her manic hair. "Radiant."

"Messy. Out of control."

"Angelic."

"Oh, no, don't go there. I'm not angelic."

"I hope not. I can't say I have much use for the whole idealized angel thing. Anyway, as I said before, I think there's some witch in you. But to have hair that forms a corona like this... never let it go, Mel. It's you."

She laughed. "Been this way all my life, so I don't suppose it's going to change now."

She bent and picked up one of the long sheets of paper. He took the other end and between them they got it folded. Chatting comfortably, they dispatched the horrid brown paper into the recycling bins behind the store.

"I have to go, Adrian."

"Thank you for being here. Planning this place wouldn't be the same without you."

"You're a pal. And thanks for breakfast. I haven't lived this well in years. What's next?"

"Next is I go on cleaning and making the deck upstairs safe and working on the list. You come back—you will, won't you? Wear something grubby, and we'll start sifting through this mess." He gestured at the overflowing shelves. "It'll take a while, but there's no rush."

With the paper gone, the challenge of cleaning up the ground floor was less daunting. Besides, she'd had fun this morning, and was beginning to envision the future bookstore in full color. "Saturday morning?"

"I'll feed you, then we'll work. And work it will be, I'm afraid." Adrian looked at the shelves with a mix of dismay and anticipation.

She nudged him with an elbow. "I'm not afraid of work. Let's do it."

He turned to her and gave her an enthusiastic, but brief, hug. "Let's."

At home that afternoon, Mel pulled out a box of magazines and tape, and took a collaged picture on card stock off her fridge door. Her vision board, her treasure map. Her picture of the future she wanted. She studied the images she'd cut from magazines and put on the page.

House, check. Kids, check. Dog and cat, check. Happy redhead, check. She hadn't updated her own image in years. It showed her as she was, in jeans and a bright teal top, relaxed and casual.

Husband, not check. The image on the board had dark hair.

Mel had made frequent changes to her vision board over the years. Since it was basically the same vision every time, she didn't make a new one; she simply put the pictures on the board with tape so she could replace them as needed. Now she got busy with a couple of magazines and found a picture of a blond man in a business suit.

Yeah.

The dark-haired man came off, the blond one went on. Mel next replaced the children with blond or red-headed kids. The rejected images went into an envelope in her box; she wasn't putting all her hopes on one blond man quite yet.

She studied the board. Perfect. A happy family in a comfortable house, the kids, the animals.

Was the paper husband stuffy? Or did the wife look too casual? Was there a mismatch here?

No. They just didn't know each other that well yet. She had no doubt that Ryan was hot, hot, hot in jeans. He'd wear jeans when he cut the lawn on Saturday mornings.

She'd be at the bookstore again next Saturday morning.

The bookstore thing wasn't likely to last all that long. It was a diversion, but...

Actually, the bookstore puzzled her. It seemed to exist outside the realm of the probable. As if she suspended her ordinary life when she set foot in Adrian's territory.

Adrian was a nice guy. He was fast becoming a friend. She'd had a fun morning.

She wondered if Ryan made breakfasts. That would be nice, getting up to find the husband and kids around the table, digging into pancakes. Then they'd take the kids to their activities, do some yard work, get a sitter and plan an evening out. Yeah, nice image. Perhaps she should collage that one, too.

Mel knew all about dreaming in Technicolor. But after last night? Maybe it was finally working, and the vision board was going to be reality.

And the man could kiss. Oh, yeah. Skilled.

Skilled, but... not quite the thrill it should be?

Based on one date?

Mel put away her supplies, put the vision board back on the fridge, and made a short grocery list. Not very exciting, but necessary, since she and Julie were meeting for hors d'oeuvres at her place before heading out to Calter Creek's most popular club that evening.

Thank God for the deli, huh?

What a night.

The next Friday night, their second date, she hadn't stayed over at Ryan's, but it had been a narrow victory of logic and long-term planning over, well, good old desire. The night filled Mel with dreams and rainbows, not to mention frustrated lust. Only the thought of breakfast got her out of bed Saturday morning.

They'd kept it simple, dinner and a movie at Creekside Mall. Ryan did indeed look hot in jeans, not that it mattered. She'd enjoyed the movie, but missed significant chunks of it. He certainly made good use of his hands in a movie. Then they'd gone back to his place, where she'd once again found herself on Ryan's sofa. Doing… things.

Things she'd put a stop to, again. Second date wasn't unheard of, but not this time. She needed to keep her wits. She was going for the long game, especially after what he'd said about respect, and marriage.

Marriage…

This was it. She was sure. Ryan Pope had the stable career, a plan for the future that meshed with her own. Not to mention the looks. He met her criteria, and the physical thing was great.

Actually, the physical thing was good but… kind of ordinary? So far, nothing that took her right out of her skin. Mel suspected that only happened in romance novels. She wasn't about to sacrifice present happiness for an impossible dream.

Ryan knew about her Saturday mornings at the bookstore, but he hadn't shown any interest in the details. She had the sense not to burble about the breakfasts—waffles with blueberries and sausages this morning—or the excitement that crackled between them when she and Adrian dove into the vision that, increasingly, she shared.

She emerged from the bookstore around one o'clock Saturday, as grubby as Adrian had promised. They'd barely made it through one side of one shelf of the old books. At this rate, they'd spend the entire summer sifting through them.

Walking to her car, she wondered what Adrian did the other six days of the week, why he wasn't tackling the bookshelves alone. But she'd seen his ever-growing list. Everything from plumbing and electrical, to the staircase, to whether the downstairs flooring needed to be replaced instead of refurbished, to what kind of cash register to use. She was happy to leave all that to him. The messy stuff, like worm-eaten books, was enough for her.

At home, she phoned Julie. "Want to go for a walk?"

Julie was reliable and predictable. "If you mean walking the corridors of Creekside Mall, sure."

She didn't, but she'd take it. "Pick you up in half an hour."

Over coffee at the food court in Creekside, she told Julie all—almost all—about the night before. "He is *so* the one, Jules. He has everything going for him."

"Mmm. What'll happen when he's transferred?"

"Oh." Mel paused. "Hadn't thought about that. But he wouldn't have to accept a transfer, would he? I mean, he could choose to stay in Calter Creek."

"More to the point, is he working toward that transfer? How ambitious is he?"

"He's ambitious. But he's applied to join the Country Club. An investor he knows through the bank recommended him. That sounds like roots to me."

Julie slurped the bottom of her mocha frappe. "Hope so. Just thinking ahead, since you aren't."

"Am too. Constantly."

"Through lust-tinted glasses. Let's go browse. I need sandals before the weather gets any warmer."

"Early June? By now the selection's been picked over. You'll be lucky to find anything." Mel tossed her paper cup in the waste bin.

They ambled down the broad corridor bisecting Creekside Mall. "So what's going on at the bookstore?" Julie asked. "I was at work last week when the paper came off the windows. You looked like you were having the time of your life, but I don't see any change inside."

"It's going to be slow. We worked through a twentieth of the books this morning. Most of them will be trashed, but Adrian got excited when we uncovered two or three of them, as if he'd struck gold."

"You're enjoying yourself. What does Ryan say?"

Mel shrugged. "Haven't discussed it. Does it matter?"

"His current love interest spending hours every Saturday morning closeted in a closed store with an eligible male? At least I assume he's eligible."

"Adrian's a friend," Mel said defensively. "And now that you mention it, I don't know if he's eligible or not. He could have a wife and a dozen children stashed somewhere. Not likely, since he's fixing up the apartment on the second floor, but I've never asked."

"Maybe you should before that goes any further."

"What do you mean? It's not going anywhere."

The conversation came to a halt while Julie selected sandals to try on. Mel sank into a chair and watched. Boxes stacked in front of her, Julie picked up her theme. "I mean, if he's eligible, he's noticed you. Hasn't he? Has he put any moves on you?"

"No. He's not like that. It's not like that."

"Careful, you might be treading on thin ice there."

"Friend, Julie. Friend. Remember that word? Adrian's a friend. He is," she mused, idly watching Julie work her way through the stack. "It's as if I've known him forever, even though I've never met anyone even remotely like him."

"Trust?" Julie's voice was muffled; she was bent over, fastening a sandal.

49

"Totally. I was a little nervous the first time I went in, but since then? It's fun to be with him."

"Going to introduce him to Ryan?"

"If it ever comes up, sure. Why not?"

"Just speculation on how that would play out. Not bad," Julie said, straightening and sticking a foot out in front of herself to admire the sandal. "You've gone from no men to two in two weeks. Not asking you to share, though. I doubt either of them is my type. I mean, I've told you I'm cool on Ryan, not that he isn't a good guy. I've seen Adrian coming and going occasionally. It's nice to work right downtown, I see everything."

"I miss everything. The disadvantage of a warehouse in an office park."

"Seriously, back to Ryan. Is he jealous? Is he likely to be?"

"Not because of anything I do."

Ryan, jealous…

But Adrian was a pal. They shared a growing friendship, and that was part of what made her life so rich. Ryan had to learn to enjoy her friends, or at least tolerate them. Her life worked for her. Ryan and Adrian existed in different spheres, so she wasn't really worried about the intersection.

Tuesday morning, out of the blue, Ryan called her at work. "Are you busy tonight?"

Even if she had been, she wasn't now. "No, I'm not. What's up?"

"An open house at the art gallery across the street from the bank. It's worthwhile dropping in, since we do business with them."

"Like an opening? A new exhibit?"

"Wine and cheese. It could be a valuable source of contacts, plus we need to upgrade the artwork in the managers' offices. If they have paintings we can use, it'll be mutual promotion. Will you come with me?"

"You bet."

"I'll pick you up at seven. Mel?"

"Hmm?"

His voice dropped. "I haven't been able to not think about you. You're... I mean..." His voice sank even lower. "... I probably shouldn't say this, but you're so... you're getting hard to resist. I'd like... I hope you'll find out soon enough what I'd like. Okay?"

Okay? Mel's voice dropped to match his. "Yeah. Me too."

His voice clicked back to normal, but she detected a trace of huskiness. "Good. See you at seven."

"Mel." She heard Amanda calling from the inner office, sort of, but didn't quite get her brain in gear to answer before her boss appeared in the door separating their offices. "Mel?"

She realized she was still clutching the telephone receiver. She glanced at Amanda, saw nothing terribly urgent, so sat back and sighed. "I've been blindsided."

"By a man?" Amanda's eyebrows went up.

"Yeah." She stretched, long and luxuriously. "The new bank manager at DCO downtown."

"I think I've met him. Chamber of Commerce. Last name Pope? Blond?"

"Damn, but he's hot."

"You and a bank manager."

Mel ignored the faint note of incredulity in Amanda's voice. "I told you. Blindsided." She returned the receiver to its cradle and executed a full rotation in her chair.

"What on earth has he done? I've never seen you approaching a swoon before."

Mel grinned. "Can't tell you. It's probably against company policy."

"But that was him on the phone?"

"Yeah." Mel gave a luscious sigh. "Oh, yeah."

"Jacob's excellent at telephone sex," Amanda said coolly. "Very imaginative."

Mel turned scarlet. Amanda and Jacob? The most straight-up, conservative couple she'd ever come across?

Then Amanda laughed. "I never thought I'd see the day."

51

"Oh, you're rotten. It was only the teeniest, little bitty bit, honest. More like a promise."

Having thrown her for a loop, Amanda returned to business. "Unfortunately, I have to drag you out of your reverie. I need you to cobble this report together, remember. A ton of statistics to condense into something readable."

"Sorry, I'm off balance. I don't know which end is up half the time."

"Statistics, Mel. Can I leave the numbers with you? You've done this often enough before. Have it ready for three o'clock?"

"It'll be a relief, working the numbers. That man's got himself into my head, and I need to get him booted back out, or I'll go crazy. Maybe I'm already crazy."

"Was that ever even a question?" Amanda returned to her office.

Mel treated herself to another lusty sigh, then settled into the task at hand.

Once again Mel faced the battle of the wardrobe. She wanted to get it right. A little flamboyance would be fun—this was an art gallery, after all—but she'd been there before and the place fairly screamed staid and restrained. This was business for Ryan, and she was determined to be the perfect partner. She settled on her standby burnt orange pantsuit, with shirring on the modest ivory blouse.

She sent up gratitude to the universe for her job. Thanks to the responsibilities she had at SI, she could talk business with almost anyone. Could she talk art? Not so much, other than the stuff they imported. But SI dealt in gift shop chic, not paintings worth thousands of dollars. At least she knew when to be modest and keep her mouth shut.

Ryan's greeting at her door was enthusiastic; Mel settled into his arms and welcomed his exploring mouth and wondered if going to the art gallery was overrated. But Ryan was a man on a mission this Tuesday night. "We have to go," he said, his mouth an inch from hers.

"You sure?"

"Very." They dis-attached. He helped her with her jacket, and they headed down the stairs. "I like that outfit, Melanie. It suits you, and it's professional."

"Thanks. This is my entertaining clients outfit." It was also the one she'd worn on their first date. It went well with her hair and skin tone without calling attention to itself.

"Appearances are so important," Ryan mused as they drove into Calter Creek. "Some call it shallow, but how you present yourself does matter. The way people perceive us can make a difference in my business."

"You're always immaculate. Makes me want to muss you up."

He flashed a grin at her. "Muss me up all you want, later. I'm youngish for a bank manager, you know. Right now it's about the image."

"I like the idea of later."

Ryan shook his head. "I meant later in the week. I have a ton of meetings tomorrow."

"Now I'm disappointed."

"Yeah, me too."

The gallery was bustling when they arrived. Mel saw several people she knew. That was the benefit and the curse of living for a long time in a small town; you were bound to be seen, and it was impossible to keep secrets. Ryan touched her back to escort her in the general direction of the refreshments. White wine in hand, they began circulating, with only an incidental study of the paintings on the walls.

She supposed that it was inevitable, given the crush, that she and Ryan would get separated. She found herself next to a heavy-set man in a severe suit, so she smiled and offered her hand. "Mel."

He took her hand briefly. "Peter. Are you a purchaser?"

"A browser. I'm one of those dreadful people who doesn't know much about art, but I know what I like. Don't you hate that?"

He laughed. "Take this one." He gestured at the painting closest to them. She and Peter fell into an easy discussion. After a couple of minutes, she felt a familiar hand on her back and turned.

"Ryan, there you are. Please meet Peter."

The men shook hands. "We've met," Ryan said easily. "How's business?"

The man named Peter was more interested in discussing the ups and downs of commerce in Calter Creek than the painting, so Mel once again drifted off, wandering through the crowd, looking at the pictures when she could get close enough to them...

... and collided with Adrian. She'd never seen him in suit and tie before. He appeared as comfortable in them as he did in his sort-the-books wardrobe.

"Mel, how delightful," he said when they and their wine glasses had stabilized. "I was wondering if we might want this for the coffee shop. What do you think?"

She immediately felt guilty, because the décor of the coffee shop had been the last thing on her mind. She studied the picture he'd been admiring. It portrayed two women in long dresses and large hats, drinking coffee from tiny cups and talking at a small bistro table. Light poured through a window into the room where they sat.

She turned to Adrian. "Yes. It's perfect."

He smiled at her. "It doesn't fit any of our concepts, though. It's an older scene, but it's a modern painting. We'd need to consider eclectic. But it makes a statement about what a coffee shop is meant to be, don't you agree? I think we should have it."

Delight turned to dismay. "Oh, but..." Mel's fingers brushed the subtle tag under the painting. "It's expensive, Adrian."

"But it'll set the tone, and I'm quite in love with it."

She heard a throat clearing beside her. She and Adrian had unconsciously moved closer together as they considered the painting. Ryan stood right at her elbow.

"Mister Pope." Adrian offered his hand.

There was a very slight hesitation before Ryan took it. "Purchasing some artwork?"

"I am." Adrian must have spotted one of the gallery owners because he waved, then turned his attention back to Ryan. "For the store. We discussed the plan in broad outline a few weeks ago."

"Yes, we did." Ryan had gone tight lipped. "This painting's a bit extravagant, isn't it? For a small-town bookstore?"

Adrian shrugged. "Depends on what you're building, I suppose." He excused himself to negotiate the purchase of the painting.

"Time to go." The crowd was thinning out. Ryan took her arm and steered her away.

Driving home he was quiet, not the comfortable kind of quiet, and Mel wondered why. Remembering Julie's words, she addressed his unresponsive profile. "You don't like Adrian, do you? That felt stiff."

"I neither like nor dislike him. His plans for that place don't show good business acumen. But he seems to appeal to you."

"He's a nice guy, and a friend."

"It bothers me that you're getting yourself involved in that place. The man doesn't know what he's doing, and your savings might be in jeopardy."

She chuckled. "It's not like that. He's made it very clear that he doesn't want my money. And I'm not that much of a fool. I'm not about to invest in a business I don't know anything about."

Ryan glanced over at her. "I'm glad to hear you're cautious."

Mel frowned. "The size of my savings and investments does suggest that I'm sensible where money's concerned. Plus at work I deal with financials all the time. I'm not a blind innocent ripe for a scam."

"I never implied that you were."

I think you did.

"But to buy that painting?" Ryan shook his head in disbelief. "When you have a commercial establishment, you go to a warehouse and you get prints. A bank is expected to spend

55

money on things like paintings for the executive offices. It's another thing entirely for a bookstore. You don't put up original art, or at least not of that quality. I'm relieved I never approved a loan for your Mister Forsythe."

"He's not mine, and did he ask for one?"

"No, it never came up. I don't have a clue how he's financing that thing."

Mel figured the bookstore's financing was Adrian's business. She'd been around him enough in the last three weeks to realize that he knew more about what he was doing than he let on. He was at home with rare and old books, for instance. His work on the store was more orderly than she'd thought at first. It was his mind that was out of control, not his actions.

And she was thrilled to think of the painting on the wall of the coffee shop. In her imagination she could see exactly where to hang it.

She didn't mention that to Ryan.

At her door he said, "You did me proud tonight. Peter Bailey is a big client of the bank, and he's a member of the Country Club. He liked you."

"Glad to help out."

Ryan finally smiled and put his hands on her arms. His deep blue eyes radiated sincerity as he looked at her. "It's important to have a helpmate. Someone who's gracious and says the right things. Who understands decorum, but isn't stiff with it. I suspect you'd be an excellent hostess."

"As long as the hostess doesn't have to cook. I've co-hosted receptions at SI for years. You set high standards."

"I do. Thank you for living up to them tonight."

They kissed and clung until he disentangled himself. He'd already told her he wouldn't stay. And once again, she didn't think the time was quite right to invite him to.

Adrian was downstairs when Mel arrived at the bookstore the next Saturday morning. She had a niggle on her mind. She and Adrian were friends, she was sure of that, and she was starting to get an idea of what refurbishing the store

56

was going to cost. The picture was wonderful, but surely he couldn't re-do the entire place at that level of luxury. Could he?

She stopped at the top of the stairs. He went around her—doing the perfect-gentleman thing, he'd followed her up the stairs—and disappeared through the door to the apartment.

Adrian had been busy. The large room was clean, although there was still plenty of work ahead. Proper lighting fixtures, patching and painting the walls—not the side walls, which were brick, but the front and back ones… the list went on.

He'd had the big windows washed. A table and two chairs stood in the coffee shop corner, with a red tablecloth and mismatched cloth napkins, a pink one and a blue and green plaid, in keeping with his mismatched china. The painting hung on the brick side wall, overlooking the table.

"It's perfect," she called.

"Marvelous." He appeared in the door to the apartment. "I'm beyond glad to hear that. I've been in here in body or in mind for the last twenty-four hours, planning how it ought to be. The picture?"

"Right where I'd imagined it. I didn't expect you to bring it over yet. I thought you'd leave it at the gallery until the place is finished. There's still a lot of construction and mess ahead."

He rolled a serving cart to the table with cereal, yogurt, milk, berries, juice, honey, coffee and tea, in the expected mishmash of containers, then held her chair for her. "It'll be going back, but I wanted you to see it. I wasn't convinced you were as certain as I was. On the other hand, I'd been standing there studying it for a good fifteen minutes before we collided, so I had a head start."

She wrinkled her nose. "Don't know where you got that idea. I loved it from the moment I saw it."

"Eat." This was another granola morning. He picked up the plastic berry container. "Sorry to lower the tone. I hope you don't mind."

She gave him an are-you-kidding look; she'd already dug the spoon into the granola. Sitting across the table from her, he fit perfectly under the picture. He was in the grubby old clothes again, but despite that there was an air about him. Worldly? Elegant, she decided. As if he could inhabit any upscale bistro and make it his own. Possibly it was the gray hair.

After she'd constructed her bowl of cereal and taken a sample bite, Mel got down to business. "There is one thing, though. It's none of my business, but it's been worrying me. About the picture."

"Go on. Whatever you want to know."

"Dangerous, Adrian."

"Not so very dangerous. I don't have any secrets I wouldn't share with you."

"Oh." She reflected for a moment, wondering if there were anything she'd keep from him. Then she plowed in. "I guess I worry about how much this is going to cost, and whether it stands any hope of paying for itself. The picture, and just upgrading the stairs and the elevator, the new fittings and stock and the coffee bar..."

He put a hand over hers. His was warm and firm. "Let me think a moment, how to explain this." He took his hand away, and they both ate granola and berries. Mel watched him while she ate; he caught her eye once and smiled, at ease with the answer he was formulating.

"I could say blame my family, I suppose," he said eventually. "When it was obvious that the family business and I were extremely unhappy bedfellows, they decreed that I needed to find something to focus on. There was a certain desperation involved or I might have ignored them, but I expect they were right, I do tend to ramble in my head and never get to any conclusions. So I started building this picture in my mind, a way to surround myself with a world that would delight me, morning to night. This is what I came up with. Coffee?"

"Yes, thanks. Given that you'd rather drink tea, you make incredibly good coffee."

"Quality of ingredients."

He poured, and she listened.

"I've told you my family are convinced I'm out of my mind, but I'm doing this for myself, certainly not for them, and not particularly for off-the-street clientele, although I hope they'll love it. And I don't want you to frown at me, so yes, I can afford it.

"Furthermore, I do have a business plan, and it's solid. I'll show it to you one day." He turned serious. "I believe the place will earn its keep, maybe not from walk-in traffic but from online sales and rare books, yes. It already is, in fact, if marginally. I admit it's driving me crazy, trying to locate what people believe I have in the disaster down there. Orders come in every day. And to set your mind more at ease, I had a professional go over the store's accounts before I bought it, so I knew that the rare book thing was the Morrisons' bread and butter."

She'd followed him, but the pieces still hadn't come together. "It's going to be an enormous outlay. Are you rich, Adrian?"

He grinned. "Rich enough, I suppose. My family, you see."

"No, not really."

"And so you worry. Please don't. Remember the Philadelphia Forsythes? My own needs are pretty small. I'll be fine."

If possible Adrian was more of a mystery than ever.

She let it go. "This is heaven." Mel stretched out her legs and leaned back in her chair, watching dust motes dance in the sunbeam coming through the upper half of the windows. "I can't see any scenario where people wouldn't choose this over the Coffee Shack."

"Oh, yes, the Coffee Shack. I took your advice. It's nothing like what I hope for here. No warmth. Regimented." He shared his impression of the downtown branch of the popular chain, then together they cleared up the breakfast things. They didn't linger in the kitchen. As soon as the milk, yogurt, and berries were safely in the fridge they headed downstairs. Mel twisted her hair into an elastic to keep it out of her face, and they approached the next shelf of books.

"It's these against us," Adrian said. "A pitched battle."

"I hope I don't chuck anything valuable."

59

"You won't. You know I check." He reached up and pulled out the first dozen or so books. "Here we go."

Mel sneezed.

Time drifted by. They were in a section of children's books, and she enjoyed flipping through the old pages, looking at the illustrations.

"Aha!" Adrian unexpectedly pounced on a book. "*A Natural History of the Hamptons,* eighteen eighty-seven. There was a query about this one a few days ago. I said I'd get back to the man, but I wasn't optimistic. I wonder how it got filed here. Do you want to guess its value?"

"Mmm... a hundred bucks?"

"Closer to a thousand. Look." They stood elbow to elbow as he showed her the still taut binding, the lack of markings on the pages, the author's signature. "Not authenticated, of course, but I expect it's real. I'll research it this week. It might not normally be worth that much, but the heirs have been in the market, trying to snap up every copy they can find. Probably that's two or three copies, no more. So the value gets pushed up."

"A thousand dollars? I'm astounded." Mel could feel her eyes widen.

"Flabbergasted?"

"Dumbfounded?"

"Gobsmacked?"

They both laughed. "I told you we're already self-sustaining." He carried the book over to the old counter.

Someone knocked at the door.

Mel glanced at her watch. "Oops. I have to go. Ryan's picking me up. That'll be him now, I bet."

Something flashed across his face that she couldn't interpret. "I concluded you're seeing him."

"Sure am."

"You're lit up under the dirt. He makes you happy."

"This could be the one," she blurted, then stopped herself. "Sorry. This is big for me." She raced for the front of the store.

"I'm sure he's a fine man. I wish you joy, Mel."

"Thanks. Hi," she said as she opened the door.

Ryan stepped in, immaculate in dark slacks and sport shirt. He looked her up and down. "What on earth happened to you?"

She looked for, and failed to find, some indication he was happy to see her. "It's surficial. I'm running late, and I still have to change. Okay if I use the upstairs bathroom, Adrian?"

"Of course." Adrian hadn't moved from the counter, his hand protectively on *A Natural History of the Hamptons*.

"Won't be but a sec." Mel grabbed the bag she'd left near the door and bolted upstairs.

When she got back down, the air had become… formal, she decided. As if Ryan and Adrian both were on their very best manners. But Adrian appeared considerably happier to see her than Ryan did.

"Next week?" she asked, her hand on the knob.

"If you can face it." Adrian grinned at her, breaking the frost that had settled over the room.

"I'll look forward to it." She put her other hand on Ryan's arm. "Let's go. We're only a little late."

The men nodded to each other. Ryan hustled her to his car, parked on a side street a block away, as if he couldn't get her away from the bookstore quickly enough.

He'd rebuffed her attempts at conversation as they walked, but Mel wasn't one to let things fester. "Tell me what's wrong," she said. "You look like the face of doom. I'm sorry I was running late, but we'd found a treasure in the books, and Adrian was explaining why it's valuable. I forgot the time."

There was a longish pause before he spoke. "The Davies are important, Melanie. He's on the Board at DCO, and he's a director of the Country Club. It's bad form to be late."

"It's a backyard barbecue. It's not that formal."

"Nevertheless, first impressions count. And seeing you so filthy…"

"I'm not now."

"No, you're lovely, as always."

They rode in silence for a minute. "Quite apart from a perceived risk to my savings, you don't approve, do you?" Mel finally said. "My spending time in the bookstore. Why not?"

"I'd rather not have this conversation right now, if you don't mind."

"I think I do mind. It's on the table, and I'm not going to be happy or comfortable until I know what's bothering you."

They were driving through a ritzy subdivision, so she figured they had to be close to the Davies' house. Ryan pulled the car over to the curb and threw it into Park. He kept his gaze on the road ahead and positively radiated impatience. "All right. It's a beaten up old building and he has to have an appalling business plan, if there even is one."

"There is," she interrupted. "I haven't seen it, but there is."

"The point is, people will assume you have a stake in that place, and frankly, it's doomed. It's not good for business for me to be associated with an obviously poor investment."

"You're convinced Adrian's going to fall on his face, and you don't want to be taken down with him. I'm not sure that makes any sense. You're not invested in the bookstore."

"I'm connected through you." Ryan's voice was flat.

"You're jealous."

"Don't be ridiculous."

"Then look at me." When he'd turned his gaze from the road to her she said, "He's a friend. You'd like him if you got to know him."

"I seriously doubt that, and you barely know him yourself. My impression is that there's something a little off. He's odd. I just hope he isn't dangerous."

Dangerous?

Mel studied him. This was her man, he was upset, and she was defensive. If she could make him understand… She banked the agitation and put her hand on his. "I enjoy working in the bookstore. I'm learning new things about retail and marketing, and that has to be good, given my job. Plus, it's exercise, believe it or not. With the paper off the windows, it's hardly private, so no one could possibly think anything's going on, if that's what's troubling you."

Ryan humphed. "I'm aware nothing's 'going on', as you put it. The man's almost certainly gay."

Something that had never crossed her mind. She filed the gay comment to mull over another time.

Mel squeezed his hand. She was flattered that he might be jealous, but wanted to make sure he understood he didn't have to be. "I agree Adrian's a little strange, but the more I talk to him, the more I'm convinced he knows what he's doing, at least in the big picture. I don't believe anyone's going to gossip, especially as it relates to you. The whole town knows me. A few people have even said they envy me, getting to help with the store. I've certainly been picking up excitement on the street. Everyone's curious."

"A bookstore in the downtown core doesn't stand much of a chance. Fixing up that dump… you'd have to do it on a shoestring to ever make it pay. The way he's doing it—"

"—is his call, I guess. Now, can we go to the Davies and wow them? Honest, Ryan, I'm right where I want to be, right now."

He seemed to collect himself and returned her pressure on his hand. "That's a nice dress, Melanie. You're very attractive today. I'm sure they'll be delighted with you."

"I'm sure they'll love you."

"I don't want them to love me. I want their respect, though. That's why it's so important—"

"No more. I hear you. Now, let's go before we're later than we already are. We're on time to make an entrance." She giggled.

Tentative peace restored, they drove off.

5

Mel caught on to the pattern of the afternoon quickly. The men formed a loose group in the yard, the women gathered at the patio table. The food had been catered or was from a good deli, so there wasn't much to do in the kitchen. She was younger than the other four women by at least ten years.

Maureen Davies, her hostess, introduced her around the table. "What can I get you to drink?"

A scan of the table told her that drinks tended to cocktails, not beer, which she would have preferred. Even the men held highball glasses. She was a little tired from her work at the bookstore, and stressed from her conversation with Ryan, so she took the prudent route. "Could I have a sparkling water, please?"

Maureen raised an eyebrow.

"It's hot, and I have a low tolerance. A cocktail sounds wonderful, but even with a wine cooler I'd risk being useless for the rest of the afternoon."

"Good for you to respect your limits. Make yourself at home, I'll be right back."

With her water to sustain her, she settled at the table and listened to the other women. The conversation swirled around a new restaurant on the old Columbus highway; one woman's diamond pendant, an anniversary gift; gossip about people she'd never heard of; and a tennis competition at 'The Club', which she assumed meant the Meadowlands Golf and Tennis Club, the one Ryan had applied to join.

Maureen turned the conversation to her at one point. "You and Ryan aren't married?"

"I suppose that makes you... partners?" She'd swear the woman called Jane shuddered delicately. "It seems to be the way things are done these days, all this shacking up and not bothering with marriage, I mean how can you build a solid family—"

"We're dating. It's a new relationship," Mel said hastily.

"Ryan's an asset to the community," Maureen said. She winked at Mel before adding, "We need more young men who have a sense of civic responsibility."

At least Maureen recognized Mel's attempt to head Jane off before the conversation got awkward. "Yes, he's solid, isn't he?"

"And you, dear, what do you do? I assume you don't have children?"

The inquisition. Digging into her life in the politest, most formal way. "No. I've never been married."

"Not that that stops some women," Jane put in. "No sense of propriety."

"It can be circumstances," Mel said. "I have a friend who's a single mother. She adopted a child from Eastern Europe."

Jane shut up. Maureen said, "I suppose you have a career, then. In banking?"

Mel smiled. "I didn't meet Ryan at work, no. I'm executive assistant to the president of Sinclair Imports."

"Executive assistant. Is that like being a secretary?" Jane asked. Her tone implied that Mel had been demoted from contender to placeholder.

"No, it's not. I do pretty much the same things my boss does, other than decision making. My job's to take some of the load off of her shoulders. I'm involved in marketing, finance, sales, the works. It's a rare day when I type a letter for Amanda. She does those herself."

"I see." Jane mercifully chose to let the subject drop.

A pushy woman called Denise interrupted to direct the conversation to more interesting channels. "The boys leave for camp in a week, thank heaven. Once school's out it's impossible."

65

"Mine are in the tennis program at the Club."

"Are you still considering Newhaven Academy?"

"Ashley's writing the entrance exams next week."

The conversation left Mel behind, although Maureen made occasional gestures to keep her involved, throwing questions her way. The attempt at a third degree had left her grateful to sit back and listen, with nothing to contribute to these alien women.

The subject of the renewal of downtown Calter Creek arose. "Imagine if a boutique women's wear store opened."

"Better than Creekside Mall. You'd swear teenagers were the only ones who ever shopped, for all the selection they offer."

"I don't suppose Calter Creek could support an independent shoe store."

"Maybe when Landmark opens."

Mel listened. This conversation would matter, to Ryan and to Adrian.

"I heard that a bakery's going into the store at the corner of Fifth. The one that used to be that little pharmacy?"

"I wonder if they'll serve coffee. A decent coffee shop that isn't a Coffee Shack would be wonderful."

"You're going to have one," Mel said. The conversation stopped and four sets of eyes looked at her. "A friend of mine bought the bookstore. The plan is to put a coffee shop on the second floor—it's amazing up there with those enormous windows. It'll be classy and unique."

"I'm glad that dump of a bookstore's gone. It was spooky, going in there. Filthy, too."

"Anything could fall on you. I heard there were bats…"

"I sort of doubt that," Mel said. "I've been helping with the cleanup, one book at a time. Some of those old books are valuable."

"It won't be a chain, will it? Like The Bindery? They're all the same. And far too much stationery and knick-knacks."

"No, definitely not a chain. I suppose The Bindery does what it has to, to stay in business, given the economy."

"Personally, I prefer my e-reader. Never set foot in a bookstore anymore."

"All that technology stuff leaves me cold. Anyway, who has time to read?"

"Are you going to the fashion show at the Club Wednesday?"

"I haven't seen the lunch menu yet. I hope they present better lines than last year."

"At least they try. There's new blood on the social committee..."

And so it went. She didn't talk to Ryan the entire afternoon, but listened and sipped, and willingly helped bring trays from the kitchen for their dinner. By the time the sexes converged over food, the party had become louder. Mel did a quick mental estimate of the bill for alcohol and whistled internally. These people were serious about enjoying their wealth. She sat next to Ryan at the patio table, ate, and wondered how many of these afternoons were in her future.

Still, she recognized the value of schmoozing. If this was important to Ryan, important for his career or even for his admission into the Country Club—in her mind the two were related—then she'd play her role.

His future was her future, after all.

It was after nine o'clock before they finally thanked their hosts and left. By then Mel was exhausted, and Ryan, she noticed, was on edge.

"Are you okay to drive?" she asked. "I've been sticking to sparkling water, so I can be designated driver if you want."

"I'm fine."

"Don't snap. I wasn't criticizing, just asking."

By then they were in his car. "Suppose someone saw us. How would it look if we changed places?"

"Like it was an alcoholic party and we're sensible. Maureen seemed to approve that I stuck to water. But with the sun and the long day, I would have ended up with a killer headache. Ryan, do you have any idea how tedious those women are? Talk about fancy schools and jewelry and tennis competitions..."

He pulled away from the curb and pointed the car toward home. "Stop living in your own little world, Melanie. That's not tedious to them. That's their life. It's what life can be, when you finally make it. Personally, I'd love to know where they send their kids to school. It's information we may need down the road."

"Then I'm sure that down the road we can ask them."

The conversation had spiraled right out of control, and Mel shut up. She longed to laugh about the dismal afternoon, but Ryan wasn't laughing. The men had probably talked business and sports, or compared lawn care companies. Ryan had fit right in.

And she was uncomfortably aware that she hadn't. At least she'd had the sense to be quiet, to listen well, to not make waves.

They drove back to her apartment in silence. Mel was sorry, and wasn't sure where to take things, but she wasn't taking them where she'd hoped. Ryan had drunk too much, he'd snapped at her, and he was holding himself tight as a drum.

They kissed at her door. She went in alone.

Mel's doorbell rang at eleven o'clock on Sunday morning. She checked through the security peephole, then opened the door, quickly.

Ryan charged in as if he was in a fifty-yard dash and she happened to be the finish line. He couldn't have glimpsed her ultra-casual clothes, her messy hair, because he locked her in his arms before she even got the door closed.

"I'm sorry, Melanie. I'm so sorry," he murmured into her hair.

This was a change of pace she wasn't ready for. She'd been thinking half the night about the tension when they'd parted the previous evening. And about the tedious backyard party and what it portended for their future.

Portended. Foreshadowed. Signified. Adrian would enjoy that one. She'd have to work it into the conversation next week.

Mel snapped back to the present. She and Ryan were so locked together they might have been one creature. His breath tickled in her hair; he rested his cheek against her head. She wiggled loose to close the front door, then looked at him. His nose and forehead were a little sunburned. "Sorry for what?"

"For the way we said good night. I was in a mood, Melanie. I shouldn't have been. The afternoon went very well."

"You'd had too much to drink and too much sun. Not good for anyone. Let's forget it, shall we? Do you want coffee?"

"Yeah."

He followed on her heels into her little kitchen. She aimed an elbow at his midsection. "Back, boy. Give me room to work."

"You're not mad?"

She shrugged and occupied her hands with measuring coffee into the filter. "I was upset last night. This morning, not so much. It was stressful, being with those people for so many hours. We just have to learn to deal with it."

He was silent, thinking. Then he said, "Yes, I agree about the stress. I didn't realize it at the time. I guess I need you to keep me in touch with what's really going on. You didn't have a good time, though."

"Not great, no. To me it was like business socializing. You do it, you say the right things or nothing at all, you hope you make a good impression." The coffee started, she led him back to the living room.

"Once they're a regular part of our lives, you'll find more in common. And of course we'll meet some of the younger members of the Club. Assuming I'm accepted."

"You will be. You're personable, respectable, a leader in the community, and solvent. What could go wrong?"

He dropped onto her sofa and pulled her down on top of him. Once again he wrapped her up against him. "Thanks," he whispered. "It means a lot to me. Sometimes I get overwhelmed…"

She spoke into his hair, quietly. "If we stick together it'll be all right."

69

They spent a few minutes exploring each other, touching, tasting... *reassuring*. Like partners do. Like a wife would do for her husband.

Like he'd done for her, rushing in, not making a formal speech, just holding her tight and showing her how he felt. Her mouth free for a moment, she sighed.

He was upright in an instant, looking at her. "What is it?"

"Nothing. You need to learn to recognize sighs of happiness." She got her fingers tangled in his hair, moving his mouth to where she wanted it, and showed him in the best way she could think of that she'd put last night behind her.

The coffee had been ready for several minutes before they got around to pouring mugs and settling at her little table. He meshed the fingers of his free hand into hers. "I'm so glad I found you," he said. Straight out, not particularly romantic, a statement of fact. Coming from Ryan, that gave it all the more credence.

"Me, too. Are you busy today?"

"No. Bank stuff, but not much."

"Then let's do something. I don't care if it's going out to the state forest or going to a show or vacuuming. I just want to hang out with you."

"Once we're in the Club we'll be playing tennis and golf and swimming all summer."

She clicked her mug against his. "The state forest and the vacuuming will still be there. Don't want all our eggs in one basket."

"I increasingly want all your eggs in one basket, Melanie."

She knew what he meant. Their eyes met. "I think," she said slowly, "they pretty much are."

He nodded. "But today you want to go to the state forest, right? I'm learning to read your signals. We'll have to call in at my place for my hiking shoes."

"And at a deli for lunch. There's a good one out the highway."

"A hike and a picnic. I'd enjoy that."

"I'm going to get changed. Stay put. Finish your coffee."

He grabbed her hand again as she walked past him, but said nothing. They looked at each other for a long moment. Then she gave his fingers a squeeze and escaped to her bedroom.

Mel sat on the edge of the bed for a second or two before digging in her closet for suitable clothes for a walk in the forest. The dream was back. *How,* she asked herself, *how could it get any better?*

You know how.

Yeah, she did. She wanted the lovemaking. Whenever, wherever. She wanted Ryan in her bed, or his bed, or any bed, or somewhere kinky like the kitchen counter. Or all of the above.

Because he was the one. No doubt about it.

The next Saturday evening she sat on Ryan's patio and enjoyed an excellent T-bone steak. She hadn't seen him since the previous weekend. The forest walk had gone a long way toward mending bridges between them, but she still felt a little off balance when she considered the tension and the uncomfortable Saturday barbecue at the Davies'.

Ryan was in high spirits. "Maureen Davies phoned me, Melanie. She loved you. Thought you were a breath of fresh air, and such excellent manners." His voice, consciously or not, imitated Maureen Davies' intonation. "She says you're a real asset."

"I'm glad. Good steak, Ryan."

"Thanks. You don't know what it means to me that I can trust you to make a good impression."

"Always happy to help."

Ryan sipped his wine, another Merlot. "That's what a marriage is. It's a partnership, two people working for a shared vision, a common goal. We pull together so well." He reached over and squeezed her hand. "You've done me proud."

Mel swallowed a bite of salad. "I was trying to be polite through a tedious afternoon. I'm still not sure why the Country Club's so important."

71

"The Club's only a part of it, a piece of the puzzle." He put his knife and fork on his plate and leaned back, cradling his wine glass. "It's an affirmation. Saying we have what it takes."

"Like social climbing?"

Ryan shook his head. "No," he said adamantly. "Building for the future. I won't be at the bank forever. Knowing the right people can make a world of difference to my career. Once we have a home and a couple of kids..." His eyes took on a daydream quality. "We'll have friends we can rely on, who share our goals. And information, like the women talking about private schools."

Mel stared at him while her mind engaged a few previously idle cogs and raced to catch up. "The house and kids?"

He snapped out of his reverie and sat up straight. His eyes met hers. In his she saw complete confidence that his life was unfolding exactly as he intended it to. "Well, yes. I haven't made any secret of my intentions. It's early to talk about it, but we both know where this is heading."

She'd hoped. Now she knew. For once wordless, Mel cut another bite of the perfectly tender steak.

"Come on. Tell me you're thinking the same thing."

She looked back up at him and turned pink. "Maybe. But we haven't even..." She flapped a hand between them. Mel had what she considered a reasonable quota of experience in the realm of lovemaking, but an unexpected flood of shyness hit her.

"Made love yet? We will, and very soon, I hope. It's driving me crazy, waiting, but I told you before. With you it's too important to be just another affair."

That 'very soon' got to Mel in private places that itched for attention; she squirmed. And then grinned at him. "You're good. You've planted that idea in my mind, and now all I can think about is getting my hands on you."

Ryan laughed. "Glad to hear it. That's where I want your hands."

Mel fiddled with the stem of her wine glass. "I've dreamed of the house, the kids. The Country Club was never a part of it, though. It's fun to throw a Frisbee around in a municipal park. Hamburgers at Joe's Café."

"I've been known to venture into municipal parks. It's another option, sure. It's good to vary our activities, it'll keep us from getting stale."

Ryan stood and offered her a hand. When she accepted it he walked them both inside to his sofa, where he pulled her down on his lap. He put his hands on, not in, her hair — *taming it* — and kissed her. Then he cradled her against him, settled their joined hands on his chest, and talked. About the sort of house and neighborhood he wanted, private schools for their children, horseback riding lessons, and for them the golf and tennis, the social occasions at the Club.

There wasn't a thing she could argue with. It sounded idyllic.

Then he added, "And we'll always have this, too."

He shifted so that his mouth was on the back of her neck, and the whole nature of the evening changed, fast. This time neither of them had any interest in keeping things under control. He ended up on top of her, sprawled on the sofa. Their mouths fused, tongues imitated what they both wanted, and hands went wherever they chose to, which was pretty much everywhere. He gasped, "I don't want to take you home tonight." Then he continued to show her why.

If she'd wanted to get her hands on him before, well, the reality was that Ryan naked was perfection. Ryan naked and next to her, naked, and touching her, driving her to where her whole body was desperate to go, was the stuff of dreams.

Later, sated, she lay next to him and watched him sleep. He had loved her with passion and tenderness. And skill; the man knew his way around woman's body. She was well satisfied, a little sad when it became evident there wasn't going to be a repeat. Grateful that fate had finally, *finally*, offered this gorgeous man to her. They agreed on the important things, they had a future.

Although...

If she was honest, it hadn't been much different from her other sexual experiences. The fireworks rating had been about the same.

But it was the first time with him. If she had expected anything else, like coming right out of herself and it happening over and over all night long and deep soul connections, well, she had to be more realistic. She was in love with a deeply conservative man, with solid values but not much flamboyance.

Was he too conservative? Flexibility wasn't exactly Ryan's middle name. But they'd both adjust. She could tone it down and he could ramp it up.

He looked so innocent, so trusting. Lying there watching him sleep, she reflected on the other things they shared. The ones you build a future on. Because that's where it was going, and they both knew it. He'd said it. Destiny had picked this man for her husband. And good unions were about compromise.

She didn't want to wake him, but she risked putting her hand on his chest. Fast asleep, he rolled away from her, taking her with him so they were cradled together. Mel settled her forehead against his back. What could be better, what could be more intimate, than holding her sleeping man, keeping him safe? She drifted off.

Sunday morning they had toast for breakfast, then at her insistence Ryan drove her home. She couldn't explain it, but with morning she felt unsettled, as if a vital contract had been signed, and the terms sounded excellent, but she'd missed something in the fine print.

The expectations, the dream? No, that couldn't be it. She had what she'd dreamed of for years. A more conservative, more upmarket version, but her dream nonetheless.

The sex? Ryan was an attentive lover, and she'd been well satisfied. That niggling sense of not-quite-right... *So what do you want? A big smarmy seduction scene?*

Maybe.

She had to stop reading romance novels.

She hauled a load of laundry to the communal laundry room at the end of the hall, cleaned her bathroom, and thought, but she couldn't pinpoint the problem.

Because, you twit, there isn't a problem. He's perfect for you, and he's into you, and you love him, and you're finally going to have the happily-ever-after you've longed for.

But she'd expected to be over the moon. She wasn't. She'd have to work on that.

Things couldn't be much better, Mel figured. The Fourth of July, meeting the gang at the park for touch football, beer and barbecue later, then fireworks… Mel loved fireworks, the sheer beauty of them.

With her man.

Since that night two weeks ago, the one that just missed being magical, she and Ryan had found time for plenty of practice. They'd spent nights at his house and at her apartment, where they'd laughed, cuddled, and talked about the shared dream. Touched and kissed and made love. If sex with Ryan meant once a night, well, Mel supposed grand passions involving multiple orgasms were fine in the romance novels she loved—and Ryan subtly disapproved of, but that was his problem—but probably didn't happen in real life. In fact, they both needed their sleep, there was no refuting the logic of that.

She loved the feel of him, too, when they were out together and he put his hand on her back or laid a casual arm across her shoulders, claiming her.

Neither of them mentioned her Saturday mornings at the bookstore. She knew he wasn't pleased about it, but she wasn't about to let him dictate who her friends were, or in what circumstances she saw them.

So the last two weeks had been great, and her spirits were high. She met Ryan at the door to her apartment in her favorite holiday outfit, a pair of white shorts that lived up to the name 'short' and a red top that didn't quite make it to her waistband.

She could see his reaction in his face, and it wasn't good. He came in and shut the door. "Melanie, sweetheart, you look like dynamite, but—"

"What's wrong?" She almost stumbled on the words as her mind processed his obvious disapproval—and discomfort.

75

He hesitated before he came out with it. "I haven't had a chance to tell you yet. I was invited to a party this afternoon at the Grants' place, Jenna and Duncan. They're in our demographic, Melanie, it'll be good to get to know them and—"

"And we already have a plan," Mel interrupted. "We're meeting Julie and a bunch of the others at the municipal park downtown. We agreed."

"Of course, but Melanie... honey, your friends will understand. This is important for me. Just for a couple of hours? Then if we can get away without making a fuss we'll go to the park." He paused, watching her as if gauging her reaction. "Duncan Grant runs the tennis ladder at the Club, his wife's an investment consultant, they're well-to-do and well connected. I promised we'd be there."

She was aware of a feeling she didn't want to experience where Ryan was concerned—blind anger. "And besides trashing our plans, I'm not dressed well enough for them, is that it?" Ryan had on conservative khaki slacks and an open-neck shirt. He certainly wasn't planning on touch football, dressed that way.

"The shorts are..." He waggled a hand.

Furious now, Mel raised her voice. "Your new friends won't be chasing a football around, and my friends can wait. And suddenly I'm expected to dress modestly for a backyard cocktail party instead of a casual picnic. Without any warning."

He had the grace to blush, but he didn't back down. "It's for us, Melanie. One more little step." He put his hands on her arms, stroking gently up and down.

"You didn't even check with me."

"It was last minute. Duncan was in the bank late yesterday. I was flattered to be asked, to be honest."

Mel sighed and tamped down her indignation, which unfortunately threatened to clog up her throat. He could have talked it over with her. There had been plenty of hours between late yesterday and right now. The idea that he didn't even tell her, never mind consult her, infuriated her. "I'm... I can't even find the words. I've been looking forward to hanging out with my friends all week. It's important to me for you to get to know them, too."

"We will. I promise." His hands continued their gentle brush on her arms. "As soon as we can get away without embarrassing our hosts, we'll go."

"I hope you didn't tell these people we'd be there at a certain time. Because it's going to take me a while to change." She could change in two minutes. She was damned if she'd do it.

Acting out, Mel.

It might be childish, but this once, she'd allow herself to be.

"I'll help."

"No. I'm perfectly capable of choosing the right outfit for the occasion." Mel shrugged his hands off her arms and stormed into her bedroom, closing the door behind her.

When she came back out twenty minutes later she'd changed into white slacks and a conservative top with three-quarter sleeves, and white sandals. She carried a bag with her original picnic clothes in it. "I phoned Julie to let her know we'll be there later. Let's go."

In the car Ryan apologized, stiffly. "Perhaps I should have consulted you. But I know we'll have a good time, and I was sure you'd see the importance."

"There's no 'perhaps' about it. Of course you should have asked me. And to be honest, no, I don't see why it matters so much. It's not rude to say you have a prior commitment, if it's true."

Ryan didn't answer. His tight expression told her he was no longer willing to be conciliatory. They drove the rest of the way in silence.

At least at this barbecue everyone hung out together, Mel wasn't exiled to an island of women. But within ten minutes she'd been exiled anyway.

"What exactly is an executive assistant?" Jenna Grant asked during the round of introductions.

"I provide support for the president. A lot of the record keeping, reports—"

She didn't get a chance to finish. Another woman in the group talked right over her, and the conversation turned to other, no doubt weightier, matters. Like the stock market, and the latest theories of raising teenagers.

Always nice to play second fiddle to hog futures and rude skateboarders.

But she got it. These were six 'professional' women and men — she mentally added the quotation marks — and no matter how much responsibility she had, the word 'assistant' in her title and the lack of wedding ring and children told them she wasn't worth their consideration. They were polite enough, on the surface, but they didn't listen.

Mel stayed on the outside of the conversation and drank ginger ale. Two hours into the afternoon — that is, around the time Ryan said they could leave — some man named Jim actually hit on her. She walked away from him.

At the three-hour mark she went over to Ryan, who was engaged in an energetic debate on federal policy and oil extraction, and raised her eyebrows at him. There was no question that he knew what she was asking, but the discussion continued unabated. They weren't going to make it to the party in the park. She stuck with Ryan, occasionally adding a comment. She could have killed him where he stood, but at least by allowing him to assert ownership, so to speak, she kept the lecher named Jim away.

It was clear to her that Ryan relished every minute. He fit right in, had plenty to say on every topic, and was a good listener, a good questioner. She could see his stock going up in everyone's eyes. *Good for him,* she thought sadly.

Driving home, too late for the municipal fireworks, Mel found herself close to tears. In fact, in tears. She kept it quiet; she didn't want comfort from Ryan. Not right now.

At her door she tried to make an escape, but failed. Ryan came in with her and pulled her down on her sofa. It wasn't a cool night, but she wrapped the cerulean throw from the back of the sofa around her, like armor. "We should talk about it," he said.

"Talk if you have to." Her voice was flat and sulky, but she didn't care. She felt hollowed out inside, left with nothing.

"You got quiet. You stopped smiling."

The anger mounted again. "Is that a criticism? Because if it is, I'm not accepting it. I was humongously disappointed, and I was ignored except for that Jim guy, the one who tried to feel me up." She twisted to look at him. Her stomach picked that moment to cramp, but she ignored it. "I can discuss politics and the economy. I have opinions and I can back them up. You know what I hate? I hate when I say something, and it's ignored, and ten minutes later someone else says the *exact same thing*, and everyone's all over it like it's holy revelation. That happened twice today. *Twice.* They disrespected me, Ryan. So yeah, I wasn't very happy."

"It felt good to me, having you close."

"You made a great impression," she said wearily. The cramp wasn't going away. She wanted a cup of herbal tea. She didn't want to fight with Ryan. She just wished he understood.

He pulled her back down and encircled her with his arms again. "We both did. Together. But Melanie, you know what the problem was, don't you?"

She struggled out of his arms and stood, taking the cerulean throw with her. Her face felt frozen. "You're saying I was the problem."

"No, honey, of course not. It's that you have a job, not a career. People have a hard time seeing beyond it. It doesn't buy you any credibility." He grabbed her hand, keeping her close, looking up at her. "Listen. Don't fret about it tonight, but listen. You've said that you could do Amanda McKinnon's job. That you understand Sinclair Imports' business that well. But you stay in a position that's... well, it's administrative. It's subservient."

"It is *not*. How can you say that to me?" The tears were coming back, tears of disappointment and Ryan not understanding and life unraveling. She shook off his hand, let the throw slide to the floor, and headed for the kitchen.

He followed her. Once she'd started the kettle he pulled her into a hug. "Don't cry, baby."

"I missed my friends, I had two texts from Julie wondering what the hell. And they ignored me. Those people didn't even try to find out who I am. Right now I'm tired and I'm annoyed and..."

79

She gave up and turned away, but he didn't let go. He let her turn in his arms, then pulled her back against him.

"Listen, sweetheart. You've got the ability, so why aren't you heading one of those departments at SI? Think about it. More money and respect. Status. Meeting people on an equal footing."

She wanted to argue. She wanted to say that with her friends she was on an equal footing. That at SI she was liked and respected, her opinions mattered.

She didn't say any of it. Instead, she sighed. "Let me get the tea, Ryan."

"A cup of tea will do you good. Let's drop it for now, but consider what it would mean, for you, for us."

She didn't invite him to stay. Even cuddling, after the tea had worked its magic on her stomach cramp, didn't cheer her up. In fact, she did her best to hustle him out the door.

She lay awake late that night. She'd expected growing pains, but these were almost too painful. She'd fallen for this man, she loved him, and he'd made his intentions clear. But they couldn't seem to find the same page, despite shared goals.

6

The post-July-Fourth workday was always a busy one for Mel. A day skipped during the week meant a pile-up of work, as if the stuff multiplied during the day off. But equally important, as far as she was concerned, was catching up on the news. Mel looked forward to her colleagues' holiday stories.

She didn't say too much about her own July Fourth, although a little casual checking around told her that she'd hit a jackpot, society-wise. The people at the Grants' gathering were big shots.

Just not much fun. And their manners could use polishing.

However that might be, escaping for lunch and meeting Julie and their friend Bryony Green at Joe's was at once a relief and a challenge.

Over a slice of pizza from the take-out window, Julie said, "So what happened?"

"I tried. I swear to God I did. Ryan was determined we had to be at this society backyard thing." Mel took a bite of her pizza wedge, then slurped her root beer.

Bryony was censorious. She was always one to lay it on the line. It made their friendship both awkward and valuable, since when Bryony was around, no one got away with anything. "Everyone wondered. Is he a cold fish, Mel? It's rude to accept another invite when you already have plans."

Julie could be just as blunt, but today she was in peacemaker mode. "What's the story on this other thing? We all kept expecting you to turn up."

"A point I made. I wanted to have fun," Mel said. "Instead, I was stuck with discussions about the Middle East

81

and oil pipelines. Plus they were snobs. Ryan said we'd leave after a couple of hours. I should have seen through that one."

"He probably tried." Julie was doing her best to be supportive. "It can be hard to get away."

"I'm still not getting it," Bryony said. "It's never *that* hard. Especially if you've told them up front you have another commitment."

"Fireworks once a year, and we missed them." Mel thought it was safer to emphasize the fireworks. Going too far along the dissatisfaction path felt disloyal to Ryan.

"We had fun. Touch football, hamburgers, beer... your book seller was there."

"Adrian?" Mel sat up on their picnic bench.

"Yeah," Bryony put in. "He's okay. I was braced for him to be weirder. He talks kind of funny, is all."

"Not always. I'm glad. I had half a worry in the back of my mind, what he was doing for the holiday." It felt strange to picture Adrian with her friends, outside the bookstore. She regretted not being there even more. It could be that she was growing proprietary about Adrian.

"He's kinda cute. Is he spoken for?" Bryony asked.

"Not as far as I know. He's never mentioned a significant other." The suggestion that he had a life, friends, possibly someone special, outside of the bookstore... she had no right or reason to be possessive, but it made her feel odd.

Julie said, "So, tell us about life in the fast lane."

Mel gave an accurate, but not overly detailed, description of her afternoon. The filet mignon instead of hamburgers. The champagne instead of fireworks. She hadn't seen the point of champagne.

"But you felt like an outsider?" Julie had polished off her pizza wedge while Mel talked. Now she licked her fingers before doing a final cleanup with her napkin.

"Ryan says it's because of my job. Because I'm 'just' an executive assistant no one will ever believe I have a brain in my head. Do you think that's true?"

"Of course not," Bryony said with some force. Bryony was always ready to be indignant for a friend. "You've got a headful of brains. Anyone who listens to you for two minutes… I mean your vocabulary's amazing."

"Must be all the dictation I take. All the documents I file," Mel said with a shade of bitterness.

"Yeah, must be. Come on, when was the last time you took dictation?"

"I don't even know how. I do file sometimes, though." Mel raised her eyebrows. Both women burst into laughter.

"You're not dumb," Julie said. "They're blind. It's rotten of Ryan to subject you to that kind of afternoon."

"Enough said. He's a man on a career path, and that means cultivating contacts. I hope that once he gets into the Country Club things will settle down."

"After you're married, maybe you could invite me to the restaurant at the Club?" Julie asked. "I hear they have a fantastic buffet Wednesday evening."

"Happy to." Her good mood restored, Mel cleaned her fingers the same way Julie had, and the three women separated to return to work.

The bookstore was unlocked. She opened the it to the tune of voices. It sounded as if Adrian had been doubled and was talking to, and occasionally talking over, himself.

She paused in the doorway, then let herself the rest of the way in, shoving the door closed behind her.

The voices stopped. "Hello up there," she called.

"Mel. At last." This voice was Adrian's. It had his lilt to it, his sense of anticipation, as if he'd looked forward to her arrival.

She'd made it to the foot of the stairs, in fact had one foot on the bottom tread, when they appeared above her. Side by side, Adrian and—she paused. The man with him had to be the brother he'd mentioned, the resemblance was so strong. The same long, limber mouth. The same shape eyes. The new man had light brown hair and stood up straighter. Both lanky frames were clad in khaki slacks and short-sleeved knit shirts. Only one possible interpretation. Mel was about to meet another Forsythe.

Adrian broke up the tableau by bounding down the stairs and taking her hand. "Come up, you're just in time—or a little early, I've barely begun the breakfast yet but there *is* coffee. Nearly."

"Hi," Mel said to the new man, who hadn't followed Adrian downstairs but stood watching from above.

"Hi. Glad to meet you."

"You too."

Adrian released her and followed her up. At the top of the stairs, Mel held out her hand. The stranger shook it, then kissed it. Old-fashioned gallantry ran in the Forsythe family. Up close she could see that the newcomer's eyes were a deeper, richer blue than Adrian's gray-blue ones

"Mel, please meet Houghton."

She guessed at the spelling, since he pronounced it 'Howton'.

"Which neither of us could say when we were young, so he's been called Huff all his life." Adrian led his guests to the kitchen. "It's generally agreed that I won the name sweepstakes, even if I lost a few others. Huff, this is Mel."

"About whom I've heard," Huff said. "I must say, you live up to billing. Gorgeous hair." He smiled and held out a chair for her. Adrian, who seemed somewhat manic, brought the French press over to the table.

"The brother," she said.

"Yes," Huff said.

"More than," Adrian confirmed.

She raised her eyebrows. The two of them were like a Mutt and Jeff routine at the moment and she'd be grateful for an answer or two, but this was the bookstore, after all, where enough weird things had happened that nothing surprised her.

"Twins, I'm embarrassed to admit," Huff said.

"Fraternal, which lessens the bite." Adrian was at the stove with his back to them. Mel smelled bacon and assumed he was working on eggs.

Huff sat and fiddled with the French press. "How long for this thing? I'm desperate."

"Four minutes." Adrian looked over his shoulder and winked at Mel. "You can suffer that long."

"You see how little sympathy I get. Just because he's older."

"Are you?" Mel was amused. Huff seemed older. She'd be willing to bet he acted older, too. More serious. Even in a golf shirt and khakis, the man had a gravity that Adrian seldom aspired to.

"My privilege," Adrian said. "Not that it ever mattered very much. We're so different that it wasn't a case of competition."

"Other than running the company," Huff put in.

Adrian sighed. "The Philadelphia Forsythes, remember? But who got to play in the company sandbox wasn't actually up to either of us."

"Dear Papa...," Huff gave the word an accent on the second syllable, "... had his own ideas."

"Which thankfully have been put to rest." Whatever Adrian was concocting was making Mel's stomach feel growly. She loved Saturday mornings since she'd stumbled onto Adrian's breakfasts.

Obviously not willing to wait any longer, Huff started pushing on the plunger of the coffeemaker. "Cream and sugar, unless I miss my guess," he said, looking at Mel.

"Black, unless I miss my guess."

Huff laughed. "God, Adrian, she's already one of us."

"Told you." Adrian appeared with plates holding cheese omelets, roasted tomatoes, and bacon, then retreated to bring over the teapot.

Mel looked from one brother to the other, concluded that this morning was no stranger than most mornings at the bookstore, and tucked into her omelet.

Later they toured the store, and it was quickly evident that Huff knew books as well as Adrian did, although he didn't care as much about them. "And he's got you working, going through this dump?" he said. "You're a courageous woman."

"It's kinda cool. I'm learning, anyway. And he promised, no Franco-Prussians."

"A brave promise, in the face of this mess. Adrian, is there any chance we could get more coffee down here?"

"So you can talk about me while I'm gone?"

"Yes, in a word."

Adrian shrugged and disappeared back up the stairs.

"So," Huff said, "my brother."

"What about him?" Mel wasn't sure where this was going.

"Good man."

"No argument. Are you trying to tell me something?"

"Not really, unless there's something you want to hear. This is your chance. What do you want to know?"

"About what?" Mel's mind, having been on overload for the last hour, went temporarily blank.

"Men like Adrian don't come along every day. You must wonder about him."

Mel shook her head. "Not a lot. He has this vision, and helping has been... it's hard to describe. Like an enchanted kingdom. If I wanted to know anything, I'd ask him. We're friends."

Huff's face grew more serious. He leaned against the end of one of the double shelves of books, studying her. "He'd tell you, too. You're seriously enjoying this? It's a little mad, renovating this place. Not as utterly insane financially as it appears, but that's my brother."

They shared a silence for a minute, eyeing each other. Then Mel said, "Okay, here's a question. What did you mean earlier when you were talking about running the company? A family business? Adrian used to run it?"

"That sums it up. Our father had a heart attack, a minor one, but it completely freaked Mom, so she needed a scapegoat to take over while she hauled Dad off to some Caribbean island to recuperate for a year or so. I was interested, but I had another commitment. Adrian wasn't interested—"

"Be honest." Adrian's voice joined them as he made his way down the stairs with a tray. "On paper I had the skills, but I was never cut out for big business, any way you try to soft pedal it."

"True enough. But you were the resident son. Problem was," Huff went on, "while Adrian was almost desperate not to do it, I wanted it. It drove a wedge between us for a while."

"It shouldn't have, but it did," Adrian confirmed. "Thank heaven, you might say, my health took a beating. I got out, and Mom and Dad saw the error of their ways. We're all better off." The tray held the newly charged French press, mugs, cream and sugar. He set it on the old checkout counter and joined them in the middle of the room.

"Your health?" Adrian certainly had nothing wrong with his health these days that she could detect.

"Old story," Adrian said dismissively.

"No secrets?" Huff countered.

Adrian glared at his brother, although there wasn't much weight behind it. "I wasn't very robust as a child, not like the jock here," he said, tipping his head at Huff. "Missed a lot of school. Then when I was twelve I got a nasty flu that felled me for a year. There is a theory in the family that that accounts for... well, for whatever it is that I am. Left too much to my own devices, our father says. Made me strange."

"You're not strange," Mel said.

"Are you kidding?" Huff asked her. "You can say it. My brother is not conventional."

Mel grinned at Adrian. "No, conventional, you're not. You don't strike me as sickly now." She'd been ping-ponging back and forth between the brothers all morning; her head was reeling. "So where does the family company fit in these days?"

Adrian flushed. "So, after a couple of years..." He glanced at Huff, clearly uncomfortable. "Okay, I said no secrets. The thing is, we're fairly well to do. Not Fortune 500, but I don't have to worry about buying pictures for the coffee shop." He stalled.

"Talk," Huff commanded.

Adrian scowled, but he talked. "Mel, our family owns The Bindery."

Mel's eyes grew wide. Everyone knew The Bindery. It was the premier bookstore chain in the country. Adrian *owned* it?

87

Adrian had *run* it?

"Yes," he said, with that uncanny ability she'd noticed before to anticipate her thoughts. "Or at least the family does. These days Huff's in charge. But I was president and CEO when we had to close forty-two stores."

Adrian turned from them both and looked out the front door, into the bright daylight. "It still gets to me. Hundreds of people out of work, people with families, commitments. There I was, a wealthy man, and no way to save the livelihoods of so many people. I signed the papers and closed the stores. Then I went home and quietly fell apart."

"Poor Mother was distraught," Huff said. "First the flu when he was a kid, then this. He wouldn't even let us in the front door for weeks."

Mel ignored Huff. She could see it so clearly, from the pain in his posture. Making a hard decision, but sacrificing himself.

After a silence while everyone regrouped, Huff spoke to Adrian's back. "You saved the company. It might not have looked that way at the time, but when we go back and reconstruct it, it's so obvious. We have well over a hundred healthy stores now."

"I know. I knew it then. That wasn't the point. Anyway," Adrian said, turning back to them, "I'm pleased to report that Huff came out of the whole debacle on top of the world, and on top of the company. He was finally getting to do what he should have been doing all along."

"And you finally have this bookstore," Huff retorted. "Coffee, Mel?"

"I could use a cup."

Adrian squeezed her shoulder. "Don't let us overwhelm you. The Forsythe brothers' routine is more than most people can take over a sustained period of time. We can be exhausting."

Huff put a cup of coffee into her hands. "Think of it as a test. An audition. If you can handle this morning, you can handle anything."

"I've enjoyed this morning."

Adrian said, "Once you two have finished swilling that stuff back, let's tackle one of the shelves, then we'll go find lunch."

Huff looked dubiously at the dusty books, then at his immaculate clothing.

"Yes, you must," Adrian said pre-emptively. "You owe me. And I did warn you."

Mel drank half her mug, then took Huff's mug away and put them both back on the tray. "If you have any more deep dark secrets," she said, "please don't tell me. I don't have the energy for them."

Adrian and Huff exchanged a glance. "Works for me," Adrian said. "An air of mystery... I always wanted to be a mysterious sort, but it's never quite worked out."

"Shut up, brother," Huff said.

"Good idea. Sorry, Mel." Adrian went to the storage room in the back and came out with several cardboard boxes, and the three of them set to work.

Mel weeded out the worm-eaten books and passed likely candidates to one of the brothers. The room had fallen quiet, as if even for Adrian and Huff the banter had become too much. As if they were both trying too hard. She sensed an undertone, something that wasn't being said, despite their promise to answer questions.

Huff was as likable as Adrian, but he was clearly the more conventional of the brothers. At times she got the feeling that he was determined to look after Adrian, make sure he didn't go off some undefined deep end. And Adrian—he welcomed Huff, but with an edge of defiance that suggested Huff challenged his right to live the way he chose. There was a dynamic between the two men she didn't get.

"In case you're wondering," Adrian said out of the blue, "yes, we almost read each other's minds. The effect of being *in utero* together, even if not from the same egg. Or so we've always believed."

"Drove the parents crazy, the way we'd know what the other one was thinking," Huff said.

"Drove us a little crazy, too," Adrian muttered.

"Insights into my brother's mind? Definitely crazy-making," Huff said.

"So if you're picking up vibrations between Huff and me," Adrian continued, "please don't worry about it. We live with it."

Mel looked at Adrian, who stood holding a book and frowning at it. "You pick up on my thoughts, too. I've noticed it before."

He smiled at her, an affectionate smile. "As you do mine. But we always have, you and I." He spoke quietly, as if he didn't want Huff to hear.

"It's spooky," she said, and went back to her side of the shelves.

But it gave her even more to consider. Perhaps he was right, and she did fit in with these unusual brothers.

Over lunch at Joe's—Club sandwich for Adrian and her, beef dip for Huff—she learned more about Adrian's brother. That he was happily married, with kids eight and ten years old. That he'd taken to running The Bindery like a duck to water. That they had a background of country clubs, tennis camps, and Ivy League schools. That got a groan out of Adrian. "You'd think they might have—"

"No point speculating where the parents are concerned," Huff interrupted. "They're a force of nature."

So Adrian was from a rich family, and had been well educated, and was weak and ill as a boy. And here he was now, in Joe's Café in Calter Creek.

Well, maybe country clubs could work out, she concluded, extrapolating to her own situation. If that type of life could produce men like Adrian and Huff, it couldn't be such a big deal. Maybe Ryan was right.

When they parted ways at the door of the bookstore Adrian held her back a minute. "I won't be here next weekend, Mel. I have to do duty at home."

"Cousin Agatha is getting married," Huff put in. "Aggie would kill him if he didn't turn up. Literally."

"We don't mess with Aggie. So no work next weekend."

"There went breakfast," Mel said. "I'll miss you. Have a wonderful wedding."

The brothers groaned in unison.

Mel wished Huff a safe trip home and said goodbye. Adrian looked drained. It was clear that while he loved his brother, Huff's presence had worn him out.

Or possibly it was how much he'd revealed about himself. Things she'd never even thought to ask. With Adrian, she accepted him as he was, here and now. Where the Philadelphia Forsythes were concerned, she'd had no real curiosity, because it hadn't mattered. Adrian so fully filled up the present that the past simply wasn't relevant.

Well, that had changed. She turned it over in her mind, driving home. This new perspective of Adrian. His money. His corporate career. His close tie to his brother. The unspoken secrets? Did he make more sense, or less?

Interlude

Huff located Adrian on the deck, where he'd propped himself on the surrounding rail, looking out over Calter Creek. "Nice," Huff said.

"Yeah."

"You want to talk?"

"Not much."

He settled in next to his brother. The skyline occupied them both. "I like Mel. She's just the way you described her. And she's one of us."

Adrian laughed shortly. "I don't get much work done Saturday afternoons, as a rule."

"Does she know?"

Adrian didn't answer.

"Okay, let me make a wild guess. Besides the store closures, you're still blaming yourself for Deanna. You know how many years ago that was?"

"Fifteen. Don't go there."

"What hurts you hurts me. It's self-preservation on my part."

The skyline of Calter Creek occupied both brothers for a few minutes. "What's next, Adrian?"

"Can't you ever let things lie?"

"Are you kidding me?"

Silence. Huff knew exactly what his twin was thinking. But he wanted to hear it.

Finally, Adrian said, "Next? Nothing."

"Won't work, Brother. I can read you like a book."

"She's taken."

"Bull. Apart from the effect she has on you, she belongs here. Give her another month and she'll read you as well as I do. It's possible she already does."

A note of bitterness tinged Adrian's words. "Yeah, she could be our kid sister."

"That's not what I meant."

Both men straightened. Adrian met his brother's eyes. "When she's been with him, she's radiant. Drop it, Huff."

"No. Not with your happiness at stake."

"I destroyed a life once. I'm not risking that with Mel."

Huff was all too familiar with that tight, pinched-lip expression on his brother's face. He'd seen it most recently when the stores had to be closed, but it dated to the long-ago incident with Deanna. "You're still punishing yourself."

"There are times I wish you'd go away."

"Could be worse. It could be Mom."

The sound Adrian made resembled a laugh, but there was no humor in it. "It's too late. I'm too late. She's head over heels. As long as I don't upset the cart I can spend Saturday mornings with her. Having me as a friend is important to her."

Huff frowned into his brother's face, studying him. Adrian didn't even try to break free of his brother's gaze. He wouldn't dare; they'd had a lifetime of these mutual scrutinies. "I'm glad I came," Huff said finally. "So I'm in the picture. If it gets bad."

"If?" Adrian snorted. "I'll be fine. Bury myself in work."

"You're going to make this place a success. Not as off-the-wall as the folks think."

"Of course not." Adrian turned away, gazed out across northern Calter Creek. "It's a good town. I could put down roots here."

"You ever need me…"

"Yeah." He pushed off the railing and walked away, leaving Huff alone on the deck.

7

"What do you think?"

What she thought was locked in her head. Mel was speechless.

At her side, Ryan looked dignified, but she sensed his excitement, right through the hand he'd laid proprietarily on her arm.

"It's gorgeous," she managed. Faced with the room before her, Mel felt like a ragamuffin dragged in off the street. The bar in the clubhouse at the Meadowlands Golf and Tennis Club was beyond anything she'd ever imagined, all polished wood with deep leather chairs. Plush, floor-to-ceiling burgundy curtains punctuated the wall of windows that looked out over a stone terrace and a small lake bordering the golf course. The place gleamed in the filtered evening light.

"Wait till you see the dining room," Ryan whispered.

A few groups were scattered around, but the room itself was more than spacious enough to accommodate ten times as many. Maybe twenty times.

"Come on." He gave her a nudge and led her to one of the smaller tables by a window. He held her chair as she sat. "This time of day it's bar service only. What would you like to drink?"

"I guess it's sort of old fashioned, but could I have a Manhattan?"

"You're not worried you'll fall flat on your face?" The skin around his eyes crinkled with mischief; he was teasing her.

She grinned back. "On one drink, no. It seems appropriate, sort of dignified. This is amazing, Ryan."

She watched him amble across the room to the bar, nodding to one or two people he passed.

So this is the Club. This is what all the fuss is about. Ryan had paid his dues the previous afternoon. The place was his.

He fits. His bearing, the way he dressed, the casual but polite way he greeted the people he passed... yes, the Club and Ryan were a good match. Mel was happy for him, and for herself by extension. She wasn't a la-di-da person, she reckoned, but sitting here in her lightweight ivory pantsuit, in a world of high gloss... Mel told herself to keep her excitement in check. She turned to the window and watched golf carts on the course across the pond. More groups of people worked their way toward the clubhouse.

What amazed her most was the other patrons, the fifteen or twenty people who looked as if they were fresh off the golf course or tennis courts, and who acted as if this were just another gathering place. Mel didn't see how she could ever be that cool.

She ran a finger across the table's smooth surface, taking it in and smiling up at Ryan as he set her drink in front of her. "Scotch?" she asked, nodding at his glass.

"Bourbon. I'd heard they stock a couple of higher quality ones, the kind you don't usually find in the liquor store. Thought I'd give it a try, this once."

She lifted her glass, and he clicked it with his own. Ryan might be restrained on the outside, but she picked up on his excitement; it was almost palpable. He spoke quietly, for her ears only. "We're here, Mel. We're going to love this place. There's a buffet on Wednesdays, and dances and social events on weekends. I'll get you a copy of this month's calendar."

"I'm always up for a buffet."

"My hungry girl," he said affectionately.

A busboy came over with a plate of tapas, or appetizers, or whatever the Club called them. Mel looked a question at Ryan.

"Not me. Must come with the service. I didn't order them."

"No bowls of peanuts? This is a whole new level."

"Yeah." Ryan leaned back with a contented sigh.

Mel sipped and raised her eyebrows at the liquid in her glass, making a mental note to go slow. She hadn't actually known what went into a Manhattan, it just sounded fitting. Pure alcohol, she concluded. She was more of a beer woman, and a serious cocktail could, in fact, find her flat on her face after one drink.

"I plan to sign up for golf lessons. I've played a few times, but not well. If I want to be a good companion on the course, I have to improve. You could take lessons, too."

"And then we'd play together?" She was doubtful that she wanted to golf at all. "Do they do that? Sort of like mixed doubles in tennis?"

"I'm not sure, but we'll find out. You can play in a ladies' foursome, get to know some of the other women."

"Maybe." She drew the word out while she turned it over in her mind. The idea of playing golf with Jenna Grant and her cohort didn't give her warm fuzzies.

Rally, Mel. She gave herself a shake. "Okay, I'm up for new experiences. I can always drop it if I don't enjoy it, right?"

"It'll be fun, you'll see. And an enormous social asset."

She wrinkled her nose at him. "Not a good enough reason, Ryan."

"Trust me."

They sipped in silence for a few minutes. Mel did her best to take in the opulent surroundings while her mind struggled with the total implausibility of golf being a real part of her future. And yet here she was, entitled to be in this incredible bar, with Ryan making no secret of his intentions regarding *their* future.

"I want to take you to the dining room tonight. We won't be able to do that on a regular basis, what with saving for a house and all, but it's sort of a special day."

"I'd love to." She'd have to be careful. The sheer romance of this incredible place could swallow her alive, at least until she got used to it.

Get used to it? Ever? Are you kidding?

If the bar was impressive, the second-floor dining room knocked her on her figurative fanny. "I'm not sure I can ever live up to this," she whispered. The ragamuffin, kid-off-the-street feeling crept up again.

"You're perfect," he whispered back as they followed the formally suited maître d' to their table.

The room gleamed with crystal and silver against dark, polished wood. Chandeliers provided light—but were unnecessary at the moment, given the floor-to-ceiling windows facing the golf course. Tasteful, restrained. She sat up a little straighter, resolved to skip wine since the Manhattan buzz was sailing through her veins, and did her best to look at absolutely everything without goggling like a country bumpkin.

Ryan was thrilled. She knew him well enough to see through the blasé veneer. Over menus, watching the sun settle toward the horizon through the smoked windows, talking over sole and pork tenderloin, they shared their mutual amazement. *We're drowning in this place,* she thought. *It dominates our senses, our conversation.*

On their way home, Mel took a deep breath, as if she needed to get normal air into her lungs after the rarified atmosphere of the Club. "It's so *big.*"

"Beyond the obvious? What do you mean?" Ryan glanced briefly from the road to her.

"It's a whole new world, where you don't know how the natives live or what they do or expect. It's exciting, but it's kind of overwhelming, too."

He smiled at the windshield. "You'll get used to it, sweetheart. It's just trappings. The people are still people." She wondered how he pulled it off. *It's as if he grew up in country clubs.* But his background was as solidly middle class as hers.

"To you. To me they're exotic birds. They don't speak my language, based on experiences so far."

In front of her apartment building he switched off the car and turned to her, gathering her up as best he could across the console. "You'll understand them better as you get to know them. You'll adapt."

The across-the-console interlude grew more interesting and intense, so it was several minutes later when he escorted her to her door. "I won't come in tonight, Mel. It's been a big day and I'm tired, plus the auditors are here tomorrow. But I wondered, have you given any more thought to the suggestion I made? About taking on another role at SI?"

She had, lots, but hadn't convinced herself it was a good move. "Not enough."

"Let the idea grow on you. Some day soon we'll talk. Perhaps I can help you in your search for the ideal career." He kissed the end of her nose. "Love you."

"Love you, too."

As happened every so often, Mel felt disconcerted and restless that night. She supposed it was the Club. For a woman with her beer-and-pretzels tastes, it was a foreign land, although Ryan was probably right, she was overawed by the trappings.

She gave herself a mental kick. If she was uneasy, she was well aware what the problem was, and the Club had nothing to do with it, at least not directly. It was the suggestion that Ryan could help her find the ideal career. She *had* the ideal career. Sure, she'd be capable of taking on more, Mel didn't doubt that, and she knew Amanda agreed. But that wasn't where she wanted to go. Her work life suited her perfectly.

But it wasn't good enough for Ryan. His bringing it up again tonight made that clear. He was comparing them to Robert Davies and Duncan Grant and their friends, with their *professional* wives, and he wanted the same. Executive Assistant didn't have the same cachet—now *there* was a good word, she'd have to remember to try it out on Adrian.

Stop that!

Ryan wanted what was best for her. He was willing to push where she chose to coast. She should be grateful that he wasn't content to let her be less than her best. Shouldn't she?

And realistically, her job didn't have the same earning power she could command if she moved into management. Because it must cost six months' rent and most of her yearly clothing budget to join the Club.

She opened her laptop and pulled up the Club's website. Tucked discreetly behind several other pages, so you had to dig to locate it, she found the membership fees.

She really was in a foreign world.

With a whole collection of foreign expectations.

She and Ryan had skipped the Wednesday buffet, agreeing that after dining at the Club on Tuesday it would be overkill. Mel was still struggling to absorb this new reality.

And was still ambivalent, if truth were told.

Instead, Friday evening she and Ryan explored the men's and women's change rooms—marble stalls, she noted— then reunited and got sandwiches at the snack bar. They sat on stools at a long table facing the window—the place hardly had solid walls, there were so many oversized windows—and watched the action on the tennis courts. The snack bar was at least lower key, although still ritzy; Mel felt more settled in her surroundings with a sandwich and a beer.

"I picked up the lesson schedule." Ryan hadn't calmed down in the three days since she'd seen him. His energy engulfed her, as if she were a moon being dragged along by his greater gravitational pull. "Golf, Melanie. You'd be amazed at how many doors it unlocks. Have a look." He pulled a printed sheet out of a pocket and put it in front of her.

Mel put her shrimp and avocado wrap on her plate and picked up the schedule.

He'd circled the Saturday beginners' group lesson. "You can enroll in this class, and I'll pick up a few private lessons at the same time. Then we can go for a swim or head out."

Saturday morning? She looked at him. Had he planned this? Was it a test?

But Mel had been on her own since she turned twenty and got her Associate's degree. Head-over-heels or not—and she assuredly was—she wasn't prepared to sacrifice her independence, or her friends, or the activities she enjoyed. Not that compromise wasn't possible, at least she hoped it was. But she refused to lose herself. It was that simple. So she said, "It's a good plan, except that I'm busy Saturday mornings."

Ryan's face tightened. "You can see how perfectly this schedule dovetails. It makes sense."

She put her hand on his arm and swallowed. Hard. Closer to a gulp, in fact, but she had to say it. "Ryan, I appreciate you want all this to happen. But working in the bookstore means a lot to me. I'm learning things about the book trade. I'm expanding my marketing knowledge. And I'm having fun. But mostly, it's what I choose to do."

If a voice could sound stiff, Ryan's did. "And I'm trying to build for our future. I'd assumed you'd want to support me in that. Melanie, the bookstore's a dead end, it's irrelevant to you and me. And frankly..." He trailed off, as if uncertain he should go that route. "Frankly, we're moving up. Together. I wouldn't presume to choose your friends, but—"

"Are you suggesting Adrian doesn't measure up? I don't pick my friends based on their social ranking." Mel wasn't going to use her newly acquired information about Adrian's background to boost his status with Ryan now. Besides, her hackles were up. She did her best to smooth them back down, while part of her brain wondered what a hackle was, and made a mental note to look it up when she got home.

A glance at Ryan's pinch-lipped face told her she wasn't getting through. She studied the sheet. "There's another beginner's class on Tuesday evening. I'd rather sign up for that one."

"Whatever you prefer," he said tightly.

Her hand was still on his arm; she gave it a little shake.

There was a longish pause, the kind of pause that stretches and becomes an eternity. Mel removed her hand.

The tension left Ryan's face, replaced by resignation. "There's a tennis ladder Tuesday nights. I might see if I can get a spot on it, if it isn't full yet. Then we can come and go together."

"Good idea." Mel sipped her glass of beer and returned to her wrap.

After a few minutes of a meal that tried to be companionable, punctuated by commentary on the doubles match on the tennis court closest to the snack bar, Ryan plunged in again. "Have you talked to Amanda yet?"

"Your timing's not great tonight. No, I haven't. I'm not convinced I want to. I like what I do."

"And you like learning new things. A new role would give you that challenge, and it might suit you just as well."

She smiled at him. "I'm still thinking." She shrugged. "Change the subject. How were your days with the auditors?"

Ryan took a swallow of his beer. "The usual. They swoop in and go through everything, then they leave and I deal with shattered nerves and other staff upsets. It's good to have the certainty that nothing's slipping through our branch procedures, but it is a major disruption. I took them to the Madison Inn for dinner Wednesday night. I would have invited you, but you would have been bored."

"Talking about audits? Sounds like a barrel of laughs."

Finally he smiled again. "Next time they come I may bring them here. Might as well get the use out of this place."

"I'm not seeing that as a problem at the moment. Although I'm not convinced I'll ever get used to it, I'm so completely out of my sphere. This is *way* more luxury than I'm used to. Not to mention the cost."

"I'm glad you've got a practical streak. I've been thinking about that. Expenses could get out of hand in a hurry. There's an initial investment, the things we'll need to do to integrate well, like the lessons. Above that though, I'll put together a budget so we won't get off track."

"That reminds me. Ryan, how much are these golf lessons? I have some money for recreation, but it's not infinite."

He shook his head. "I'll pay. You keep on building your savings."

"My savings have mostly been for a home. Julie and I plan to look at condos."

"Look all you want, but it might be better if you didn't invest yet." His voice dropped to a more intimate level. "It's something we might want to consider doing together."

Mel stared at him, then grinned. "You give me shivers."

"When you finish your sandwich, we'll go home, and I promise you more shivers."

She squirmed. Just what she needed, a mental image of Ryan naked in the middle of the Meadowlands Golf and Tennis Club. *Holy crow.* Mel felt her face heat up and huffed out a breath. "I've eaten enough." Sacrificing a quarter of a wrap and the last few swallows of beer was a good trade, given how tense Ryan had been only a few minutes before. Besides, a better feast awaited. She dropped her voice to match his. "Possibly I can give you a shiver or two?"

"Possibly you can." He'd already signed the chit—money never changed hands at the Club—so he took her hand and hopped her off the high stool.

They detoured by the pro shop and put their names down for lessons. Mel did her best to appear enthusiastic. She'd tried pitch-and-putt a couple of times and was convinced golf wasn't her thing. But Ryan might be right. It could be she believed she wouldn't like it because she hadn't given it a fair trial.

Might that apply to changing her job, too?

Mel spent the drive back to his place is a state of pleasant—no, make that nearly agonizing—moist and quivery anticipation.

Saturday morning felt strange. She'd been going to the bookstore for a couple of months now, sharing breakfast with Adrian, planning and dreaming, getting grubby plowing through the old books. Adrian's dreaded cousin Aggie's wedding left her Saturday morning blank, as if a chunk were missing from her life.

At nine o'clock she phoned her sister.

"Of course you're welcome, if you enjoy grocery shopping," Cassie said. "Come on over."

"Who's going with you?"

"Just Betsy. Lulu's got dance class. Move your butt, Mellie, we have to be out the door in twenty minutes."

103

'Just Betsy' meant her four-year-old niece would be the center of attention, but at least she and seven-year-old Lulu wouldn't be fighting over the honor. "I'll be there in fifteen."

Fortunately, this was Calter Creek. She could be at Cassie's house in seven minutes flat, if there wasn't any traffic.

Two little girls met Mel at the door, both of them with several weeks' worth of news to report. During the ensuing babel, she and Cassie got everyone herded into the car and on the way. It wasn't until they'd dropped off Lulu and were sharing a careful perusal of the deli department at the supermarket that Cassie said, "So, what's up? You look tired."

Mel shook her head and picked up a packaged quiche to study the label. "Not tired. Just, well, mix of good and—"

"Not so good? Talk to me, baby sister."

Betsy grabbed her hand and swung from it, then scampered down the aisle.

Mel dropped the quiche into their shared basket. "He's so amazing, Cass. He's gorgeous, he's ambitious—"

"He's good in bed?" Cassie added, *sotto voce*.

"Oh, yeah. Last night we started whispering to each other in the snack bar at the Club, and it got more and more—"

"Hot?"

"By the time we got home we were ready to tear each other's clothes off."

"Not to change the topic before we get to the hot stuff—"

"We're not getting to the hot stuff. You may be my sister, but you're not my confessor."

Cassie laughed. "But I caught the casual way you dropped in 'the Club'. I take it Ryan's membership came through."

Mel was in line at the deli counter by then, waiting to buy shaved chicken. "The bar and the dining room Tuesday night. The snack bar last night. I'm signed up for golf lessons, but I'm not so sure I'll like them."

"They won't even let you in the front gate, dressed like that." Mel had on bright orange jeans with an aqua T-shirt.

"I bet there's a membership rule book. I bet there's not a single shirt in the place that cost less than a hundred bucks, then they get sweaty on the golf course. I mean, in the bar the glasses are *crystal*. What does that tell you?" Mel's turn at the counter came, so she dropped the diatribe to order her chicken.

"That most of the people there have nannies who take the kids to the pool while Mom and Dad play? Is it really that up-market?" They worked their way along the canned goods aisle, where Mel grabbed a single can of tuna and Cassie picked up a whole flat.

"I don't know yet. But it is intimidating. I'm afraid to risk being the real me, because I'd be hopelessly outclassed." She filled her sister in on the Davies, the Grants.

Cassie frowned and roped in Betsy, who'd danced ahead of them into the potato chip aisle and come back with two bags. "It doesn't sound like your scene. But these people must let their hair down sometimes. You just haven't found that time yet."

"Ryan's so suave. He seems to know how to behave by instinct. He comes from the same kind of family we do, but somehow he gets it. And the man's positively glowing, as if Meadowlands is the pinnacle of success."

"Around Calter Creek, in certain circles, I suppose it is." Cassie sounded noncommittal, possibly because she was absorbed in choosing peanuts and pop.

Mel added tortilla chips to the cart. "It's a big learning curve."

"So this is the not so good? Joining the Country Club? You need to rethink your priorities."

"Not all of it," Mel said glumly. She'd wanted to talk this over with her sister, but sort of didn't want to at the same time. While they worked their way through the freezer aisle, taking turns restraining Betsy, Mel filled Cassie in on Ryan's reservations around her work at the bookstore.

Cassie drew the basket to a halt, causing a minor traffic jam in the dairy department. "What do you gain from the bookstore, Mel?" she asked. "I mean, I really want to know, because I don't get it, either. It's not as if you've got a stake in it. You're not even an employee. In my opinion, he should be paying you for what you're doing now, since the way you describe it, it's physical labor, and not always very nice."

"Yeah. Worms." She hadn't seen a worm, only the evidence of insect destruction, but it was worth trying to get a rise out of her sister.

No luck; Cassie ignored the worm comment. "So you like this Adrian guy, but back to the question. What do you get out of it?" She cocked her head questioningly at Mel, then added two gallons of milk to the cart.

Mel shoved the cart into motion after grabbing a six-pack of yogurt and a measly pint of milk. Watching Cassie's shopping habits, she was getting an economic lesson in the difference between single-and-footloose and married-with-children.

But she didn't have a ready answer. So she was quiet, other than bantering with Betsy, until they were in housewares.

"I have fun. Adrian's interesting."

"Has he come on to you?"

Mel shook her head. "No way. He's a friend. I've never had a close male friend before. Anyway, he knows about Ryan."

"But fun, how? Nothing you've described sounds like fun." Cassie picked up a big container of laundry detergent.

Fun, how? She couldn't explain what it was that kept drawing her back. She just knew that when she stepped through Adrian's door, she left her usual life behind. It was freedom, and discovery, and a respite. After a few hours in the bookstore on a Saturday morning, the world, when she re-entered it, looked brighter, fresher, as if it had been polished up. And she herself felt ready to take on any challenge.

Then there were the breakfasts.

"I don't know how to explain it." By then they were in juices. Mel added a single vegetable cocktail, Cassie snagged four dozen individual cartons of apple juice.

"Then, Sis, maybe you should give it some thought, because you're going off in two directions at once. I mean, if you can't even tell me why you like that place, why fight with the man you love about it?"

All good questions. "I won't let him pick my friends."

106

"He'd better not try. If he's half the man you say he is, he won't. But Mel, you don't want to mess this up. You've got to be flexible. Is Ryan spending time with friends you don't know, and you're not part of his life with them?"

"Point."

Mel was aware that she wasn't hearing what she'd hoped to hear from her sister. She certainly had new perspectives to consider — as if she didn't have enough already.

Betsy was on her back now, pretending that Mel was a horse, and Betsy's mother was choosing broccoli. Mel tossed in a package of cocktail carrots.

"Change of topic. Could you move into another role at SI if you wanted to?"

"Yeah, if there's a position available. Amanda's told me she believes I'm capable of doing more than I do, taking on more responsibility. But I love my job, Cassie," she said a bit plaintively.

"I know you do, hon. But you've been doing the same work for years. If it meant extra money, trust me on this, it can be a godsend, especially once you have kids."

Cassie pulled Betsy off Mel's back and gripped her hand before she could escape to explore the nearby bulk bins.

There was a lively mother-daughter discussion involving whether to buy chocolate anything-at-all, Betsy wasn't particular. The outcome was never in serious doubt, and Cassie added a bag with exactly six chocolate covered almonds to the cart. Three for each daughter.

"Ryan's always planning for the future. Saving, judicious spending, and that includes golf lessons, apparently — and Cass," she said, excited again, "he said not to go buying a condo, because we'd want to house hunt together." Mel hugged herself. "He's just so perfect. You'll see."

"When I finally meet this paragon," Cassie said dryly. "But you're radiant, so who am I grouse?"

Mel dropped the rapture in favor of seriously mature. "I know we have stuff to work out."

"All I'm saying," Cassie said while they waited in the checkout line, "is don't be too fixated on the way things have always been. Because they're going to change. Be careful to weigh it in the balance."

"I guess. Thanks, Sis, you've given me food for thought."

"That's what big sisters are for. To puncture balloons." Cassie grabbed Betsy by the neck of her T-shirt and held on. "Just think, Mellie. Thinking is good. And it's always been one of your strong points, but sometimes you need to be reminded."

That evening, Mel and Ryan stayed in, at Mel's place. That was fine with Mel, who was at saturation point with the Club; for every venture into the hallowed halls, a week of recovery hardly sounded like enough. Besides, she enjoyed doing domestic things, puttering in the kitchen with her man. This was the sort of thing they could spend their whole lives doing; normal, in a word.

And, she could put her hands where she wanted to, without worrying about the optics or the propriety of it.

They both had cooked for themselves for years, and they were learning to work in the same small kitchen space and not trip over each other. Between them they produced oven fried pork chops, baked potatoes in the microwave, and mixed stir-fry vegetables. While the fare wasn't as gourmet as the dining room at the Club, it was also not as rich, therefore more easily digestible, and tasted fine.

Over supper she commented on it. "You know, this is my dream. The Club overwhelms me. This is everyday. Comfortable, like a bathrobe you've had forever."

Ryan laughed. "Are you comparing me to a bathrobe?"

"No, not exactly." She swatted at his arm to make the point. "It's not you, silly, it's the situation. At home on a Saturday night. Do you want to put some music on?"

Ryan had moved part of his old CD collection to Mel's, and it wasn't long before a classical piece involving violins came from her speakers. "Okay?" he called into the kitchen.

"Perfect. You see? Little domestic things. You could keep a pair of slippers here, to follow up on the theme."

Ryan was padding around the apartment barefoot, as was she, since it was a hot night. Mel's ceiling fan was earning its keep.

"I'm glad," he said between bites of pork chop. "I've envisioned this, too, you know—of course you know, I've told you often enough. Two people who are where they want to be. Together."

That simple word sent a thrill through Mel. She swallowed a bite of potato and heaved a sigh, the good kind that says all's right with the world. "I'd almost given up on dreaming. I'd tried so many strategies to bring my dreams to life. I even tried an online dating service for a while."

Ryan shuddered. "Not for me. I'd feel like so much packaged meat."

"You don't, when you actually do it. I met a few nice guys, and one or two creeps. But not the one I'd want to make pork chops with for the long haul."

He put down his fork and sipped his wine. Mel had picked up a bottle of Shiraz at the grocery that morning, in a move to break Ryan of his Merlot habit. He swirled the wine in his glass and nodded. "I don't want to sound vain, but for a while, well, it wasn't hard to meet women. Nice when you're in your twenties, but by my age..." He gave her a helpless little shrug.

"I'm sure they came crawling out of the woodwork, given you're so handsome. I mean, you stopped me in my tracks, the first time I laid eyes on you."

Mel's frank assessment, plus her equally frank gaze over him, made him blush. She was glad he wasn't hung up on his surfer god appearance.

"I wasn't sure. I thought you were quiet, that's all."

Mel grinned. "And now you know better."

"You don't chatter a bunch of nonsense. I like listening to you."

Ryan had polished off his meal. She'd learned he liked simple cooking, straight up meat and potatoes. She agreed. The extravagant fare at the Club was for special occasions.

He leaned back and studied his wine, smiling across the table at her. "Thank you for this. I suppose you thought I was in a rut, always choosing Merlot."

"Maybe a little."

"I guess you're right. Once I find what I like, I'm not all that big on experimenting. You're good for me, pulling me out of myself."

"Talk to me," Mel said. "I know you do outdoor things, hiking, skiing. What do you do around a fire in the winter? Scrabble?"

"Winter's the furthest thing from my mind. I'm looking forward to a swim tonight, it's so hot."

"Good idea. Come on, Ryan, think snow, fires, cocoa. Jigsaw puzzles?"

He made a face. "It's been years. I remember wondering what the point was."

"It's sort of romantic. Crazy storm outside, cozy over your puzzle inside."

"I'd go for Scrabble before a puzzle. Dream for both of us, Melanie, but be warned, I'd never do a jigsaw puzzle without prodding."

Mel grinned. "Let me guess. You'd rather read the latest book on bank administration."

"Actually, yes." He recognized the tease, though, and grinned back at her.

"I guess I'm going to have to teach you the joys of pointless activity." She turned her attention to her meal.

He reached over and took her hand, playing with her fingers. "Life's too short for pointless."

"Even golf has a point, every time? You'd never play it just for fun?" Mel extracted her hand to cut another bite of pork chop.

"Sure, I would. I'm just saying that if there's another reason as well, why not take advantage of it? Building relationships, for instance."

"Fresh air's a good reason. I want you to stay healthy."

"I schedule gym time for fitness."

She knew that. Ryan's physique was, well, flawless.

"And is it fun?"

"I don't mind it. I like to push myself, and I feel good afterwards. But fun? Maybe not so much." His eyes met hers, and his held an expression she recognized.

"You're not thinking about the gym."

He shot her a devilish grin, while his finger traced a line from her lips right down her front, snagging on the scooped neckline of her peasant blouse. "A physical activity that's more fun than the gym. Can you guess?"

She just grinned, catching her lower lip in her teeth.

"Anticipation is the 'fun' part of fun and games." He broke their eye lock and withdrew the finger. "So, about jigsaw puzzles."

Mel groaned. Anticipation, huh? The man didn't need lessons for this particular game. He was excellent at driving her crazy.

"Suppose, instead of wasting that time, you took a course at the college, something useful for your career."

Mel got a grip on her libido and told it to settle down, since the payoff down the road would be worth it. "It's both-and, not either-or. I wouldn't mind going back to school, if they offer any business courses I haven't already taken."

He reclaimed her hand. "I didn't mean to imply you couldn't do both. I meant that if you want that promotion, having a couple of recent courses under your belt wouldn't hurt."

Mel sipped her wine. "Thing is, my work's varied, it's exciting, and best of all, I can leave it behind when I go home. Amanda's always taking work home—less so now that she's married and with the baby coming, but she still does. For me, there's too much else going on in life."

"Are you saying you don't want the responsibility?" He frowned.

"No. I carry a lot of responsibility. It's just trying to keep the balance. Besides, it suits me," she said somewhat helplessly. Why couldn't Ryan get it?

He smiled, the smile that said he could feast his eyes on her all night without regrets—other than the lingering anticipation. "I understand. I don't want you to lose that enthusiasm."

Her sister's words popped into her head. *Don't be too fixated on the way things have always been. Because they're going to change.* But how much change was she comfortable with? And how much would be a sacrifice?

How much should she expect Ryan to change?

He already is, her nagging voice said. *He's building a future. With you.*

On his terms.

He's learning. You won the golf lesson discussion, didn't you? And the Shiraz.

Won?

Mel didn't want it to be a case of winning and losing. She caught Ryan's fingers and squeezed. "Cassie said something today that made me think. About things changing, and not being too hung up on how they are now."

"Your sister's a wise woman."

She laughed. "My sister's a harried woman with not quite enough money and two daughters who run her ragged. But switching careers... that's big for me, so don't push, okay? I hear what you're saying."

"I'm sorry." He sounded like he meant it. "I don't want to railroad you into anything you really don't want. I just know you could do so much better—"

"Ryan."

"Right. Sorry."

"I'm curious. How do you see your life changing? If we're on this path together, do you see compromises to the way you live?"

She stood and began stacking plates. His gaze went somewhere far away before he turned back to her. "That's a tough one. Having someone else in my life, someone to take care of, knowing my decisions affect another person. What we both want lines up so well with the way my life's going. And it's falling into place. What did you have in mind?"

"Well, for instance, what if you got transferred to another branch of DCO? Would you take it? I don't ever want to live anywhere but Calter Creek." Her apartment had an open pass-through between kitchen and living room, so Mel spoke while she scraped the pork chop bones into the compost bin.

He shook his head. "I've told you, I don't plan on being with the bank forever. Between Calter Creek and Columbus, I'll find the opportunities. I'm working hard to establish a base here. I'm not throwing it away."

"Well, suppose I wanted to learn... oh, I don't know. Bridge, for instance." Mel leaned on the counter, watching him.

Ryan grimaced. "We'll see about that one. There may be good reasons to learn bridge."

"You're thinking contacts. Contributing to your social network."

"*Our* social network."

"You're still fighting doing anything for the fun of it, aren't you?"

Now Ryan looked puzzled. "Be fair, Melanie. It's perfectly possible to enjoy something and still find it useful. Cooking supper on a barbecue is fun in its own way, but it feeds us, too. I don't see why things shouldn't have a practical purpose."

"Like golf." Full circle. She'd have to make sure Ryan learned it was okay to give himself a break and enjoy an activity for no particular reason.

"Come on." He carried their wine over to her sofa as she emerged from the kitchen. "It's almost too hot to snuggle," he said, "but I want my hands on you. Hard to manage at the table."

"It's not that hot."

"Yes, it is." He lowered his voice and dropped an arm over her shoulder, allowing his fingertips to graze her breast. "It's about to get hotter. I don't mind getting sweaty with you, Melanie. We could... play? Without purpose?"

She leaned forward, breaking contact just long enough to set her wine on the coffee table. She took his glass from him and put it next to hers. "You're getting the idea," she said.

That ended intelligent discussion, for which Mel was grateful. Later, lying next to her gorgeous man, a cynical part of her mind remembered that once upon a time, and in some parts of society, lovemaking had been for procreation only—it had a purpose. Was there a practical reason to be making love on a hot summer evening?

Later they went downstairs to her apartment block's swimming pool to cool off. He laughed and splashed with her, proving her point. She was making too big a deal out of this whole fun thing. It was there, it was just their definitions that were at odds.

She put the thought aside and enjoyed the evening under the stars with the man she loved.

Amanda was staring at her as if she'd grown a second head.

"Just exploring the options," Mel said.

"You're exploring an option you've specifically rejected at least twice that I recall."

Mel had spent the week obsessing about Ryan's encouragement and Cassie's little lecture on change. No one was immune to change. She was comfortable in her role at SI, but when had she stopped stretching?

Going back to school, beefing up her skill set, was tempting. She'd face the Jenna Grants of the world without a qualm, nose to nose, qualification to qualification. And with the extra money that came with a promotion, she'd be pulling her weight as they built their shared dream, hers and Ryan's.

Counterbalancing all of these were the downsides. People who'd always been her friends would report to her. And a new position inevitably meant a larger workload, possibly taking work home.

No. that's where she drew the line. She might work late occasionally, but her evenings at home were sacrosanct.

By Friday afternoon she'd decided to put out feelers. And now Amanda stared at her as if she'd composed her thought processes along with the table scraps.

"I have reasons." Mel had stood—why, she wasn't exactly sure—in front of Amanda's desk to make her initial pitch. She sank into one of the familiar guest chairs. "I've been in this role for a while. I worry that I'm stagnating. And my

115

life's on a different trajectory now, and... well, it might be good to try something new, stretch myself a little."

"Taking on new challenges when everything else is changing isn't always a good idea," Amanda countered. "Ever hear of overload?"

"My perspective's changed, and my priorities. My future."

"And unless I miss my guess, that future involves Ryan Pope."

Mel couldn't help it; she flashed a grin. "Oh, yeah."

"Okay, still blindsided, I see. Does he have an opinion?"

"Totally on board. He's very encouraging."

Amanda's pen traveled from one hand to the other, but her eyes stayed fixed on Mel. "I rely on you. Seriously, Mel. You're a godsend more often than I can tell you."

She blushed. "You've said so before, and I love working with you. But sometimes I wonder if I could handle a job that doesn't include fetching coffee in the job description."

Amanda laughed. "You fetch coffee because you want to, or because it's a crisis. It's not in your job description, and you know it." She grew serious and aimed her capped pen at Mel for a moment. "It's who you are. You love people, and it's your nature to be supportive. Everyone loves you. It's nothing to do with your work."

Mel's heart flickered between ecstatic and discouraged. "So, if there were a position open, you wouldn't consider me?"

"Don't be obtuse. Of course I'd consider you. Leave this with me for a while. I'll mull things over and we'll see where it goes. Bear in mind," she said as Mel got to her feet, "if this happens, you'll be training your replacement. Thanks to you, I'm used to high standards."

"Yes, ma'am." Mel headed for the door. Before she left she stopped and turned back. "I appreciate this, Amanda. I'm not a hundred percent on board with it, myself. It helps to know what my options are."

She returned to her desk and the report on quarterly sales stats she'd been compiling, but her mind wasn't on her work.

Half of it screeched, *What have you done?* The other half cheered, *You go, girl.*

She wished Amanda had been more encouraging, but Mel saw the situation from her perspective, too. At least the odds were that nothing would happen for a while, so she'd have time to figure it out and stop sending mixed signals. The SI workforce was stable, and employees rarely left. She needed breathing room to be absolutely sure she wasn't chasing a vision that *might* prove interesting, *might* be a good move.

Still... Mel spun away from her computer and stared out the window. She flashed to an image of herself among a group of professional women, on the terrace at the Club sipping a Long Island lemonade, discussing whatever women at the Club discussed. Exchanging news, sharing opinions and information. Everyone listening when she spoke. Perhaps there'd been a doubles match on the tennis court earlier. Mel's tennis wasn't great, but it was infinitely better than her non-existent golf.

Maybe they'd discuss their kids.

The daydream shifted. Their children, hers and Ryan's. In that big house she'd conjured in her mind. It was enough to give her a thrill down her backbone.

She shook her head at her own time wasting skills, spun back around, and returned to the report.

Saturday morning she and Adrian were both in shorts and T-shirts, in deference to the heat wave assaulting Calter Creek. For some reason she'd expected skinny, but Adrian's legs were muscular.

He had set up their breakfast out on the deck. Mel was grateful. Mornings were soft and not too steamy, so she was happy to be outside when she could. Today he'd provided fresh French bread, a fruit salad, sliced tomatoes, cheeses, and... "Oh, my gosh. Are those sardines?" she blurted.

"You're under no obligation to go anywhere near them," Adrian assured her. He'd come up behind her carrying the coffee and tea.

"Adrian, I *love* sardines. How'd you guess?"

117

He circled her and put the tray on the table, then grinned. "Because I do. They make up my lunch, not infrequently. Huff won't touch them."

"This is a feast." She wandered over to the rail surrounding the deck. "If I lived here I'd never eat anywhere else. Calter Creek's spread out at your feet."

He'd made a good job of the deck. A white metal railing surrounded smooth cedar planks, and pots of geraniums softened the view of the rest of the roof, which was black and industrial looking. He'd added a large flower-print umbrella over the two-person table to ameliorate the effect of the sun.

He leaned on the rail next to her. Adrian seemed relaxed and loose. His trip home to Philadelphia, spending time with his family, had been good for him. "You'd change your mind in a hurry if you came out here at noon. It's an oven."

"Spring and autumn, anyway," she conceded, and turned to the table. "A summer breakfast feast."

"One of my favorite kinds." He held her chair, then poured her coffee before sitting across from her. "What have you been up to? It's an eternity since we last spent time together."

"My whole world's topsy-turvy." Mel filled her plate, buttered her bread, and stirred sugar and cream into her coffee, then launched into a description of the Country Club and all its implications.

He listened—she knew she was prattling, but she couldn't help herself, and Adrian would understand—without interruption, his expression neutral.

"You paint a tempting picture," he said when she wound down and bit into her bread with tomato and sardine. "Not that your description isn't swoon-worthy for anyone normal. Since I grew up in an environment like that, it doesn't attract me in the same way."

She studied him. "No, I guess it wouldn't. Still, you're living and breathing proof that a kid can survive The Club and come out just fine."

"Thanks. Huff's fine. No one's sure about me." Humor danced in his eyes.

"I am." Mel felt a burst of indignation on his behalf, then immediately let it go. Adrian was at home in his own skin, as much as anyone she'd ever known.

"So, golf lessons. Explain the appeal, please. I've never understood it."

"You don't play?"

"Huff does. My brother's very conventional. I know the rules, that's all."

Mel swallowed a bite of fruit salad. "I'm not sure I'll like it. I'd never have taken it up on my own, but if that's the kind of circle we'll be moving in, I guess it could be an asset."

"I will definitely find you a book on golf. In the meantime, try to explain to me why you'd want to spend hours of your free time doing something that doesn't thrill you." Adrian had grown serious. He turned his focus from her to a hummingbird exploring the geraniums.

"I have no intention of doing any such thing. If it doesn't work for me, I'll drop it. Easy."

The hummingbird flew away, and his smile returned. "Good. You're fine the way you are, Mel. Don't force yourself into a mold, for any reason. Please."

"People who eat sardines for breakfast aren't easily molded. This is paradise."

"I agree. Makes me wish not to mess around with the books at all today. We could linger out here until we start to roast."

"Then let's do. What else do we have on the list?"

Adrian had his tea poured by then and was idly stirring honey into it. "Speaking of forcing into molds, or not, you see what you've done to me? I was always a purist where tea was concerned, and here I am, polluting it with sweetener—"

"Not just any sweetener," Mel pointed out.

"True. Manuka honey." He tapped his teaspoon on the jar. "Straight from New Zealand. I read that Manuka is the best honey for antibacterial and anti-inflammatory properties. They say it makes an excellent emergency treatment for scrapes and such. Isn't that an appealing image? You're out in the woods and get a scratch, so you scrape some honey off your peanut butter sandwich and glom it on. Sounds sticky to me. But the thing is, I find I like tea this way. You've corrupted me from the straight and narrow, woman."

"You? Straight and narrow? Doesn't fit, Adrian. Try again."

"You never saw me in my sober company president suit."

"I saw you at the reception over at the art gallery. I'm glad you're not a president anymore. It must have been horrible for you."

He shrugged. "I have the skillset. But you're right, never again."

Neither of them said much for a while. When they'd both eaten their fill they gathered up the plates and leftovers on trays and carried them back indoors. Adrian disappeared for a minute and re-emerged with a sheaf of papers.

"The list never shrinks. In fact, it's taken on a life of its own, growing tentacles while I sleep. Getting away gave my mind the space to add several more pages." He sighed. "This is one big job. I had no idea. At The Bindery there was a department and a standard plan for renovations. I probably should have borrowed the outline."

"Those stores are always in malls, not beaten up old buildings. This is a new ball game. Let's see the list. And tell me about the wedding."

He handed her the pages. Standing by his kitchen table, Mel flipped through them but mostly focused on Adrian as he told her about his visit with his family, which gave a new meaning to the word 'extended'. Huff was his only sibling, but there were cousins galore, and everyone in his generation was busy producing the next generation. That he was invigorated by the family weekend showed his capacity to care for this large and diverse bunch.

"And Aggie?" she prompted. "The reason for the get-together?"

"Gorgeous in her gown, which I was told was satin brocade. Must have been sweltering. Before we got that far there was a wrestling match," Adrian reported glumly. "She pinned me."

"Seriously?"

"Yep. Not for the first time, I suppose I should add."

"I mean, you know how to wrestle? I thought you were sickly."

"Once I was on my feet again, I took up wrestling and suchlike to build up strength. Unfortunately, Aggie was on her college wrestling team. I'd guess she takes me three times out of four. Huff won't even fight her."

"Good Lord. The Forsythe boys, wrestlers. That I'd love to see."

"You just want to ogle my brother in a tank top and shorts."

"Nah. I've already got you in shorts. You guys are twins, so what more can he offer?"

"A better tan?"

Mel waved a hand at her pale legs. "Tans aren't something I can afford to love, I'm afraid."

"Good. We'll skip the lecture on the horrors of melanoma. Bring the papers, I've got the juice pitcher." They made their way back outdoors.

They drank juice and debated the bookstore, the coffee shop. Adrian did most of the talking, as if his weekend away had left him with an entire vision dammed up in his head. Mel watched his face as his ideas flooded out. He had always shared his thoughts, but today she sensed a different level of openness as he painted his vision for her.

Finally the sun, cooking the black roof surrounding the deck, chased them inside to the future coffee shop. He'd had the second floor space sanded; the wood would gleam once it was varnished. She supposed there hadn't been time for that before his trip to Philadelphia.

"A gathering place, Mel," he said. "Not somewhere you go just because there isn't anywhere else. A place to meet friends or be alone, but comfortable. Conversation, ideas. *Not* to plug in your laptop and put in your earbuds and tune out your surroundings, but I thought we could have one long table, right here…" He paced off a stretch of the empty room along the side wall. "We can put electrical outlets in the floor. I've already

121

talked it over with an electrician, the guy who was in a couple of weeks ago for the wiring. And I've found a carpenter."

"You've been busy."

Adrian's eyes danced behind the glasses. "I've been back two whole days. You'd be amazed, the people who come and go around here during the week. It must seem quiet to you Saturdays, but it's not always."

"I like it. It feels sort of deserted and mysterious, like a secret. Does that make sense?"

His grin changed to an outright laugh. "Not much, but then I live here. I'm glad just the same. It's that witch in you fighting to come out. Who knows what history this old place has? For all we know a coven met up here monthly at the dark of the moon, casting spells."

"Are we going to sort books today? If we are, we should get started. I still have grocery shopping and a few other things to do before Ryan picks me up."

"What's on your agenda?" Adrian led her down the stairs to the bookshelves.

"Hopefully a swimming pool. Then meeting another couple for drinks."

He dropped a box at the end of a shelf. "Are you up to Franco-Prussians?"

Mel couldn't believe how happy she was to be back in the bookstore bantering with Adrian. "I'm up to throwing a worm-eaten book at you if you even suggest them again."

He made a face. "A fate worse than death, but have no fear. These are books for teenagers, mostly. Let's find us a treasure."

By the time she left the bookstore to head for the grocery, Mel was dirt-streaked, sweaty, and happily aware that she hadn't obsessed about her career choices a single minute all morning.

9

It had been a great weekend, Mel thought as she dove into housework Sunday afternoon. She'd had an unusual—as usual—but definitely A-plus time with Adrian at the store Saturday. It surprised her how happy she was to see him again, like a kid whose blow-up magic castle had been re-inflated. She and Ryan had spent Saturday afternoon by the pool at the Club, Mel slathered in sunscreen and wrapped in a white dotted Swiss cover-up, before showering in the marble change rooms and meeting another couple for drinks on the terrace. Other people stopped to say hello, making her feel as if she belonged. They hadn't stayed for supper, but cooked burgers on his barbecue. And then...

Mel allowed herself to blush.

He knew his way around a woman's erogenous zones, that was for sure. She reveled in every bit of the memory. He'd used his hands, his mouth, to turn her into a quivering lump of melting jelly.

Except... wasn't there supposed to be magic involved?

If sex was a dance, with Ryan it was formal, with prescribed steps. She already knew he had a comfort zone, and there was little point attempting to breach its boundaries. So far it was exciting, but she wondered if down the road their sex life would begin to seem vanilla.

And while he was a fine lover, that special spark still eluded her.

Mel puzzled over this as she vacuumed, after Ryan had dropped her at her place and gone off to study banking reports.

Then she shrugged it off. Just because romantic fiction said it should happen didn't mean it ever did in real life.

A good weekend, with a good balance of interests. Even the housework made her happy, in the result if not in the doing.

❖

Monday, Anne, the SI receptionist, snagged her as she came in the building. "I saw you in the old bookstore when I was downtown Saturday. That guy's really renovating it?"

"Sure is." Mel could give discourses on the changes in Morrison Books. "The electrician's done a bunch of work, and upstairs has been sanded, and the interior walls have been patched up. And half the books are gone. I mean to the dump. They were nasty."

"Never can predict what you'll take on next, that's for sure." Anne slipped behind the desk at reception and poked the buttons to start up her computer. "And the love affair? You're looking pleased with yourself this morning."

"Sort of glowing?" Marcia from Personnel came through the door and joined them.

"We spent Saturday afternoon at the pool. A full bottle of sunscreen, a hat and long sleeves, and I still catch the sun. Call it a glow if you want to, though."

"Give us the scoop, Mel," Anne said.

"Not going to happen." She felt her herself go pink. "Good weekend, and that's all I'm sharing."

Anne and Marcia looked as if they were ready to exchange a high five, but they contented themselves with definitive nods. "Catch you later," Marcia said and headed for her office.

"Coffee at ten?" Mel asked Anne.

"See you there."

Mel made her way through the corridors of SI, greeting those she ran into, exchanging weekend gossip.

She found a note from Amanda on her desk. She'd never been able to get to SI consistently earlier than Amanda. But she reckoned that came with the territory. When you ran the company, you kept crazy hours.

She frowned. If she ran a department at SI, if she left her comfortable Executive Assistant position for a role with heavier responsibility, did that mean she'd have to keep Amanda's hours? She hoped not.

Mel read Amanda's scribbled note. There was a doctor's appointment, she'd forgotten about it, she'd be in later. She'd made that appointment weeks ago. Under the weight of the changes brought by marriage, instant motherhood, and now pregnancy, ultra-efficient Amanda was losing it.

Mel settled in at her desk and turned to her work. A quiet morning, getting on with business as usual.

Usual is good, she thought. It was a revelation. She'd always thought of herself as a risk-taker, ready for the next big adventure.

Trying new things, sure, but in the context of… usual. A solid base to catch you if you stumble.

After a peaceful day, Mel was wrapped in content when she answered the downstairs buzzer Monday evening. The disembodied voice said, "Mel, it's Adrian. Can I see you for a minute?"

"Of course." She buzzed him in, wondering what was going on—he'd never come to her apartment before. When he arrived at her door she shunted him inside. "What's up?"

"Nothing enormous, but I wanted you to have this." He fished in a pocket of his khakis and pulled out a key. "It popped into my mind at Aggie's wedding… in the middle of the service, actually. The woman at the gift shop next door keeps an eye on the store, but I'd feel better if someone else had access. And the obvious someone else is you."

"I'd be happy to help. Drink?"

"Ice water? It's miserable out there." The temperature was in the low nineties, and the relative humidity was the same. A few of the units in her older building had window air conditioners, but Mel had never installed one. She'd been living in front of a fan for days and relishing the air conditioning at Sinclair Imports.

She put the key on the kitchen counter, then brought two glasses from the kitchen and handed one to Adrian. They did a mock toast, and both guzzled the water.

"When I was a kid I ate the ice," he said. "Once it wasn't too big, in it went. Summer heat was a good excuse, and Mom was stingy with Popsicles."

"I heard the ice cream cart the other day. I was tempted to grab some change and run out to meet him."

He grinned. "I have Eskimo Pies in the freezer."

"I'll remember that."

Adrian propped himself against her table. "This wouldn't have been urgent, except that I'm heading out of town again. Family business, unexpected but I can't get out of it. I'm still on the Board at The Bindery, so—"

"I'll drop in and make sure everything's okay. Weird without you there, though. When do you leave?"

"Thursday, and yes, if you don't mind, Saturday morning? It's for insurance requirements, which I should have dealt with before now. I honestly doubt anyone's going to break in and cart off the worm-eaten books, although come to think of it... maybe if I left the door unlocked?"

Mel laughed. "Tempting. Save us weeks of grime. Where do you hide the good ones? Just curious."

"The miracle of old-fashioned technology. There's a massive safe in the downstairs storeroom. It's built-in and weighs a ton, so it's not going anywhere. The last thing Samuel Morrison turned over to me was the combination. Which is locked up in my safe deposit box."

"And in your head."

"Mind like a steel trap." Adrian was relaxed and happy, she noted, and realized with a start that except for that lunch with Huff at Joe's Café and their collision at the art gallery, she'd never seen him out of his native environment, the bookstore.

"Want to stick around for a while? Ryan's coming by in an hour or so, but in the meantime I have to start a load of laundry. Not the most exciting occupation."

"Happy to hang out with you."

Adrian picked up the laundry basket while Mel found her keys and detergent. She locked her door behind them, and they made their way to the laundry room at the end of the corridor. It was a pokey room with no window and only one machine, but it was convenient.

She'd just put the sheets in the machine when the fire alarm sounded. "Blast. Probably a drill, but they'll expect us to go outdoors." She tucked the basket and her box of detergent under the sorting table. "Let's go. With any luck it'll only take a few minutes—"

The power went off.

"Mel, take my hand." They groped in the dark until they'd locked hands, then fumbled their way to the door, and Mel cautiously opened it.

The lights were out in the corridor, too, although the exit sign still glowed. Half way down the hall, a fire door separated the building into two halves. As she stepped from the room, that door flew open and five or six people stampeded through, fighting each other to get out. On their heels was enough smoke to suggest the pits of hell.

Mel had just turned toward the exit when someone ran into her and knocked her across the corridor. She stumbled and collided with a wall. The air became thick with smoke, and visibility plummeted. She couldn't catch her breath or see...

"Here." Adrian's voice, and then his hand, found her. "Quickly. Don't breathe." He shoved her into the laundry room and pulled the door closed.

"Take a couple of deep breaths," he said, speaking in a hurry into the darkness. "You remember where the exit door is?"

She nodded, recollected he couldn't see her, and said, "Yes."

"Okay. We get through that door. If it's smoky on the other side, we'll have to feel our way downstairs. We stay calm. And Mel, once we're out of this room, *don't breathe.* Pretend you're under water."

She coughed. "It's coming in..."

127

"*Now.*" He must have been listening to her breathing, because the instant she'd completed an in-breath he opened the door and pulled her toward the exit.

Much later Mel tried to reconstruct the next eternity. After the collision in the hallway, when she'd lost contact with Adrian's hand, her mind had gone into shutdown.

So she didn't know how she got through the exit door and down the stairs. Smoke filled the space, drove away the air. The blackness was solid, but shifting, like a living thing enclosing her. Her eyes stung and she couldn't see, but she was afraid to close them. She looked for the exit sign, at least a glow from it, but there was nothing. Just darkness, and the shrill fire alarm, and Adrian's hand. He tugged at her, kept her moving even though she was going to collapse any moment, her legs had no strength left in them, and she didn't dare breathe but she was desperate for air. She didn't want to die in this terrifying, airless void.

Adrian had dropped her hand and locked his arm tight around her, urging her forward. It wasn't that far to the exit, her logical mind tried to tell her. But it might as well be light years, she'd never make it...

They found the door and pushed through it.

The stairwell was, if possible, even darker. She felt the walls in the narrow shaft closing in on her. Panic welled up as she realized she couldn't hold her breath any longer. Adrian heard her sharp exhale and pulled her shirt up, over her nose and mouth. He held it there as they inched through the dark, working their way down the stairs one at a time, until an eternity later they made it to the outside door.

He shoved them out. She was coughing and crying and the only secure thing in her life was Adrian. She'd reached the end, her muscles gave out and she dropped, hard, onto the concrete pad outside the door. She could hear Adrian's ragged breath, and Mel felt as if her lungs might come up with her next cough. Oxygen, she had to get oxygen...

It was still mid-summer, and not yet dark. They were free of the swirling blackness, although her eyes burned and her vision was hazy. Adrian was coated in grime, and she supposed she must be equally filthy. He grasped her hand again and tried to pull her up, but even with his help she wasn't able to stand.

So he sank down next to her. Between gasps he said, "We have to move further away, Mel. Try to stand up. Please."

It took another minute before the incessant sound of the fire alarm reached into her brain and drove her to her feet. Something crashed in the building behind her. Adrian supported her against him as he staggered across the pavement to the grass verge that bordered the furthest edge of the parking lot. There he let her go and bent over, still fighting for breath.

She dropped to the ground, her own breath coming in short pants.

He collapsed next to her on the grass, and his arms circled her. And that's when she lost what little hold she had on herself. She tried to speak, but her voice was gone. Her body quaked, and spasms gripped her. Her stomach clenched, she started shaking. Tremors ran over her skin.

Adrian pulled her against him, holding her and stroking her hair, murmuring to her. He held her cradled against his chest, protecting her from the nightmare. She drew her arms up against her middle, making herself small.

Mel was never sure how long they huddled together on the grass. But gradually she calmed, enough that she wasn't hysterical anymore, even though she couldn't control the internal shaking.

Someone came by with a clipboard and noted her name and apartment number. Her smoke-hazed mind was glad they were coming around checking. She felt weak, and sick, and terrified.

The back of the building was eerily quiet. The action was in the front. She heard the noise of engines and fire hoses and shouting as if from a long way away. It was peaceful, a few people but none of the sirens and alarms. She wiped her nose with her soiled shirt. Her body spasmed again. She could feel Adrian shaking, too, but his hands held her closer still, stroking her, soothing her.

It didn't seem possible, hovering this close to the edge of hell, that it could be tranquil. But she gradually relaxed against him.

She was finally getting her breath. She'd never take breathing for granted again.

"Melanie!"

The voice got through to her. Ryan.

"Back here," Adrian called. His voice sounded strange, sort of strangled.

Then Ryan was there. His hands turned her away from Adrian, held her face, studying her in the dim light. "Melanie. My darling, are you all right?"

She broke down again, sobbing.

"I think she is," Adrian said. "She's breathing all right. Scared, though."

"Hush, shh." Ryan was on the ground, cradling her as Adrian had done. "I've got her," she heard him say.

A hand touched her hair. "It's okay now, Mel," Adrian said. "You're safe. I'll check in tomorrow."

"Thanks," Ryan said gruffly.

"I wasn't about to let anything happen to her. Get her to a clinic."

She clung to Ryan. After a time he released her and stood, then took her hands and pulled her up after him. "We're going to my place."

"I want..." Her voice wasn't working, she was blubbering. Every muscle in her body hurt. "Adrian, where...?"

"He left. Don't you remember?" She didn't remember. It was as if the smoke had infiltrated her brain and clogged the synapses. "Let's go, Melanie. We'll get you checked over, then home. You'll feel better once you're cleaned up."

Keeping her close, Ryan led her away from her building. She stumbled her way to his car, clinging to him because she couldn't have made it on her own.

That night, after a stop at the clinic, a long shower, lozenges to soothe her throat, drops to soothe her eyes, antibiotic ointment and bandages where she'd grazed her knees when she fell on the concrete once they were outside, and a pill for her nerves, Mel lay in Ryan's bed and tried to piece it together. Her mind couldn't work past her certainty that if Adrian hadn't pulled them into the laundry room, where there was still oxygen, she wouldn't have survived. She'd lost her orientation and the air in her lungs when the panicked person in the hall collided with her.

His voice murmuring to her had soothed her. She couldn't be sure, but she thought he'd whispered, "It's okay now, my love. We're okay."

The pill kicked in. She woke once in the night, disoriented and panicky. Ryan held her until she fell asleep again.

The next morning Ryan woke her by stroking a finger across her cheek. "I have to go, Melanie."

She turned her head on the pillow and risked opening her eyes. They burned, so she squinted up at him. "You're going to work?" she whispered.

"Have to. Major meeting, head office. I told you last night, but I doubt you took it in. I'm sorry, I'm running late, but I wanted to let you sleep as long as I could."

"Do you have time to put drops in my eyes before you go? I can't see very well." Her whisper had gravel in it.

"Hold on." He retrieved the drops from the bathroom and applied them to her eyes. He kissed her, briefly. "I called your sister last night so she'd know you were okay. There's a key on the kitchen table. I'll check on you later."

Mel felt almost human, although nowhere near normal. After Ryan left she dragged herself out of bed and noted that she'd slept in one of his shirts. Her own stuff… she explored, holding onto walls because she wasn't steady. In fact, she was dangerously close to a meltdown. She located her clothes by smell, in a pile next to his stacked washer/dryer combination. She'd been wearing casual old do-the-laundry clothes, no sorting needed, so she fished her keys and change for the washing machine out of her pants pocket, gathered the lot up, and dumped them into the machine.

Assured that she'd have something to wear in a while, she wandered through the townhome, looking for a telephone. Her cell was locked up in her apartment, along with everything else she owned except a washing machine full of sheets. Mel longed to connect with her sister, her parents, Amanda. She needed to see Adrian, to prove to herself that he was okay. Eventually she had to find out if she had a home anymore.

Dizziness assaulted her from out of nowhere, although she might have expected it. Weak and wobbly, she dropped onto the sofa and put her head forward into her hands, wondering if the vision of black, inky smoke would ever leave her. She took deep, conscious breaths.

After a few minutes she went to the kitchen and found cold cereal, which made an adequate breakfast. She stuffed her clothes into the dryer, then looked again for a phone, but she doubted there was one. The only number she had for Ryan was a mobile, so odds were there was no landline.

When the doorbell rang she jumped and her heart leapt into her sore throat. She looked out the front window.

Julie. Thank the gods and goddesses. Mel yanked the door open and hauled her friend in.

"I couldn't reach you so I went over to the bank and cornered Ryan," Julie said from the depths of a hug. "How are you, honey?"

"Bad." Mel's voice sounded as if someone had run coarse sandpaper over it.

"Want me to make you coffee or tea?"

"Tea," she forced out, and then wondered why. She'd always drunk coffee in the morning. But she went with it. "Sounds wonderful. And can I use your cell? I have to talk to—"

"You're not talking. You should hear yourself, like you're finishing a two-week chest cold. Tell me who to call and I'll let them know I'm right here pouring tea down your throat and you're fine. Make a list."

Mel rummaged in Ryan's kitchen drawers until she located a pen and a piece of scrap paper. She left Adrian off the list, because she didn't remember his number. It was in her phone, but her phone was in her apartment—assuming she still had one. Julie poured her a cup of tea, then squeezed her shoulder and started phoning. Mel listened while Julie canceled her workday and reassured her family.

"The management company says it'll be tomorrow at the earliest before you can get into your apartment," Julie reported after the last call. "It was a kitchen fire that got out of hand at the other end of the building. Some of the hall carpet burned, that's why there was so much black smoke. Significant damage, but you should be okay since you're at the other end. So what happened? You didn't even grab your phone or your purse?"

Mel whispered, "We were in the laundry room. Smoke, panicky people. I wasn't sure I'd make it out. If it hadn't been for Adrian—"

"Stop right there. What's Adrian got to do with this?" Julie fixed herself a cup of the tea while she spoke.

"He brought me a key to the store. Coincidence," Mel whispered. "He saved me. Then Ryan came. I have to see him."

"We'll run into town to check in with your men. And then, how about a new outfit to get you through the next twenty-four hours? You could do with a dash of normal."

"Okay. Do I still smell like smoke? I still smell smoke. I was black, Jules."

"Must be in your nostrils. Are those your clothes tumbling in the dryer?"

Mel nodded.

"Good. When they're ready we'll head into Calter Creek. Go brush your teeth—oh…"

"It's okay. I have a toothbrush here."

"And not much else," Julie said, eyeballing Ryan's shirt.

They went into town. First stop, the bank, where they left a message for Ryan, who was incommunicado. Next they called in at the bookstore. The door was unlocked, so Julie shouted upstairs. Adrian bounded down the stairs and grasped Mel's hands in both of his. "Thank God you're okay. You are, aren't you?"

"Can't talk," she rasped at him. His voice wasn't right either, his eyes were red-rimmed and his hands were still shaking a little. She gave his fingers a squeeze. "I'm okay," she managed.

"I had to grope my way to my car. My glasses were opaque from the smoke."

They locked eyes. Something tickled at Mel's insides, something she couldn't define or even locate accurately. *He might have died with me*, she thought.

"We're going to Joe's for a burger," Julie said, breaking the moment. "Want to come?"

He nodded. "Normal and everyday sounds good. Gives me less time to think." He returned her squeeze and released her hand. "I canceled the trip," he told her. "No way could I handle a business meeting this week. My mental faculties have been smoked out."

Mel smiled. This Adrian was taking practical steps, whereas the man who cooked Saturday breakfasts lived in a world of dreams and maybes.

"From what I hear there's never a time when you're not thinking," Julie retorted. "Probably even when you're asleep. And given the state of your voices, it's either going to be a silent lunch or I'll have to carry the conversational ball. I hope you're both fascinated by the mega-mansion that just came on the market."

The meal was quiet, but mainly because Mel, for one, realized she was starving. She'd had an early and light supper, before Adrian had turned up, and only a bowl of cereal since then.

"Nothing like abject terror to build up an appetite?" he asked, sounding more like his old self. "Something I didn't know." He was making short work of his own burger, plus a pile of decadent yam fries he'd offered to share.

Mel laughed. Until that moment, she hadn't been sure she'd ever laugh again. "Thank you," she whispered.

He shook his head at her and handed her a fry.

Later, she and Julie went to Creekside Mall and chose Mel an entire new outfit, right down to underwear and shoes, which they put on Julie's credit card. She changed in the store and threw the old clothes away. She might regret it later, but at that moment she didn't want any reminders of the previous night.

At the grocery she selected a quiche from the deli. Not Ryan's preferred type of food, but Mel figured it would be easy on her throat and stomach lining. The burger earlier had been wonderful, but wasn't sitting lightly.

Julie took her back to Ryan's. She napped and again woke from a dream of being lost in smoke and blackness. She didn't risk a nap again. When Ryan came home she had the table set on his little patio and the quiche, with Mediterranean vegetable and quinoa salads, ready to serve.

Over supper she whispered, because it was important that he understand, "It was Adrian who got me out. I'll owe him forever."

He smiled at her. "You're enterprising and determined. You would have made it."

She shook her head. "I panicked. I didn't have any oxygen. The smoke in the corridor would have killed me."

"What was he doing there, anyway? And how did you end up at the far side of the lot?" Ryan's question was casual but his face was taut.

"We went out the back door. Adrian was going out of town, and someone needed to check on the store, so he came over to drop off a key."

Ryan sighed over a bite of the quiche. "I suppose I should thank him again."

Mel looked up. "He's a friend. He saved my life."

"I know, honey. Don't fret."

"He knows I'm with you." *Shut up, Mel,* she commanded herself. She wouldn't justify her friends. But she wished Ryan understood.

He'd come round. Right now she needed his strength more than she needed confrontation.

The fire had been on Monday. Now it was Friday, and Mel was no closer to moving home. She'd had the all-clear, but she wasn't ready.

"To put your mind at ease," Ryan said, "I stopped by the bookstore and thanked your friend for rescuing you." He twisted a finger into her hair, twining it, watching it spring free.

He lay on his side, stretched out next to her on his living room floor. The heat wave hadn't broken, and neither of them could face going upstairs to his bedroom, where the air conditioning fought a losing battle. They'd put beach towels over the carpet, and he'd taken off his shirt, which meant that Mel was acutely aware of his sculpted body next to hers. The ceiling fan brushed the partially cooled air over their heated skin.

She went up on an elbow and traced his lips with a finger. "I'm glad. He's an okay guy, Ryan. Honest."

"I'm sure he is. Just not much to my taste."

She hadn't returned to work until Thursday. And she and Ryan hadn't made love all week. It hadn't even come up.

"Are you okay to talk about it, baby? Why did you take the back door? I'd been looking. I was getting frantic until the guy with the clipboard told me he'd checked you off."

Mel flopped onto her back and stared at the ceiling. She hadn't had a bad dream in twenty-four hours, her nerve endings didn't fire at any unfamiliar noise, and her voice was almost back to normal, so she might be able to handle explaining what had happened. She related, haltingly, the laundry room, the swirling black, the sting in her eyes, her lungs bursting. "To be honest, I didn't have any idea where we were, just that we were out. My legs gave way completely once we'd made it out the door. Adrian must have hauled me across the parking lot." Abruptly she turned toward him and buried her face in his shoulder. "I've never been so scared. I was sure I'd die there."

"Shh." He wrapped her up in his arms. *Hang the heat,* she thought. Ryan's proximity meant stability, and a certainty that the fire demons were truly gone.

His hand smoothed the length of her, from her wild hair down past the hem of her shorts.

"You need to put it behind you," he said into her hair.

"I went to see the counselor today."

"Did it help? I've never been too sure about those guys. I've always believed you can work through things on your own, if you're focused enough."

"I know now that you can't always find that focus when you need it. Yeah, it helped. I'm going again next week."

"If that's what it takes. I don't want this to haunt you, Melanie."

"I don't mind borrowing perspective when I need it." She shifted and kissed him. "I've got this song in my head. 'It's Too Damn Hot'. Remember it?"

Ryan's gorgeous body stretched and flexed. Mel watched every muscle. She dropped her head to kiss her way down his chest, his abdomen. Smiled when she got a response.

"I don't know, Melanie," he said doubtfully. "It's sweltering." He caught her hand, kissed her knuckles.

"Good excuse for a shower." Ryan's townhome complex didn't have a pool, a fact Mel regretted. Driving to the Club didn't appeal to either of them, and in the aftermath of the fire they'd closed the pool at her apartment building.

As for her apartment, it had survived, and she'd been allowed to return home on Wednesday, but the corridor was filthy and still stank of smoke, and the stench leaked in if she so much as *thought* about opening the door. Plus the memory... no, she couldn't go home quite yet. She'd retrieved her car and some necessities and fled to Ryan's.

"I hope a cool shower's enough reward," she said into his chest. She licked his nipple; he gasped. "More?" she asked.

Oh yes, lots more. Ryan took control and showed her the true meaning of hot, sweaty sex. If she didn't keel over from heatstroke, she'd have an epic night.

Maybe it was what she'd needed.

Later, she lay beside him again, modest in a lightweight silk kimono she'd brought with her from home and marginally cooled from the shower, waiting for the day's heat to dissipate. "Can we dream a while?" she asked. "I know the big stuff, the outline, but flesh it out for me. What are the little things? What kind of house you want, what kind of yard, grass or trees or garden, where to go on vacations. A shower curtain or sliding doors on the tub?"

"Nesting?" He pulled her in, kissed her, let her go.

137

"Probably." She grew serious. "In the fire, my life didn't flash before my eyes or anything. But after, I started thinking about how fragile it all is. How important our dreams are. It's the only chance we get. We can't afford to waste it."

Ryan sat up. "I'm going to grab an iced tea. Want one?"

"I'll come."

"No need. I'll bring it." She watched him walk away and envied him. He had pulled his boxer briefs on, but other than that his toned body was there for her to admire. Men were so comfortable in their skin, not the least reluctant to wander around with next to no clothes on.

"So, you tell me." He settled next to her on the floor, leaning against the sofa. "Do you have a dream house? New? Old? Ranch or split level?" He'd wrapped paper towels around the bases of the glasses, but condensation had gathered above the paper. He rolled the dripping glass against his forehead; a drop fell onto his chest.

Mel reached over and spread the moisture, then blew on the damp spot.

"That's nice. Cooling. You can keep doing it all you want."

"If you return the favor."

He put his glass on a mat on the coffee table, then kissed her shoulder. "I love that you're planning how we'll live."

She sipped from her glass, then traced her finger through the moisture on the outside. "How about a newer home? If we're both working, we won't have time or energy to fix it up. Ranch, just because. There'll be tricycles in the yard, and a fort or a treehouse. We can rake leaves every autumn."

"We may hire a teenager to deal with the leaves. I expect the yard to be tidy. Kids' toys stowed in the garage."

"Once the kids are old enough. Before that, it depends on how much energy you and I have to pick up after them. Being a working parent sounds challenging."

"To me, too. If we have to, we can adjust your work hours so you'd have more time at home."

She sat up straighter and smacked his bare shoulder. "Or yours. Shared responsibility, Bub. I'm not raising these kids alone. No weekend-only dad."

It was clear to Mel that he'd never considered that one. He didn't answer.

"Ryan?"

"Sorry, just thinking. We'll figure it out. But I've always believed that the mother has the primary responsibility for the children. My career is vital, I can't afford to slack off there."

She moved her forehead against her glass. "And I might not have the option of reducing my hours. I don't expect to be a stay-at-home mom, even though some days it sounds good."

"What else? Vacations?"

Mel was happy to change the subject. "I'd like to go camping. We could take the kids into upstate New York, for instance. Or Kentucky."

"Don't you think camping's kind of messy? Bugs and no sanitary way to wash dishes? But I meant just you and me. What do you dream of, Melanie? Help me out here. Imagine..." He paused and took a breath. "Imagine it's a honeymoon. Tell me what you'd love."

She could hear the way her voice went faint. "Honeymoon?"

"I'll ask you formally another time, somewhere that isn't the living room floor. We can start planning, though."

"Planning." Not dreaming? A guy thing, she concluded. Mel fell silent while her mind turned to days of fun and exploration, mild evenings, long, languid nights under a full moon. "Somewhere with an ocean," she said. "Maybe the Caribbean? With good snorkeling. And luxurious. For once, I'd love luxury."

"You'll get it, baby. We may not be able to afford another gourmet vacation for a long time, so I'll make sure our honeymoon's everything you dream of."

She reached over to set her glass on a mat on the coffee table, then kissed him, brushing her hand the length of his chest. She looked the question at him. But Ryan shook his head. "Too hot, remember?"

And the unspoken, once-a-night rule. Mel pulled back and imagined a yard full of kids, and camping, and sighed to herself.

But he was Ryan, and he loved her, and he was stable. So *damn* stable—but that was the trade-off, wasn't it?

She settled against him, for five seconds, then reached out for her iced tea.

It was just so hot.

10

Like returning to work, stepping into Adrian's domain brought a sense of returning normalcy to Mel's life. She felt as if the building embraced her and welcomed her home. She was late getting to the bookstore, but at least she had her phone again so she'd been able to alert Adrian. She'd gone to her own apartment that morning, after sleeping uncomfortably next to Ryan in his roasting bedroom. She couldn't explain why, but it didn't feel right to go straight from Ryan's bed to the bookstore.

She was too late for breakfast, but they shared tea and scones before they set to work. Adrian didn't look the worse for wear, but he seemed more tentative, not quite his usual effervescent self.

Over tea he took both her hands. "It was beyond scary," he said without preliminary.

She nodded and choked up. After a week of struggling to keep it at bay, now, suddenly, the emotion came flooding in again.

"How have you been, really? I worried myself half sick about you. I couldn't tell you when you came in with Julie. Too close to the bone."

Because this was a personal worry, not one he was willing to make public. Mel got that. He'd shared the most cataclysmic event of her life. If anyone understood what the past week had been like, it was Adrian.

She tightened her grip on his fingers and received an answering squeeze. "I didn't believe I'd make it."

"You had no choice. I'd move heaven and earth before I let anything happen to you." He released her hands and concentrated on buttering his scone. "Not that I was entirely comfortable that I'd be able to move heaven and earth," he said with a note of the old humor. "I was more frightened than I've ever been in my life."

"I'm glad you didn't tell me. You were the only thing that kept me going." She claimed one of his hands again, needing the contact. "I don't have enough words to thank you. I was hopelessly disoriented. You got us out the door and down the stairs. I've taken those stairs hundreds of times, and I didn't have a clue how to—"

"Stop. Please, Mel. I did what I had to do, and so did you. We escaped. We're here."

"We are. I believe in miracles."

"I always have."

They returned to their tea. "I saw a counselor last week," she said.

"Good. So did I, as a matter of fact. It isn't wise to deal with trauma on that scale without help."

"We came through it."

"We're here, and eating—what shall we call it? Brunch?—together. I'd say we're on the mend. Sharing food with you is part of my definition of the good life, in fact." He looked at her, serious. "I hope you believe that if things ever fall apart, I'll be here for you. You're important to me."

"You're just about the best friend I've ever had. It's so great being here, working on the store."

He grinned. "Eat your scone. I'm getting antsy to finish the book sorting, so I plan to stress test that enjoyment today."

She didn't grin back. She'd been debating with herself all week whether to bring this up. Bottom line was, she wanted to know. Maybe she just wanted reassurance.

"Adrian…"

"You're troubled. What is it?"

"Just something that's… not exactly bothering me, but… when we were out there, on the grass… what did you say to me?"

"Say to you?"

"You were sort of mumbling into my hair. Crooning."

He shook his head. "I don't know, Mel. Nonsense, I expect."

She swallowed. "It sounded... in my mind it sounded like, 'It's okay now, my love'."

She caught a deer-in-the-headlights expression that vanished before she was convinced she'd seen it. Then he looked thoughtful for a minute. "You know, I probably did. It's the kind of thing our mother might say to us, when we were hurt or frightened. It makes sense."

"As if I were a little girl with a scraped knee?"

"You'll never be a little girl to me. A sprite, maybe, but not a child. But given the stressful situation, to use those words to make it better, when I needed to be the strong one—not that there was much of that, I felt like a wrung-out dishcloth, only dirtier. Did I worry you?"

She smiled. "No. I felt safe. And cared about."

Cherished, she thought. Adrian had made her feel cherished.

"You are. Now... books?"

Mel took a final gulp of her now tepid tea. "Let's do it."

She had to cut short her bookstore time, because she and Julie had plans that afternoon. Driving to her apartment, filthy and sweaty and comfortably full of her half of the chicken and sprouts sandwich Adrian had produced part way through the day's quota of books, Mel considered the sense of satisfaction that always traveled with her whenever she left the store. It was as if she'd started to own the renovation. And yet it wasn't hers, in any way.

Sure, Adrian filled her in on his decisions. She'd talked over the more interesting aspects of the plans—he didn't bother her with things like plumbing. He'd made her a copy of his master to-do list, and encouraged her to annotate it. She'd come to believe that he honestly did value her opinions. She'd chosen the tiles for the downstairs washroom and even knew where the mystery safe was.

Still, it wasn't hers. Why, she wondered, should she feel so personally invested in the renovation of Morrison Books?

Well, whatever, she was proud of what they were doing—what *he* was doing, she corrected herself. She was looking forward to the opening, to seeing it all completed, sometime in the fall. And she'd begun to sense how much she would miss the store, once she wasn't involved anymore. No more plans, no more breakfasts. Perhaps she could work there, at the cash register or serving coffee, on weekends?

Yeah. Ryan would really love that.

Mel regretted the mood of near-defiance that came over her when she thought of Ryan and the bookstore. He wasn't willing to discuss it, that was obvious. The whole business was like a thorny hedge cutting through an otherwise beautiful relationship.

But it wasn't up to him to choose her friends.

Mel was uncomfortably aware of how little time she'd spent with her gang, other than Julie, over the summer. Ryan occupied her free time. Possibly she was due for a correction, a change in the flight plan. With any luck there'd be a party or barbecue somewhere this weekend. She'd take Ryan. She was integrating into his world and wanted him to integrate into hers.

At home she checked her email. She wasn't an enormous fan of computers and spent all day, five days a week, working on one, so her laptop was a convenience, not a toy, and as often as not she ignored it.

There it was. In Danika and Sven's back yard, on Sunday afternoon.

She sent a tentative "yes" and phoned Ryan. "Tomorrow afternoon there's a barbecue. I want to go. You'll come, won't you?"

A longish pause. "I hoped we might go to the practice green."

"We could putt from two to three, then drive over to the Larsens'."

Another pause. "Melanie, I can't help but wonder if it wouldn't be better for you to see your girlfriends on your own. At the mall, for instance. They're not—"

"They're not what?" Mel was annoyed. "This isn't just my girlfriends. And you haven't even met them."

This conversation so far held more silences than talking. But eventually Ryan said, "You're right. It's just that I can get a little flustered if I don't know the people I'm with well enough to understand them."

"I recognize the feeling."

"You? You're so comfortable socially."

She remembered the Davies and the Grants. "You think? But I've known most of these people for years. They won't bite."

"And you really want to go to this?"

"Yes. I do."

The pause on the other end was a beat too long. "Then we will," he said at last.

"Good. I'll phone Danika and confirm."

"When will you be here this evening?"

Mel planned to stay at his house again. "Seven? Julie and I are going out looking at condos, and then I need to squeeze in some cleaning. The fire smell's everywhere."

"We can pick up something from the deli for dinner."

"Cool and easy." Happy again, she gathered up throws and pillow covers to take to the laundry room on the third floor—her own hadn't reopened yet. Later on she'd mop the floors. Once the smell was out of the hallway she'd have to have her sofa and rugs cleaned. In the meantime, at least she'd do what she could to sanitize her place and erase olfactory reminders the fire.

Spending nights with Ryan worked for her, and he'd made it clear he was perfectly content with the arrangement. Soon she'd have to decide when, and whether, she wanted to start sleeping in her own apartment.

Julie arrived at three o'clock, as promised. Mel laughed to herself as she headed downstairs, dodging barricades around the main entrance and damaged west wing. Of course Ryan was happy to have her stay with him. It wasn't even a question.

"Just so we're clear," she said when she opened Julie's car door, "I've warned you, I'm not buying. I might never be buying. I hope this isn't wasting your time."

Julie had a sheaf of listings in her hand. "There's nothing else going on today, so let's look. I've lined up a bunch of open houses, so no one's inconvenienced."

"It's probably voyeurism, but I love looking at houses." Mel climbed into the car.

"It helps me, too. Gives me a chance to see what's on the market. I'm putting my time to good use, so stop feeling guilty."

In the car Julie continued. "So, it's hot and heavy with Mister Pope, huh?"

Mel blushed. "You could say that. You know I've been staying at his place. He's really getting into barbecuing, so he did chicken last night."

"Sounds perfectly romantic, except for the heat."

"It is. Or perhaps it's the Club," she joked. "It's drool-worthy."

"The high life turning your head, huh?"

"Nah. The truth is, the Club's a distraction. I don't need it. Still, it's amazing, Jules." Julie had heard it before, but Mel went over the wonders of the Club again during the short drive to the first open house, a two-bedroom, third-floor condo. The two women looked it over, shook their heads, and moved on.

"You can do better."

"I'm thinking four bedrooms, large yard…"

"Your lust is raging ahead of your logic, girl."

"So much more than lust, Jules. But the man works out. What's under the business suit is fine, believe me."

"So invite me over for a swim one day and I'll ogle."

"I will, once the pool opens again."

Julie's love life wasn't half as rich as Mel's, but she had caught the interest of a man named Chris who worked with kids and seniors. Mel tried to plumb Julie's ambivalence as they drove, but for once Julie was oddly reluctant to discuss the latest man in her life. Maybe she was finally figuring out that hot guys didn't have to be dangerous as well? Mel crossed her fingers.

As they pulled up in front of the next place, Julie summarized. "Townhome. Almost new, on the edge of your price range, but it has granite counters."

"Don't see how I've lived for so long without granite counters."

"Behave."

It was a nice place. The owners had a flair for color; the living room had a rich terra cotta wall, one bedroom was a deep blue. Mel toured it once, then went back through, more slowly. She could see herself here, her furniture in these rooms, her odds and ends on the mantelpiece, her pictures on the walls.

She sighed.

"What?" Julie demanded.

"Ryan's townhome. All neutrals."

"Yours is all neutrals."

"Yeah, but I don't have the right to paint. He does."

"Worthy of a conversation, perhaps?"

Yes, it was. She didn't plan to live with neutral.

They looked at two more condos, but neither of them did anything for Mel. Not that it mattered. That four-bedroom house with yard was looming large in her imagination.

Ryan's deck faced north and mercifully had some shade. He looked delectable in a pale yellow polo shirt with cargo shorts. Over supper she brought up their earlier phone conversation. "You really get uncomfortable around new people? That surprises me."

He shrugged. "I guess… yeah. I keep it to myself. It's about the image. To get ahead, you have to be confident. Possibly it's being an only child, no siblings, always pressure to be the best."

"I'm glad you told me." She ran a finger up his forearm. "Thank you. That's why…" She took a breath. "That's what makes you matter to me."

147

"I couldn't have shared something that personal if I didn't love you, Melanie. Or if I didn't believe you cared about me."

Time froze. They'd both said 'love you' in passing, which meant more or less the same thing as 'take care' or 'see you later', but he'd never before used those words with intention, dropped so casually over their smoked meat sandwiches. Mel's heart rate doubled. "You do?" she said faintly.

Ryan gave her an uncertain smile. "You must have known." His look was intense. He turned his hand over to twist his fingers into hers. "I may not say it very often. I don't find it easy to talk about things like that. But don't doubt it."

"I don't."

"When I couldn't find you, the night of the fire..." He took a rough breath.

Mel's insides were out of control. Her heart had gone into a wild, tap dancing kind of thing. Her stomach clenched, then released, to her embarrassment, a largish belch. "Oh, God," she moaned, and pounded her head on the table beside her plate.

"Come here, you." He stood up, hauled her to her feet, and held her, held her as tightly as the two of them could fit against each other. "Last time I tell you I love you when you've been eating dill pickles," he said into her ear. "Unless you're carrying my baby."

She looked up at him, at his eyes laughing at her, and dragged his head down to her mouth. This was one deli dinner that wasn't going to be finished any time soon.

After their lovemaking she snuggled up to him, despite the heat, and said, "I love you, too, Ryan Pope. You swept me off my feet and I forgot to say so, earlier."

"Good," he said. "So good."

Mel's world was complete.

The putting green Sunday afternoon was kind of fun, like mini-golf without the noise and chaos. She missed more than she sank, which was fine with her. Sinking the putts wasn't the point. The point was meeting Ryan half way and sharing an activity they both enjoyed.

When they got to the Larsens', Mel was welcomed like a long-lost friend, which, she reflected ruefully, she was. Twenty or so adults stood around the back yard chatting, drinking beer, and preparing food. They'd been her pals for years, and she realized with a pang how much she'd missed these casual gatherings.

Furthermore, her gang swooped Ryan into the proceedings as if he'd always belonged there. In no time at all he was standing by a flowerbed, engaged in a discussion on begonias or slugs or something. Mel watched from her own conversation, woman talk about frustrations trying to get pregnant. She'd prayed he'd fit with these people. She could sympathize with his uneasiness in new situations, but surely he'd find her friends easy to hang out with. Wouldn't he?

Later Ryan sank into a chair in a patch of shade and tugged her down next to him. "Sven Larsen is an electrical engineer," he told her, seeming mildly surprised.

"His wife teaches sociology at the college."

She watched him looking around. Her friends were laughing, noisy. The kids present had a badminton game going with a few of the parents. Chicken produced stomach-awakening aromas from the barbecue.

Julie wandered over with Antonio, who managed a neighborhood pharmacy west of town. They pulled up lawn chairs. "How's the bookstore, Mel?" Antonio asked.

"It's a disaster area downstairs, but it's coming. I'm filthy when I get out of there. The plans are fantastic."

"Those of us who work downtown can hardly wait," someone said. "There's a lot of excitement about the coffee shop. Heaven knows there's enough pent up demand. Right now we only have the Coffee Shack and the Madison Café."

A couple more people drifted over. "And Joe's," another person said.

"For morning coffee? Ugh. You come out smelling of hamburgers."

"Best hamburgers in the state. Where's Adrian today?"

"He said he couldn't make it," Danika reported.

"Too bad. But Mel can fill us in."

Mel was surprised. While she'd been busy with other things, it seemed that Adrian had become a regular with her group of friends. They spoke as if they knew him well, and everyone was excited by what he was creating. And she hadn't had any idea.

How would Ryan have reacted, if Adrian had been here?

No, she scolded herself. These were her friends. Ryan had to adjust, even if he was, well, stiff on the subject of Adrian.

Sensing that the conversation was going in a direction Ryan wouldn't be comfortable with, Mel reached over and took his hand. "Yes to the coffee shop. He chose this amazing painting for the brick wall. And the light, with those gigantic windows. Cleaning out the worm-eaten books, pretty yucky. There'll still be lots of second-hand, though."

The conversation meandered. A few people pulled up chairs, others sat on the lawn. After a while everyone migrated to the tables to eat hamburgers and chicken. Beer flowed, the baseball season was dissected, mortgage rates and lines of credit were touched on—Ryan shone there—and kids ran in and out.

Mel sensed that Ryan wasn't completely at ease in this crowd, especially after the Adrian bomb. But fair enough. She hadn't been at ease with the Davies or the Grants. But he wasn't rejecting them, either. Yeah, so Sven and Danika had impressive sounding jobs. Julie was a real estate agent, another friend clerked at a store in Creekside Mall while she put herself through school, another was an auto mechanic. Mel's friends came in all shapes and sizes, so to speak. Ryan would get that, once he was used to them. She was sure of it.

Anyway, he loved her. The night before had been dreamy, even if all they'd done after that spontaneous burst of lovemaking had been to finish their supper and go to sleep. Even sleeping with Ryan was something she could do forever.

Later they had a moment to themselves and she said, "I didn't know Adrian was a part of this group now. I'm glad, but I don't want you to be uncomfortable."

"It's fine, Melanie." He hugged her to him, staking a very public claim. "It was interesting, getting a broad perspective on the bookstore. The word on the street can be useful. The coffee shop might prove to be a bigger draw than the books."

"Adrian's getting that message. He's thinking about expanding the coffee space."

Mel cuddled against him and sighed, a deep, contented sigh. She sipped at her beer and held Ryan's hand, watching the activity swirl around her. This was her clan, these were her people. Ryan was okay here, and life was good.

11

"Sit," Amanda commanded, waving Mel toward the small, round conference table tucked in the corner of her office. "Let's talk."

"Is something wrong?"

"You tell me." Amanda eased into a chair with all the grace of a six-months-pregnant woman. On her way down she grimaced; Junior McKinnon must be practicing acrobatics. A protective hand hovered over her little baby bump as she settled. As usual, she had her fountain pen handy, twitching between her fingers. "Mel, have you thought any more about changing positions?"

Actually, she hadn't. Between the fire and Ryan's declaration, her mind was on overdrive as it was.

"I'm still uneasy," Amanda said. "Not because you couldn't do the job, but because I'm not sure you'd be happy."

"Something's come up." Mel heard her own voice, the flatness of it, as if she was facing a jury verdict she couldn't avoid. She gave herself a mental smack; this could be her opportunity, not a trip to the gallows.

She should have given the whole thing more thought. But vacancies at SI were so rare, she'd expected to have months.

"I need a manager for the search team. Paul's moving to Milwaukee to be closer to family."

"I see..." She listened while Amanda outlined the position. The search team went around the world, sourcing the treasures that made Sinclair Imports the highly regarded distributor of giftware it was. She'd known Paul for years and had a reasonable understanding of the nature of his job. He didn't travel himself, but coordinated, analyzed and assessed, tracked expenses and handled snafus, judged the suitability and sales potential of the items the search team found.

She could handle it. She knew SI's inventory, she had a good eye for the types of things they looked for, and she knew what sold. And she was familiar with the business end, shipping, customs, estimating probable revenues and so forth.

On the other hand, any shift in position entailed outranking someone. Having the responsibility for managing the team, judging the team members, made Mel uneasy. She'd been a pal to the whole company for too long.

Other than that, it was a match made in heaven. And at least this team wasn't based in Calter Creek. The two men and one woman lived overseas and came to the office once in two or three years. Mel hadn't even met one of them.

Speaking of which... "Boy or girl?" Mel blurted. Amanda hadn't said.

Amanda shrugged. "We decided to not find out."

"Now, that would drive me nuts."

"You're changing the subject. The position's open. Here, take this." She handed over a printed summary of the job. Mel scanned it, her eyes widening when she saw the salary.

Amanda's voice softened. She'd become a bit of a mother hen since acquiring a stepdaughter, and it was more pronounced with the baby on the way. "I'm serious. It's part selfishness, because you and I have such a strong working relationship. But it's more that I don't want you to jump if you aren't sure. There's no going back."

"Yeah. I've thought about that." The idea of someone replacing her as Amanda's right hand gave her a pang. "How long do I have?"

"Next Monday? That gives you a week. And come talk to me any time. Any questions or concerns. You can handle this one, Mel. I'm just uneasy."

"Don't be. This is sooner than I expected, but I'll give it plenty of thought before I jump."

"Good. Now, I have an appointment in Inventory Control, and you were going to do something with departmental budget tracking, I think?"

"Yes, ma'am." Mel's mouth twisted in a grin. "If I take this position, I'll never have to do budget comparisons again."

Amanda laughed and stood. "Wrong. Given the unstructured nature of the search team, you'd spend half your life with your departmental budget. Ask Paul."

She kept the grin; this wasn't really news. "Well, darn."

Mel went back to her desk and the departmental budgets. She truly had no idea which way she'd jump.

Then there was the matter of telling Ryan. She knew his opinion already. He'd be ecstatic. And it worried her, because he'd think it perfectly proper to encourage her, even push her toward the new position.

Maybe she'd keep it to herself for a while. This was her decision, after all.

She could talk it over with Adrian on Saturday. He was a businessman, and he'd be objective. He could help.

Tuesday evening. Mel took her stance, bit her lower lip, held her breath, and swung. She hit the ball, more or less; it went ten feet, hopping across the ground.

The golf instructor seemed pleased. Mel had seen the cartoons with hunky golf teachers coaching their pupils by locking them in a muscular grip. Not this time; the instructor teaching Mel and two other women how to swing a golf club was perky, blond, and decidedly female.

Oh well.

After an hour of trying to get the club to connect with the ball, Mel revised her estimate of the level of fitness involved in golf. Her triceps were going to be immovable tomorrow. Still, it was a lovely evening, and it was a lark, out there on the practice tee, trying to hit the ball instead of topping it.

Ryan turned up as they were finishing and met her with a hug. "Fun?" he asked as they walked over to the terrace.

"Not sure yet. Different. But I suspect I'm doomed to failure. I foresee scores in the mid two hundreds."

He laughed. "Maybe we should go to the driving range. Then you can keep hitting balls without having to find them."

"Finding them's not the problem. They're never more than twenty feet from where they started." She turned to the young man hovering at the table and ordered a white wine.

Ryan was in his element, she thought. He exuded content. The heat wave had finally broken, and a drink on the terrace was the perfect way to wrap up a balmy summer evening. A drink with her man, in this lovely setting, after an adventure into the world of sports.

"Hey, Dreamy." He nudged her hand.

"Doesn't get much better, does it?"

"Not much, no." He lounged in his chair, watched the people arriving for a late meal or heading to the pool for the sunset swim.

She could conjure up ways it could be better. For one thing, yesterday, after Amanda's bombshell, she'd decided to move back into her apartment. She planned on making the move that evening. She needed space to think through her job offer, and being with Ryan didn't give her that space. That wasn't a positive thought. But they both had to navigate the shoals of togetherness, so they'd learn.

Ryan had been neutral when she told him. Perhaps he also needed a little separation. Theirs was, after all, still a new relationship.

Their drinks arrived. "We were so busy last weekend, I haven't even told you about my house hunting jaunt," she said, looking at him over the rim of her glass. In fact, she knew instinctively that Ryan wasn't all that interested in her time with her girlfriends, so it hadn't come up.

He leaned forward and cradled his G-and-T. "I'd forgotten. It was just for fun, wasn't it? Give Julie a chance to assess the market? Did you find something you liked?"

"That's why we met, remember? Because I wanted to buy a place of my own?"

He sipped his drink. "Melanie, you wouldn't seriously consider—"

"Not now. Things have changed. But it's fun to look." She put a hand on his arm to drive her point home.

He relaxed again. "Tell me what you saw."

"Nothing tempting, except there was this one townhome." Her mind diverted from golf swings and SI management, and she felt excitement building up. She squeezed his arm. "Ryan, what they'd done with the walls, the way they used color to bring out the furnishings, the light… I got so many ideas for decorating."

He grimaced. "It's jarring when one room's green and the next one's pink. I've always thought if you need color, you could add it with pictures or drapes."

"You know I love bright things. I don't want neutral walls."

"You have them now."

"Only because I rent. In this house, one wall in the living room was a deep terra cotta. It was magnificent."

"Just one wall?" Ryan sounded skeptical.

"One was enough. An accent. They had this giant African mask hanging on it. It looked great. There was a bedroom in indigo, too, but it didn't work for me. Soothing, but too dark."

"It sounds awful, to be honest."

"It wasn't awful, but not what I'd choose. It was somber, not cheerful."

He reached for her hand on his arm and held it between them on the table. "I suppose we might be able to compromise on one wall. As long as it's not something like primary red."

She laughed and shook her head. "I outgrew that years ago. I'm not an unsophisticated kid anymore. And kitchens… nothing popped out at me. Lots of granite counters. Stainless appliances—you'd spend your life wiping off fingerprints. Amanda's kitchen before she got married was a light yellow. It always looked like sunshine, even when it was miserable out."

"I don't know." Ryan's voice conveyed more doubt than confidence. "It sounds sort of country."

"No way, not Amanda. The kitchen's the heart of the home, where everyone wants to hang out. A friendly place."

Ryan was thoughtful, sipping at his drink and looking out over the fairway. "I like the look of stainless appliances. And dark wood."

"Sophisticated, in other words."

"A kitchen you'd be proud of."

"You're imagining a frumpy kitchen from the fifties with café curtains or something. I see a room that's happy to have ten kids in it for a birthday party. Indestructible, cheerful. We'll figure it out."

Compromise, Mel. Ryan wasn't sold, she could tell. Maybe she'd been too enthusiastic, too fixed on her own vision. She'd never considered that he might be equally attached to his own. But she wasn't going to let a discussion about a kitchen that didn't even exist yet spoil this perfect evening.

"One day we'll go looking together," he said. "Then we can discuss what we've seen."

"Good thinking."

A couple stopped by their table, and everyone chatted for a minute or two. It was a good way to break off the conversation. He freed his hand and draped his arm over her shoulders. She sipped her wine and relaxed.

A storm had rolled through on Friday, bringing a sparkling Saturday in its wake. On Adrian's deck, over a breakfast of scrambled eggs with spinach and feta cheese, Mel told Adrian about the job offer. "It's been on my mind all week. I don't know what to do."

"Be warned, I have my own opinion of the corporate ladder. Huff and I are a perfect example of how what's a gorgeous view from the top for one person is pure vertigo for another. In the end, only you can make this decision, but I'll help you work through it, if you want. Which hat should I put on? The ex-CEO one or the friend one?"

"Could we do both?"

The last few days had been miserable overall. She hadn't wanted to discuss the job offer with Ryan, because she knew what he'd think, and she suspected he'd sway her to his opinion. So she'd bitten her tongue on Tuesday when they had after-golf-lesson drinks, and used moving back into her apartment and the need to clean, clean, clean to avoid him the rest of the week.

Avoiding Ryan was the last thing she wanted to do, but she needed to be clear in her mind before she told him.

Problem was, she was a long way from that clarity, and they'd be together at the Club later in the afternoon. She couldn't keep it back any longer.

Adrian's voice interrupted her thoughts. "We'll start with the easy one."

She looked at him and saw him studying her over the top of his teacup. This was a different Adrian, she realized, one she hadn't encountered yet. One who assessed, did profit-loss statements, made executive decisions, despite the elderly blue shirt and khaki shorts he had on. There was something in his eyes that brought home to her that he'd once held the reins of power of one of the major book chains in the United States.

But behind the teacup, he gave her a smile. "Corporate-speak. You're qualified, the pay's a step up. I haven't seen your leadership skills in action, but I'm going to guess they're in line with the demands of the position, or Amanda wouldn't have offered it to you. You're organized and efficient. So yes, from that perspective, you should take the job."

"That easy, huh?"

He put down the teacup and gave her a fuller smile. "That easy." There was a pause and he dropped the smile. "If that's all you're looking at."

"And it's not, is it?" she moaned. "I wouldn't have just spent a week in hell if it were."

"Oh, Mel. That bad?"

"Yeah. Pretty much. Why can't I make up my mind?"

"Eat your eggs."

She giggled. "You're a yummy cook, Adrian. I haven't eaten this well in years."

"My delight."

They both ate. Mel pushed the plunger in the coffee press and poured herself a cup. They didn't stand on ceremony anymore; she knew his kitchen and made herself at home, sharing in the cleanup after one of his breakfasts.

He shifted his plate to the side. "Second hat? You ready?"

"Why do I get the feeling I'm not going to like this?"

"Because it's what you already know, maybe?"

He waited until she'd had a gulp or two of her coffee; no ladylike sipping today for her. Then he said, "What is it you want?"

"Damn. Do I have to answer that?"

"Not fair? Another context, then. What did you want three months ago? Because I'm sorry, but I have the impression that this confusion is because of Ryan Pope."

Adrian must have seen that she needed to sit with that for a minute because he became very busy clearing their breakfast plates and taking them into the kitchen. She heard water running into the sink, dishes clattering.

Mel sat alone on the deck, cradling her coffee and staring out into nothing. Did it all come down to Ryan? Dumb question. Of course it did... sort of. He had opened her eyes to another way to live her life, to exploring her own capabilities. To being more than she'd been. So in the final analysis it wasn't about Ryan at all.

"He was the spark," she said when Adrian came back out.

"Catalyst."

"Kick in the butt." She got a laugh from him. "Problem is, I'm not sure if I've been kicked to somewhere I want to be, or not."

"It's not a bad idea to be forced to take stock. You love your work. And it gives you the space to live the way you choose. The time consideration matters, because this new role's likely to consume more of it."

"But to stretch myself, spread my wings..."

"Could be good," Adrian conceded. "Or there might be other ways to do that."

"Such as?"

He shook his head. "Confusing the issue."

"It's already confused enough. I'm almost always game for new things. That's why I'm here, I guess. Plus the breakfasts."

"And my delightful company?"

"Naturally." She reached across the table to put a hand on Adrian's forearm. "You're a friend."

He squeezed her hand, then moved his arm away to pick up his teacup. "So let's go to a different starting place. Where do you want to be in, say, five years? What will your life look like? What's the dream?"

A pause. "I'm trying to come up with a big dramatic thing for you, but at heart I'm a small-town girl, I guess. Adventure's fine, but I value stability. A house, kids. What my sister has."

"There's usually a step before the house and kids. You never mention your sister's husband, although I assume she has one."

"Steve. He's never there. He's got an auto parts business that takes up his time. I guess he has to be that tied up in it, to keep them fed. That's not what I'm after." she mused. "I want a family that's really a family. Not a man who's married to his work."

"Mel..." He spoke hesitantly, peering at the little bit of tea left in his cup. "I hate to bring this up, but—"

"I know what you're going to say. Not true. Ryan's dedicated to his career, but he wouldn't be an absentee dad."

Adrian looked up at her, eyebrows raised.

"Honest. We've had this conversation."

"And it's truly none of my business, so please forgive me. For you, work and kids, that's a complicated equation, even in your current job."

"It's hard for me to imagine, looking ahead at it. I guess I want it all. Now I've got to consider the practical realities of having it all. In my dreams there's always sunshine and nothing goes wrong. Not much help, is it?"

"But this sunny image isn't tied directly to your work. It's the whole package."

"I watched Amanda for years," she said, thinking back. "She loves running SI, but for a while it seemed as if it was all she did, and it was making her sour. Then she met Jacob and now..." Mel shrugged. "She still loves her job, but it isn't everything. There's a balance. I want that."

Adrian's eyes watched his teacup as he turned it round and round in the saucer. "One more question. How stable is your position? If, say, Amanda decided to retire."

"Won't happen. Her father will step in when she has the baby, and we'll probably have a bassinet in the president's office for a while. That's the benefit of a family owned company."

Adrian chuckled.

"No bassinets at The Bindery?" She imagined Adrian or Huff in some big corporate office with a baby bed in the corner. "Maybe not every family-owned company, but that's how SI works. I'd say it's stable. I can't see the Sinclairs ever selling out."

He changed the topic. "You ready to get to work on a bookstore?"

"Good timing. It's getting steamy out here."

They stopped in the kitchen long enough to wash the dishes, then headed downstairs. The ground floor had been partially cleared. The new books section had vanished, and Adrian had taken the secondhand romances to the Thrift Shop over on Superior. He'd tossed out the empty shelves, and Mel could see most of the space without clutter. "Good light. Good vibes."

"I think so. Do you want to tackle cookbooks today?"

"Will there be treasures?"

"Most of this isn't old enough to be interesting. Probably decent recipes, but out of fashion and no one's going to buy them."

They set to work on opposite sides of the double shelf, Mel on the side facing the front windows where sunlight poured in.

"You've never told me what possessed you to start this," she said. "Is it a lifetime's dream?"

"I did tell you once. Something to delight, to focus my errant mind. So it's a dream, but not complete in itself. I've been thinking, we may have made a mistake not investing in dust masks."

"Non sequitur."

"Driven by desperation." Adrian sneezed.

"I think this place should have been gutted before you started."

"Except for the hidden treasures. Anyway, there's this redhead who kept coming in insisting on buying books from a bookstore that wasn't even open."

"Sure, blame me. I've been reading Emily Dickenson occasionally. One poem a day, like you suggested."

"Are you getting into it?"

"Not always. But it sticks with you, doesn't it?"

The silence stretched as they worked. It was pleasant after the heat of the deck; Mel was grateful for the way the ground floor of the store remained cool. "What are you doing about the temperature upstairs?" she asked.

"New insulation. Air conditioning. Keep it as natural as possible. The rare book room's going to need serious climate control. Why do you ask?"

"Just curious." She turfed books for a while. Half the books she put into boxes threatened to crumble. Then, as a stalling technique to duck his response to her job opportunity, she said, "So tell me, Adrian. What's your dream? If it's not the bookstore, what's the biggie?"

"Why don't we finish with yours first? The one that seems to be coming true."

"Yeah." She sighed, a deep, contented sigh. "This time, maybe it is."

"So the work has to mesh with Ryan, and with your own dreams and needs, and with your own expectations and plans. What does he think?"

"That I should take it." It wasn't necessary to tell Adrian that Ryan hadn't heard about the job offer yet.

"Why?"

That gave her pause. Why *did* Ryan want her to move up on SI's corporate ladder? "Same reasons. Grow, stretch my wings. Make me feel better about myself."

"Hold everything." Adrian came to her side of the shelves. "You don't feel good about yourself?" He looked troubled.

She grinned. "Almost always. Lately, once or twice I've been kind of overwhelmed by some of the people at the Club, acting as if Executive Assistant isn't good enough for them to bother with."

He went back to his side, but he was still frowning. "Give me a minute," he said. "I'm trying to figure out how to say what I want to say."

"You're wondering why should they matter to me?"

"To either of you. You shouldn't have to defend the work you choose to do. And if you love it..."

She suddenly felt miserable inside. She knew what Adrian was thinking, that Ryan was railroading her into a more important sounding position. But he *wasn't*. He was suggesting that she could be better, do more...

"Do you still want my opinion, Mel? Are you mad at me?"

"Of course I'm not mad. He's not... I mean, Ryan's not trying to push me into anything."

"I'm glad."

"So... opinion, please." She circled the shelves.

He looked startled for a moment, then said, "You have no idea what sunlight does to your hair, do you?"

"Frizzy?"

"Hard to describe. Like a nimbus. Have a seat." He waved at a precarious stack of books.

"Maybe not." Mel laughed and propped herself against the shelves.

"So, weighing it in the balance, and looking at who you are now, when you're around me... I'll say no, I don't think you should take the new position. I'm not convinced it would help you attain your goals. But bear in mind, I don't share that much of your life, so I'm not working with a full deck here."

"You know me pretty well."

"It's your dream that's important, Mel. Following your own star."

She un-propped and went back around to her side. "I still doubt the dream-come-true stuff sometimes."

"You can't merely have a dream, as my family keeps reminding me. You have to look at it, top and bottom. You have to be sure it's right and not an illusion. That it fits with who you are at heart, with your reality."

"You mean like you think you want something, then when you get it you realize you didn't really want it after all?"

"Exactly like that. It's better if you can avoid that path in the first place, not wait until you're half way down it. Otherwise you're in danger of heartbreak."

Sorrow, anguish, despair... "You know what? The synonyms for heartbreak are all components of heartbreak. None of them seems to be complete enough."

Quiet from Adrian's side. Then he said, "I think you may be right. So don't risk it. Roll your dream around on the floor, kick it through the air, whatever. Prove to yourself it's the right one."

"I have. It is."

More quiet. Mel studied cookbooks, discarded them.

His voice became lighter, the customary, ebullient Adrian. "Once you're sure, you need to put energy behind your dreams. Build up power. We could do a ritual. Throw in a candle-lit tarot reading."

"You're kidding me. You do those often?"

"Only as needed. In case you were wondering, in my mind you're the Queen of Wands."

She thought he was fighting off a laugh. This was too good to resist. Mel once again circled the shelves and looked at Adrian, who had sunk to the floor cross-legged with stacks of books around him, studying each one.

"Tell me about the Queen of Wands."

"Sure. She's self-confident, warm hearted, energetic and popular. And frequently a redhead."

"I like it, except it's a lot to live up to."

"We're talking intrinsic qualities here, not goals."

"Do you have a ritual cloak or robe or something? Does it have a hood?"

He looked up, mischief in his eyes. "Why not? I choose a robe, definitely a hood. Like monks. Do you have a color preference? Black?"

Mel shook her head. "Blue, maybe. Midnight blue. Mysterious."

"Mysterious appeals."

"You don't really have a robe, do you?"

He returned to his books. "In my dreams. But the cards, those I could manage. Put a pre-teen boy in bed for a year and there's no telling what odd skills he'll develop."

She went to her side and lifted another book from the ancient shelves. "Dreams again. Come on, Adrian, your turn. What's the big dream?"

She could hear him drop a book into his box, walk to the end of the row. She turned and there he was, lightly haloed in the dim light that filtered through the dust in the air.

"You really want to know?"

"Why? Is it a secret?"

"No. Or maybe yes. Okay, here goes." He took a breath. "It can be expanded in a number of ways, but at the core it's about being in a room full of people, and looking across the people and seeing..." He paused. "And seeing the woman I love. And remembering the feel of her hand on my chest. Something private and intimate, in the midst of all that public."

His eyes had locked onto hers; he'd taken off his glasses.

"As I said, there's more to it. Right to the home, the kids, building a life together. But that's the one image that sort of sums it up." Adrian disappeared to his side of the shelf.

Mel leaned against the bookshelf and let herself slide until her back rested against vegetarian cooking from the nineteen seventies. Her bottom hit the floor with a thump.

"You asked." He'd been serious, looking myopically at her. Now he sounded like his usual, insouciant self again.

"Cripes, Adrian."

A book thumped into his box. "Cripes? Well chosen. I haven't heard that in years, if ever." More books landed, an irregular tattoo in the quiet room.

Mel stood and went around the end of the bookshelf. He had squatted to squeeze books into a box. He looked up; his glasses were back on.

"That's one heck of a dream," she said, and sank down beside him.

"An honest one. Not that much different from yours, when you get right down to it."

"Yours is a lot more poetic. Do you write poetry?"

"Occasionally. Doesn't everybody, at one time or another? I think most people outgrow it."

"Show me, one day?"

He snorted. "Not likely. Juvenile attempts."

"Knowing you, I doubt that. It's a good dream, Adrian. I hope it comes true."

He stared off into the distance, as if he could see right through the next bookshelf. "It seems so simple. We all pine for that level of connection, that degree of intimacy. But here we are, you and I, neither of us at the starting line anymore. I keep thinking, one day. But for you—you're on your way, aren't you? You've found Ryan."

"Yeah." She leaned her head back and took a deep, pleasurable breath. "Maybe it will happen this time. Keep your fingers crossed for me, I want this so much."

He hauled himself to his feet and held out a hand. "Back to the dust and worms. This will take all summer, the rate we're going."

"I don't mind. It's fun, in a peculiar way." She returned to cookbooks.

There was silence from Adrian's side of the bookshelf. Then he said, "Oh, it is. Definitely."

❖

Talking to Ryan was a lot more straightforward, with fewer digressions.

"Of course you should accept it. Why would you even debate? This is your future, Melanie. *Our* future. Honey, chances like this don't turn up that often."

They were on the grass surrounding the pool deck at the Club. The pool wasn't as busy as it usually was on a Saturday. Possibly more people were away on vacation, or maybe it was the break in the weather. It was still noisy enough, and hot enough that Mel looked forward to the ten-minute adult swim once an hour. With her fair skin she'd never been a sunbather. Today she was avoiding the sun like the plague, huddled under a beach umbrella.

Ryan had stretched out near her. The sun didn't bother him, and putting sunscreen on his back was... yeah. Not bad at all. *Mine,* she thought, catching the appreciative glances he garnered.

But he'd sat up when she told him about the job offer, and her indecision.

"I am happy with what I do now."

"I know that." He scooted over to sit next to her. They both watched the kids cavorting in the pool. "But I also know how you react when you're with people whose jobs are... that sound more important. You want to hold your head up. You want them to listen to you."

"Yes. But..."

"I don't see any 'buts' here. Take it, Melanie. Use your first paycheck to buy yourself some clothes. Get your hair done. Start the new job with a bang."

"My hair?" Mel squinted at him behind her sunglasses. "It was just cut, actually."

"It looks fine. But... it's the professional thing again, honey. It's kind of, well... big?"

"When it's any shorter I look like Little Orphan Annie. Not a good look on me. Trust me on this."

"I guess you understand your corporate environment best."

167

The hair debate ended, thank heaven. As did the job debate, but without as clear a resolution. Ryan made accepting the new position sound so easy. Maybe he was right, maybe she was squirming around like a bug on a pin for no good reason. Why shouldn't she try new things? Earn more money? Gain professional status? Feel at home at the Club?

Mel suspected, at that moment, that she'd end up taking the position. But something inside still wasn't convinced.

The loudspeaker announced the adult swim, and the kids stampeded out of the pool, most of them in the direction of the refreshment stand. They waited until the kids were out of the way, then joined hands and headed for their swim.

The Job—in Mel's mind it had taken on capital-letter significance—became a theme for the rest of the weekend. Ryan didn't push, not too much anyway, but he clearly couldn't understand her reluctance. Ninety percent of the time she didn't understand it, either. Problem was, the other ten percent she had this sinking sensation in her stomach, the edge-of-a-precipice feeling that told her not to take the next step.

Sunday afternoon they went to the driving range, and Mel's shots started going farther than twenty feet. She treated herself to a happy dance, proud that she could succeed in a challenge. The driving range presaged good things ahead, she was sure.

"If I take this position," she said in Ryan's living room as the weekend wound down, "I want it to be because I want it for myself. Not because anyone else thinks I should do it. Even you," she added, but did her best to convey, through her hands resting on his shoulders, that his opinion mattered.

"I'm trying to understand why you're so hesitant. I guess it's a bigger step than you've contemplated before. To me it's self-evident. Especially given... well, everything. The present, the future. I have faith in you, Melanie."

"That means a lot."

But Mel spent Sunday night at her own apartment, with no more idea than she'd had at the beginning of the weekend what she'd tell Amanda Monday morning.

12

In the end she flipped a coin.

Not that she intended to go by the quarter's verdict. But she'd heard that once the coin was in the air, you'd know what you were thinking.

The coin said to take the job. Mel monitored her gut, and her gut said okay, maybe.

She took out the piece of paper where she'd listed pros and cons. There didn't seem to be very many cons, in the greater scheme of her life. That odd internal sinking feeling hadn't gone away, but could be ascribed to nerves, or excitement, couldn't it? The biggest con was the changing relationship between herself and the rest of SI. But others had accepted promotions, or had resigned for new positions, new adventures. They were like family, but they *weren't* family, were they?

In the pro column were a) more money and b) more stature, leading to c) better relationships at the Club, which mattered because her future was with d) Ryan, e) whose approval mattered most. The web of her life had changed over the summer, and it was time for her to change with it.

By two o'clock Monday afternoon Mel was the new manager of the search team.

It wasn't an instantaneous switch, worse luck. She had one job to phase out of and another to phase into, so the next month was likely to be crazy. She and Amanda huddled with Marcia, the head of personnel, and found applications on file from a few promising candidates to take over the Executive Assistant position. Mel was on the phone arranging appointments before the day was over.

She went home Monday thinking she should feel on top of the world. Instead she felt nervous, exhausted, and displaced. She phoned Ryan as she'd promised.

"I'm so glad, baby." He at least had no second thoughts.

"It feels kind of lonely. I've been in Amanda's office for years. I'm bothered that another person will be doing my job, taking my place."

"You'll be in Amanda's good books more than ever, because you'll be doing a greater service for her. You'll see."

They arranged to celebrate at the Club Tuesday night. After Mel declined an invitation to spend the night at Ryan's, she was alone with her thoughts.

It was more than Amanda's opinion at stake. Their work together had been like a friendship, a close collaboration between two people who understood each other. Sure, she'd do a good job for Sinclair Imports, she never doubted that. But it felt as if something was broken.

"My executive girl." Ryan was bursting with pride and happiness. They sat at one of the window tables in the dining room at the Club, drinks and bread before them. He'd pulled out all the stops. He'd even brought her roses when he picked her up.

Mel was feeling celebratory, too. Now that she'd had time to let the change sink in, to meet with Paul and discuss the job with the man she'd be taking over from, the idea felt more comfortable.

It just might work.

"Executive. Me?" She giggled. The mojito must be getting to her. "Unreal."

"You'll get used to it. When they bumped me up to branch manager, I don't mind telling you, I was nervous. I'd been assistant manager for a couple of years, so it wasn't that I didn't know the job. It was the new responsibility, plus relocating. Don't worry, I'll have your back."

"It's not the work, it's the other stuff. Missing being in Amanda's office. I'm jealous of whoever takes over from me."

"You'll get over that. And you'll see Amanda on a much more professional basis. Once you settle into it, you'll see how much Sinclair Imports has to offer you in return for all the benefit you bring to them."

"And suddenly being in charge of people—it changes the balance. It worries me."

Ryan shook his head at her. "Sweetheart, they'll get used to it in no time. They probably think you should have done this years ago. Anyway, didn't you tell me that the people reporting to you aren't in the office very often?"

"True, they live overseas. And most of the managers hang out with the rest of the staff. I guess I'm self-conscious."

"Hold your gorgeous head up and let them know you're proud. And that you're in charge."

Mel had virtually forgotten her mojito, or even that they were in the over-the-top elegant dining room at the Club. She reached across the table and put her hand on Ryan's. "I'll need your support. I'm liable to be a nervous wreck for a while."

"Any problems," he promised, "we'll work through them together."

"Problems I can deal with. It's anxiety that gets to me."

"Never hurts to double-check your decisions. I've been in management for a while, now."

"Not in the wholesale business, though. Just keep me from falling apart and I'll be fine."

How much did Ryan think he'd be helping her? She took a roll from the basket while she thought. She knew SI's business better than he possibly could, other than perhaps personnel issues. But she'd take a personnel question to Marcia. He wasn't thinking he'd tell her how to do her job, was he? It sounded a little like that.

No. Of course not. He wanted the best for her, and for her to do her best. She had to get over this reluctance to accept help. Ryan could be—*would be*—a fabulous asset.

Mel turned her attention to the setting, the handsome man across the table from her—a handsome man whose body she knew really well, and that she had tantalizing plans for, after this dinner—and the general state of her life. She'd never have dreamed she'd be dining at the Club as if she belonged here.

Or that she'd be one of Amanda's managers.

Well, why not? Maybe it was the mojito talking, but Mel, at that moment, felt excited and confident. Life, she reflected, might have taken a turn, but it sure was going in positive directions now.

Over their steaks Ryan said, "You're getting a nice raise. What will you do with the extra money?"

"Not a whole lot. There's nothing I particularly want. Building my savings, retirement planning, that kind of thing. I've been stashing money for a long time now, for that house—"

"It's good that we'll both be able to contribute to it."

She set her fork on her plate. "This is serious talk."

Ryan finished his bite and said, "Yes, it is. But about the kinds of things that affect our future."

"It feels funny, talking about financing 'our' house, when—"

"When it's not formal yet? But it will be. We both know that, Melanie. I was thinking, there are attractive subdivisions around. Some of them are old enough that they have mature trees again. Brandon Caine—that's the name. Major developer in the area. I haven't met him."

"As a person, I've heard less than wonderful things, but his developments are popular."

"That's what matters. You don't have to like the man, just be aware of what he can do for you. I'm looking forward to buying you the house of your dreams."

"Uh-uh. Nice thought, but *we* choose and buy the house, not you alone. Even if I weren't contributing."

Ryan looked uncomfortable. "That came out wrong. I thought… besides that I'm in banking, I guess I'm traditional. It made sense to me that I'd handle the family's finances."

"Ryan." Mel spoke quietly, but decisively. "I've managed my own money since I was eighteen years old. I've never messed up my credit rating, never been late with a payment, never owed money after I paid off my first car. My taxes are filed on time and are done correctly. My checkbook balances. I have a good investment consultant and a small portfolio that's balanced in a way I'm comfortable with. As I see it, we share. Share ownership of the house and any new cars. It doesn't have anything to do with who contributes how much."

"Melanie, slow down." Ryan had moved through uncomfortable to tense.

"I haven't thought much about household expenses. Do we keep our own incomes separate and put money into a household account?"

"I... sweetheart, I don't have an answer. I'd assumed I'd manage an account with both our salaries in it."

Mel shook her head. "You might get the job of balancing the checkbook. Personally I use a spreadsheet so it's easy and accurate, but that's a minor point. What's major is control. Ryan, I'm not turning over control of the money I've earned, or my salary. Shared, yes, that's fine. But I'm not the little woman."

Mel stopped and caught her breath, and realized she was angry. "Is this some kind of a guy thing, wanting to take charge? You've been pumping me up for this job, and now you tell me I'm not able to handle a family's finances?"

She'd insulted him. But then he'd insulted her. What did he expect?

Ryan had turned icy. "That isn't what I meant."

Peace at any cost, her better angel cautioned. This was her celebration dinner. Mel took it down a notch. "Then what do you mean?" she asked, keeping her voice calm and steady. "I don't understand. I'm getting mixed signals here."

They ate in silence for a minute or two.

Finally Ryan said, "I'd thought... well, traditionally it's the man's role to see to the business end of a marriage."

Peace at almost *any cost,* her better angel amended. "This is the twenty-first century, and I'm thirty-five years old. You can't treat me like a child."

"I'm sorry if it felt that way to you."

They finished their meal in near silence, punctuated only by comments about the food, the goings-on outside the window.

But walking back to his car, Ryan took her hand and drew her up to him. "I really am sorry, Melanie. I guess I hadn't thought it through well enough, the reality of being married, having a house and all. I didn't mean to diminish your role. Honestly."

"I know. We could have picked a better time. We should schedule an afternoon business meeting, to be sure we're on the same page."

"You are so delightful. And so understanding." He pulled her to him. "And I want you so much," he whispered.

"Your place," she whispered back. She wanted to put the two of them back on a good footing, and she knew one excellent way to do that. First, get him out of his suit and tie, slowly. Run her hands and mouth over those fine pecs, work south over his light chest hair and tight abs… drive them both nuts.

She hoped. Ryan's lovemaking was oddly formal, and he didn't like ceding control.

But she also planned to have Ryan take her back to her apartment afterwards. She wanted to spend the night in her own surroundings. She needed time to herself to think over the evening. She wanted to be close to the half dozen roses he'd brought her, now in a vase on her table. And for once she wanted no roommate.

Mel let herself into the bookstore. It was quiet; Adrian must be in his apartment, but there wasn't any of the usual kitchen clatter. "Adrian?" she called out.

Still no answer, but she picked up a sound like music, or birdsong. She went upstairs, at home now in the half finished bookstore. Through the open apartment door she could see Adrian on the deck, looking out over the gray skies that blanketed Calder Creek.

He turned and smiled when he heard her. The birdsong stopped.

She joined him at the rail. "You're playing your recorder. You've never played for me."

He showed her the diminutive instrument. "It's a sopranino, more like a piccolo. The music's called 'The Bird

Fancyer's Delight' — that's fancier with a 'y'. Written to teach your pet bird to sing."

"Does it work? Play me some more?"

"I have no idea, and another day. Look over there." He gestured to the horizon, then slotted the little recorder into a storage pouch.

His deck faced north, and far off, beyond the right corner of the deck, she could see the top of a crane. "Landmark Center," she said.

"I hear they're starting with the office complex. I wonder how much difference it'll make to downtown."

"Creekside Mall's funneled off some business. Maybe they'll steal more from Creekside than from us."

"It's innovative, from the plans they've made public. Not much similarity to Creekside. Whether it's enough to sell it to businesses..." He shrugged. "Probably so, but I'm not worried. There'll always be a market for what we're making here. It wouldn't surprise me if Huff moved The Bindery into Landmark. He's been in touch, by the way, asking questions. Could be he's protecting his investment, but I think he's wondering if there are aspects of our concept he could borrow. We've become the talk of the family."

"They know all about what you're doing, huh?"

"Naturally. Not many secrets in the Forsythe clan. Whatever, I doubt there's anything The Bindery could use from this place, it's too idiosyncratic and personal. But we — I mean The Bindery — we do need to freshen up the concept."

She looked up at him. "You still think of The Bindery as yours, don't you?"

"It is still mine, in the sense that I'm a part owner and I'm on the Board. But even if I didn't have a stake in it, it's family, so I want it to go well. How are you?" he asked in an abrupt change of subject. "You look tired."

"I am. It's been quite a week."

"So you took the promotion."

"Are you disappointed?"

175

He looked startled. "Why would I be disappointed? Mel, if it's what you want, then I wish you every joy. Have you started?"

"Both jobs at the moment. I'm interviewing to fill my old role next week, and I'm working with Paul to learn his. Long hours, brain overload."

"I bet. I think we should begin our mornings with meditation. It might help you keep things organized in that head of yours."

"The head that's reeling right now."

"Overwrought?"

"Overtaxed."

"Overcooked? Come in. It's gray out here and I have a puffed pancake thing keeping warm. It collapsed, though."

"Doesn't matter. I'm intrigued."

"Fresh berries. Sounded light and nice." Adrian pulled a cast iron frying pan out of the oven. Sure enough, the contents looked a little like a collapsed soufflé, a little like a pancake. "Voila."

Over the pancake with raspberries he asked her, "Any concerns? Worries?"

"Not really. There's a lot I still don't know, but right now it's mainly volume. I started out thrown into the middle of a crisis, plus selecting, then training Amanda's new assistant."

"Have you celebrated? I don't have a handy split of champagne, which is a pity, we could have had mimosas with breakfast. Although that might have affected the book sorting..."

"Went out for dinner Tuesday night. Steak."

"You know, steak is a strange thing. Once upon a time I knew the names of all the cuts. Now there's flatiron steak and triangle steak and Denver steak and who knows what else. Have cows invented new muscles?"

She giggled. It felt good to kick back and laugh with Adrian.

They took their coffee and tea out onto the deck and chatted for another fifteen minutes or so. Mel was grateful.

Lately it had seemed as if every minute of every day was laden with meaning and challenge.

There were only a few bookshelves left. As they tackled the natural sciences side by side, Adrian said, "Question for you."

"What? Please make it an easy one."

"It may not be. Have you given any thought to what you want to do when we're done with the bookshelves? I almost don't want it to happen, for fear that you'll disappear into the world and I'll never see you again. I'd welcome your staying involved, but I don't know what might work for you."

"Oh." Mel tossed books into her box. Sciences were easy. If it was out of date it was no good from a factual standpoint, and not much chance of finding a treasure. A lot of it was outdated textbooks. "I haven't, really. It's felt as if this could go on forever."

"Because you're happy here."

"Yeah. It's a world of its own. But once these shelves are done... do you have something in mind?"

"In fact, I do. My only concern is that you won't have time. I thought you might tackle the coffee shop."

Mel stopped tossing books and turned to him. "Tackle how?"

He dropped a stack of books into one box, set aside another book for further consideration. "Decorate. Source the tables and chairs and the bits that go on them. Food services. Figure out what to offer, find a baker, coffee and tea and so forth. Wall decorations, if any, to tone with the ladies in our picture. How to delimit the coffee shop from the rest of the building."

Mel sank to the floor. She could see the coffee shop, absolutely *see* it in her mind. But she'd never find the time to make it happen, not now.

"Sad face." Adrian sat next to her, his arms resting on his raised knees. "Not enough time, not enough energy. I suppose secretly I recommended you not take the new position so I could keep you here. But there we are. You can go on being the idea woman."

"I'd like that," she said sadly. "I'd like the other, too. I'd love it. But I don't know how I could."

"Whoa." Adrian took one of her hands and squeezed before releasing it. "I didn't mean to give you cause to worry. I hope you'll keep coming by, now that you've got your fingerprint all over this place. We could spend Saturday mornings focusing on this or that. I love where it's going, but you know that to me, it's become as much yours as mine. I don't want to break that link."

"Thanks, Adrian. When I'm here..." She trailed off and leaned her head back against the old books. "It's as if I've stepped out of my ordinary reality, as if I'm somewhere else."

"We should get out to Joe's for lunch more often. Or you could drop by weekdays when the workmen are here. That's when reality smacks you right in the face."

Mel clambered to her feet. "I don't want it to be finished. You'll have employees and a business to run. It'll be a beginning, but an ending, too."

"I'll still want you to come for breakfast, just because." Adrian stood and returned to his section of the shelves.

"Oh, I will." She spoke without thinking, so it was a moment before Ryan's probable reaction to her sharing breakfast with Adrian sank into her head. Antiquated natural sciences took a back seat in her mind to puzzlement over the future. One day this magical time would be over, the decisions and work complete. Could she bear coming to the store as a customer rather than a... a what?

"Adrian, how would you define my relationship to the bookstore?"

"Muse? Worker in the trenches? Integral, anyway. It's hard to imagine the place without you."

Hard for her, too. But it was inevitable.

She'd always told herself the store was a fantasy, a dream for the summer. A trip into a magic realm where everything was possible and worries could be set aside. Problem was, she didn't want the fantasy to end.

No point obsessing about a future that wasn't certain. She settled in to her assigned shelves of books, chatting cheerfully back and forth with Adrian. She'd take what she could and enjoy it for what it was.

Mel took her vision board from the fridge door and studied it.

Blond executive husband, check. Blond and red-headed kids, check. Casual mom in jeans, not so much.

Updating needed.

Work on the vision board was relaxing, and usually fast, which was good. Mel didn't have the time to spend an afternoon playing with her collage supplies. But on a rainy Sunday afternoon it might help her unwind.

Or maybe she was subconsciously putting off dealing with the flurry of emails she'd had late Friday. There was a problem getting a shipment out of Thailand, and her main contact there was freaking out. Legalities, ruffled feathers, deadlines... yes, definitely time to take a few minutes to play with the vision board.

Mel had acquired a collection of redheads she'd cut out of magazines over the years, in all manner of different poses and garbs. Which one to choose? The executive one or the upmarket casual one? Dressed for work or dressed for the Club?

Which of these came closest to the dream?

The one in jeans, her traitor mind grumbled. But current events had superseded that dream. This was the new reality. The new future.

These days, work took precedence, to the extent that periodically she wondered if she'd ever see the end of it. This was full immersion. She didn't believe that Paul, who was heading for Milwaukee and leaving her on her own, had faced problems like this. Or if he had, he'd never let on.

Maybe she wasn't cut out to be a manager. Because, when she was honest with herself, Mel was close to the point of not looking forward to going in to work Monday morning.

Enough. She sat in front of her collection of images, her scissors and glue at the ready. She carefully trimmed the picture of the executive redhead behind her desk. She peeled the jeans-clad redhead off the board and put the executive redhead, desk

179

and all, on it. The desk hid one of the kids, so she did some rearranging.

That summed it up. Mom behind a massive desk, there on the lawn in front of the nice suburban house. The work dominating her life. Was that her vision?

No. But it was the only executive redhead picture she had.

This redhead was cool and collected, and had her hair neatly back in a low ponytail. Not for her the wild, too curly mass Mel dealt with daily. Her hair had come up in conversation again last night, when she and Ryan got together for a movie and a sleepover.

Ryan didn't approve of her hair.

No, Ryan hadn't said that. He'd just suggested — *suggested* — that it was unprofessional.

After she'd got home from Ryan's this morning she'd experimented. Amanda had curly hair and kept it under control with a headband. But Amanda's was nothing like the wild-woman mess that Mel's hair became at the least hint of humidity. And what else was Ohio in the summer but dripping with humidity? The headband was insufficient, so she tried the ponytail next, but that was worse. Her hair wasn't that long, not long enough to be caught at the nape of her neck. And what she was able to catch formed a massive, shapeless lump back there. Horrible.

Over the years she'd grown accustomed to it. She'd been teased as a kid, but at college and in her working life, no one had ever said a word. So was it unprofessional? Or was that Ryan's bias? If she wanted to be taken seriously, did she have to tame things a bit? A lot?

Or did the opinion of the people at the Club count that much with Ryan? Did her hair embarrass him?

Mel sighed and put the vision board back on the fridge, with an envious thought to the executive redhead behind the desk, with her smooth, straight hair and her air of being in control of her life.

❖

Amanda appeared at her office door Monday morning. Having an office to herself was still a shock to Mel's system, and she was lonely in her little room down the corridor from the break room. Even though it was at the far end of the building, in Amanda's outer office she'd felt as if she was at the heart of Sinclair Imports.

"Come on in. Coffee?"

Amanda shook her head but perched on Mel's guest chair. "No time. I need a couple of reports, and you were going to make up a list of interview questions before Wednesday. Where are you with that?"

"I'm reviewing the questions with Marcia later. I'll send them over to you as soon as they're ready. What reports? I do have a day job, you know," she added with a grin.

Amanda laughed. "I miss having you next door. Be sure you add compatible sense of humor to the mix when we do the interviews." Amanda passed on the information she'd need to do the reports. "Tomorrow?"

"You'll have it. Paul's coming in this afternoon to walk me through a few last-minute questions. I gather his moving van's arriving on Thursday, then I won't be able to pick his brain anymore. It's beginning to feel real."

"You can handle it, but now that you've tried it out, if it's not where you want to be... practically speaking, this is your last chance to change your mind."

Mel shook her head. "No, I'm just trying to tie up as many loose ends as I can, while I can. I can't do two jobs indefinitely without losing my mind, so I sure hope one of these people works out."

"So do I. I'm about to land another burden on you, but if it's too much you can defer it. The college has a course in small business retail. I've seen the course outline, and it sounds good. We're not retail, but a lot of it applies in terms of selection, stocking, overheads. I'd like you to sign up for it."

"Night course?"

Amanda nodded. "Most of the business courses are. Think it over. It could help, and you might pick up something we haven't already thought of around here."

"I expect you can appreciate that now isn't the best time for me to add anything else to my life."

"I recall warning you about that. You only have three weeks before term starts."

"I'll let you know. Go away now, please."

"Have faith. It'll smooth out." Amanda hoisted herself up from the chair. "See you later."

Mel allowed herself a minute to groan before finishing the work she was doing for her search team and pulling Amanda's list of reports in front of her.

She'd had an uninterrupted hour with the reports when Anne buzzed her from the front desk. "Better come out here, Mel. You'll want to see this."

Mel checked her watch. Coffee break time, and definitely time for a stretch and change of focus. "I'll be right there."

When she got to the lobby she saw it. A bright and cheerful sunflower plant sat by Anne's desk. "Wow. Is this for me?"

"Delivery man said so. Check the card. I bet it's from your sweetie."

Ryan might send flowers, but sunflowers? Not his style, she thought. But it sure was Mel's. She ripped into the card's envelope. And grinned. "Nope. Not Ryan. Adrian, the guy who's renovating the bookstore downtown. This is so sweet of him, especially since he voted against my taking on the new job."

"So read the card."

"'Congratulations. You'll be fantastic. In fact, you already are. Adrian.' Isn't that sweet?"

"Very sweet. Want help lugging this thing?"

"I doubt it's heavy." Mel hoisted the pot, and the sunflowers nodded above her head as she carried it to her office. There near her window the plant brightened up the room. She texted Adrian, *Love it, it's perfect, thank you oodles!* She brushed a finger over the sunshine-yellow petals, feeling decidedly more sunshiny herself, then headed for the break room.

A few minutes later her phone vibrated. The text read, *"Oodles? Bunches?"*

She fired back, *"Megatons?"*

"Lots. I'm glad."

"My office is happy. See you Saturday."

Coffee at hand and the sunflower in the window, Mel settled in to work, feeling much more positive.

13

"Oh, no."

Saturdays weren't supposed to begin this way, but she knew immediately what Adrian was referring to. His voice carried absolute dismay.

"Mel, you didn't."

"I guess you don't like it?"

Getting her hair cut short—*tamed*, was the word she'd choose—was enormous for Mel. She'd spent an hour with pictures in magazines at the hairdresser's before finding a style she could live with. Not more than an inch long, easy to care for and keep under control using Amanda's headband trick. She'd had a few days to get used to it, and no longer jolted to a stop when she passed a mirror.

But Adrian... he was actually upset.

So much so he could hardly speak. "You've... damn it all, Mel. I suppose it's very up market and professional. But your hair..." He sounded both frustrated and bereft, as if she'd deprived him of his greatest pleasure.

Adrian, mild-mannered, supportive Adrian, had actually panned her choice. Mel wasn't sure if she was furious or stunned. She was sure her voice was cooler than usual, when she finally answered him. "It's my decision. As it happens, I like it. You don't have any right to criticize me, Adrian."

He'd met her downstairs. Now he sank onto the next-to-bottom step and put his face in his hands. She was so used to his presence that she rarely noticed his appearance anymore, the casual way he dressed in old shirts, khaki slacks or hiking shorts. Seeing him slumped on the stairs triggered a memory in her mind. The man she'd first seen in the doorway back in May had slouched. He didn't slouch anymore. Until this minute.

He shook his head as if to clear it, stood, and looked over to where she still hovered near the door. His face was drawn with tension. "Mel, I'm sorry. I overreacted. You look wonderful, in fact."

She wasn't done being mad. "Thanks, but a little too late. I mean, suppose all my hair fell out? You don't have any right to—"

" —to assault you like that?"

Batter? Attack?

"Try deflate."

He winced. "I was wrong. I'd never willingly offend you. And to me, even if all your hair did fall out, you'd still be you. Please forgive me."

Mel was so off base she didn't know where to go with this conversation. "It's not as if I shaved my head."

"If you had there'd be a good reason. Can I feed you? You will stay, won't you?"

What more did she expect him to do, after apologizing? "Let's drop it."

As they climbed the stairs to his apartment, he asked, "Are you on edge this morning? I sense it's more than my poor attitude."

"Maybe."

"Because of your hair?"

He was reading her mind again. Cutting her hair felt like a bigger step than taking the new position at SI. "Yeah, some. It's different for a man. Changing your appearance is scary, not knowing what anyone will say. If they'll approve or think you look like a dork."

"You could never look like a dork. Ryan likes it, I bet."

She smiled. "A lot." Ryan had in fact been fervent in his approval. They'd had Friday night drinks at the Club before going to the Madison Café for a light dinner, and he'd brought up her hair time and again, touching it occasionally. He'd even said it didn't tickle his nose now, when they made love. She hadn't considered that aspect. But anything to enhance their lovemaking...

The whole business of making love with Ryan was another thing on her mind, but she wasn't going to go into that with Adrian. Because it was satisfying, sure, but the zing, well, it still hadn't turned up. Its absence troubled her. She was beginning to doubt that she'd ever find the right time to be more adventurous. And was the absent zing even related to more edgy lovemaking? She wasn't sure.

And then there was SI...

She had too much on her mind, and this was Saturday morning. She shook her head and kicked the unwelcome thoughts out.

Before their cold breakfast—he had provided sardines again, and cottage cheese, along with fruit, tomatoes, and bread—he said, "One thing. May I touch it? Once?"

"I guess, if you want to."

He stood next to her chair and brushed his hand very lightly over her head. Then again. "It doesn't feel the same. The curls are more compact. I'm so sorry I messed this up for you. You're much more to me than your hair."

She smiled up at him. "Forget it. What are we doing today?"

"We could tackle the last shelf of books, but I'd rather pick your brain in another direction. The coffee shop's getting a fair amount of buzz." He circled the table and sat opposite her.

She nodded. "I picked up on it at the Larsens' barbecue."

"I regretted missing that. I still get tripped up with Bindery business occasionally. Have fun?"

"Mm hmm. I brought Ryan with me. It took him a while, but then he fit right in."

"You sound as if that's a milestone."

"It worried me a little, but it was good. So what's on your mind?"

"Enlarging the coffee shop. We've talked about it some. I'm beginning to see it taking up most of the second floor."

She considered. "We don't want a barn, but too small and you lose business."

"I have some informal statistics. Took me most of the week, talking to anyone I could snare. They'd see this odd looking guy coming their way and take off in the other direction, but once they got what I was after they were happy enough to talk. There could be a steady stream throughout the day, with peaks at coffee breaks."

"Eat your sardines. I bet we'll need the protein before this morning's over. And what do you mean, calling yourself odd? You're not that odd." Mel chuckled.

He pointed a fork at her. "And you just gave yourself away. 'Not that odd' means there's some oddness in there, right? Don't answer that, I know what I am."

"I'll tell you what you are. You're a nice guy. Trustworthy, visionary. Your hair's kind of long. The beads are unusual." He still wore the brightly colored beads around his wrist; she hadn't noticed them in weeks. "And you're a heck of a cook. What's your tarot card?"

"The Fool, what else? Off on quests, with innocent faith that things will work out, trusting enough, or foolish enough, to step off of cliffs."

"Except that you're no fool. Not in the usual sense of the word."

"Thanks. I'm not always so sure."

Their eyes locked for a moment.

"So," she said, snapping them out of it, "if it's all-day traffic, does that mean the bored housewife trade?"

"Is there such a thing anymore? I'll show you my notes later, but I can tell you that there must be several hundred people in town tired of the Coffee Shack and waiting for us to open. The pressure," he groaned. "Fast service, great coffee, changing menu… I didn't have a clue what I was getting into when I started this."

She spoke slowly, watching his face. "But that doesn't matter, does it? You get a kick out of making it up as you go. You've got a big sandbox, and you can build and change as much as you want to, until it's right."

Adrian folded a sardine into a slice of focaccia. "That's a nice way to put it. The budget's not unlimited, incidentally, so I can't keep changing things forever. But creating this place, it's healing and... I don't know. I needed it." He grinned. "And of course I got lucky, because I'd barely started when this muse pounded on the door."

"I'm no muse. A worker bee is all."

"Don't knock worker bees. Without them we wouldn't have much food around, since they do the pollination. And never underestimate how you've influenced this place."

She remembered his absolute certainty, the first time she came here, that she'd play a major part in redeveloping the old store.

He went on. "The other thing I'm considering is converting the apartment to an office. I've started to realize I want a back yard to entertain in, a fireplace when winter comes."

"Putting down roots. Where do you entertain when you're in Philadelphia?"

"I don't. My family provides all the entertainment I can handle. I did have a house there, small but nice. It sold last spring, so I stay with my parents or Huff. Now I'm ready for a home again, get my stuff out of storage. I'm not Bohemian enough to live in the apartment here forever."

"I'm glad you aren't planning to flip the store and leave."

He looked startled. "Did you think I'd do that?"

"Never crossed my mind until this minute. I still have a hard time keeping up with your thoughts sometimes."

"Me too. So, a larger coffee shop. Good idea?"

"I think so. Seems to me the coffee's getting more buzz than the books."

"Then let's plan." They had finished their breakfast while they talked, so they cleaned up and spent the morning in the large second floor room, talking and diagraming the floor space.

It was almost as usual, but not quite. Adrian wasn't himself, she thought. On edge. Trying to make everything feel normal—but having to try, instead of flowing with it. She wondered if she should ask what was wrong, but decided against it. The hair episode had shaken her more than she cared to acknowledge, and she didn't want another upset.

It was well after noon when he said, "One more thing to show you, if you have time."

Mel glanced at her watch. "Show me."

They went to his kitchen. He disappeared for a moment and came back with a roll of paper. "We've tossed around ideas, but we haven't named this place yet."

"I still haven't come up with anything I like. Have you?"

"Check this out." He unrolled the papers onto the table.

The first was a photocopy of an old photograph of two elderly people. "Josiah and Annie Calter," he said. "The original's in the archives at the library."

"I didn't know that."

Adrian sat and put his chin on his palm, studying the photo. "I discovered this talking to the man who owns Joe's. I knew his name wasn't Joe, so I wondered why."

The light went on in Mel's brain. She dropped into the chair across from him. "You're going to call it…"

"*We* could consider calling it Annie's. We'd have a plaque outside, and frame a copy of the photo with a history of Annie and Josiah, so it doesn't come out of nowhere. But it's only a possibility. We can play with it."

Mel shook her head. "It's perfect. The coffee shop theme is eclectic and old-fashioned. It'll make sense."

He spread out the next sheet of paper. On it was a sketch of a sign. He'd envisioned it in wood, carved, with the one word, 'Annie's'."

She ran a finger over the paper. "I love it, esthetically. But we might need to say something about books and coffee."

"Peering in the window won't be enough? Not for the coffee, perhaps, up on the second floor. Do you want to take this home and play with it?"

"I don't need to. Putting a name on it sort of makes it more real, doesn't it?"

"It sort of does."

"Can we tell people?"

"Are we sure?"

"I am. I'm excited."

189

"Then by all means. Annie's will soon be a part of Calter Creek, so let's notify the population."

They both stood and went back downstairs. Before she left, Adrian touched her hair again. "It's good, Mel. You were wise, and I was wrong."

"I needed a change, and you were shocked. Don't obsess."

"I can't bear hurting you." He was serious. She again saw stress tightening his face.

"Adrian." She turned in the door and put a hand on his arm. "We're pals. Sometimes we're going to say or do something we regret. We'll get over it. I'm over it. Don't worry."

"I won't. I'll try harder, though."

Impulsively Mel got on tiptoe and kissed his cheek. "You want the best for me. What more can I ask for? Bye."

"Bye," he answered a little faintly. He was still standing in the door, watching her, when she reached the crosswalk, turned, and waved before heading for the parking garage.

"He has no right. He doesn't know what he's talking about." Ryan's eyes were blazing, and she could sense the tension in him. He was ready to go over to the bookstore and pound Adrian to a pulp.

All she'd said was that at first Adrian had been unhappy with her hair. Pretty neutral, not worth making a big deal out of it.

They were spending Sunday afternoon at the state forest, with an old quilt to sit on, drink boxes from a small cooler, shade from a massive maple tree, and a breeze. There was talk of the driving range later, when the heat abated. She stretched out, gazing through the pattern of leaves overhead. Ryan lay beside her, propped on an elbow and idly tracing patterns in the quilt with a finger.

She'd found herself unaccountably edgy that weekend, often on the verge of tears, and didn't understand it. Was it Adrian? She'd never known him to be so far off balance.

But in the course of breakfast they'd gotten beyond that. So perhaps the whole edgy thing was just organizing and coming to terms with the new facts of her life. Besides the vacuuming and grocery shopping, she'd spent Saturday afternoon with a pile of folders she'd brought home from SI, the one thing she'd promised herself she'd never do. But until her replacement started, she was holding down two jobs. SI had overflowed into her weekend.

She'd hoped Ryan would make it better. Like a little kid with an owie? But she wasn't a little kid, she was a grown woman dealing with trepidation over new responsibilities, compounded by the minor if lingering hurt in her heart from Adrian's words, and she needed help to put things to rights.

Ryan's anger wasn't doing it.

"I guess he was shocked. I can relate to that. I'm still kind of shocked myself." Her hand went to her hair. She couldn't quite believe where she found it, so close to her head.

His hand followed. "Honey, you look sensational. Absolutely perfect. No one could help but take you seriously now. It's exactly right." His hand tightened in her short curls as he leaned in and kissed her, briefly and with no body contact.

"He did say he kind of liked it, once he got over the shock."

"He's a tactless bastard, Melanie. I don't for the life of me understand why you want to spend so much time with him. That bookstore..." Ryan took his hand away and made a helpless gesture. "It's nothing to do with you."

"You're wrong, in one sense. He says I'm the bookstore's muse."

Ryan dropped down next to her. "Which is just a fancy word. It means nothing. You're setting yourself up for a fall, and that bothers me."

She sighed. This was familiar ground. "He's a friend."

"Melanie, look at me."

Mel did, reluctantly, because she knew what he was going to say.

191

"He's got you involved in this… this *thing*, and there's no payback. I don't trust him. I don't understand what he's up to. It makes me nervous, and you deserve better."

"I have fun, and I learn a lot. We'll be plowing through catalogs for fixtures next week. Shelves and wall art and lighting and stuff."

"If he had a clue what he was doing, he'd have dealt with all of that by now. He'd have a designer working on it."

She got up on an elbow, suddenly excited. "I want you to see the old elevator, it's the kind with that folding metal gate in front of it. It's been completely refurbished and polished up, as if it's new again."

"He's throwing away his money, wherever he gets it from," Ryan muttered. "And you have enough on your plate."

"You're right there. I've told him that I can't be any more deeply involved."

"That's a relief."

Mel knew more about how Adrian was funding the bookstore than she was willing to say. They hadn't asked her to keep his background to herself, and it was bound to be on the Web, but there had been an unspoken communication that bounced among Adrian, Huff, and her, convincing her this was privileged information. In any event, she didn't choose to discuss Adrian's personal life, so she was more than happy to nudge the conversation onto a different trajectory.

Sprawled there on the quilt, her mind turned to the pile of work on her dining table. "The bookstore—it's going to be called Annie's, incidentally—there won't be as much to do from now on, and I'm swamped with SI stuff. It'll be better once Amanda has her new assistant, but…" She shook her head. "I vowed I'd never be in a position to have to take work home, and here I am facing a stack of binders. Not what I want."

"Focus on what's going to enhance your career. The bookstore's been a summertime lark, Melanie, but it's time to consider more important things."

"I've been wondering myself what will happen once it's done."

"Once he doesn't need you there anymore, I bet he loses interest in having you around." Ryan sat up. His enthusiasm washed over her. "The new position at SI's much more exciting. You'll find lots you can do differently once you understand the business. The more you grasp the work, the more innovative you can be."

"That's a goal. So far, it's interesting, but I wouldn't say fun. I've always had a good rapport with the people on the team, even though I don't know them as well as the rest of SI. They're never here, so it's Web meetings and email."

"If you ever have any problems or concerns..."

"Thanks. For now I'm fine with it." His comment bothered her—again. She didn't want him in SI business, in her business. But she couldn't explain why.

Possibly it was his assumption that she might need his help.

But you might.

It was possible, but why would she? She hadn't so far. And she could talk to anyone at SI if things went sideways.

Ryan sighed with contentment. He lowered himself onto his back so they were side by side, watching the leaves dance against the sky. His hand fished for hers and held on. "Sweetheart, you couldn't be more perfect. You're capable..."

"We'll be good partners."

"Between us we'll be able to do so much. Want to go by the Club for a drink? Show off your new hairdo?"

"After the driving range, maybe? Too hot to move right now."

His hand ran over her face, down her front, along her bare thigh. "We could go home."

She smiled. "Hot."

He moved his hand to her tank top, a finger making inroads. "You've talked about lazy Sunday afternoons. The two of us at home alone...that's a part of the plan we could act on now."

The idea had potential. Her mind ranged over the dream ranch house set in its well-tended lawn, the furnishings they'd choose together. The work done, the afternoon stretching before them. This magnificent man, not only capable and successful, but fit and gorgeous in the bargain. And hers. She pulled herself upright. "My place or yours?"

He was up in an instant. "Mine. At least we'll have minimal air conditioning. Then the driving range, then the Club."

"Can we fit food in there somewhere?"

Mel found herself scooped up into a bear hug. She could feel Ryan laughing. "My practical Melanie."

Then he took her home. Because even on a hot afternoon, they had better things to do than lie on a quilt and stare at leaves.

Cassie had Betsy and Lulu more or less contained when Mel and Ryan got to Mel's sister's house Sunday afternoon a week later. With emphasis on the 'more or less' rather than on the 'contained'; her sister's home was a perpetual whirlwind of competing female energies. Betsy at four was the baby and proud of it, demanding attention at every turn. Lulu at seven was severe and critical, devoted to her ballet and gymnastics classes and disdainful of her little sister's exuberance.

Cassie met them at the door with a weary sigh. "At least they've been fed and watered. Come on in." She shoved the door open and backed out of the way.

Two little girls heading outside, one laughing and the other furious, nearly bowled them over before they could set foot in the house. "Don't leave the yard!" Cassie shouted. The screen door slammed behind them.

"Ryan, meet Cassie. That tornado was my nieces. I'm sure you'll see them later."

Cassie led them through the house toward the kitchen. "Sit. Have an iced tea. I need a break."

From the shrieks coming from outside, she could understand why. They sat.

"Where's Steve?"

"Work."

The screen door slammed. Betsy hurled herself against Mel's leg and screeched, "Don't let her kill me!"

Everything in her sister's house came with exclamation points. "Why would she kill you?" Mel inquired calmly, peering at the hot little face.

"'Cause I gave her hair ribbons to Claus." Claus was their dog, a large and lazy animal currently sleeping on a rug on the back patio. Mel exchanged 'what next?' glances with Cassie and went to the window. Sure enough, bedraggled pink ribbons bedecked Claus's collar.

"Doesn't seem like the wisest thing to do," Mel said.

"Pleased to meet you," Ryan said to Cassie, who'd set glasses and a pitcher of iced tea on the table, then slumped into a chair.

"You, too."

"You're such a big baby," a screeching voice said. "Always running to Aunt Mel. As if *she'd* care about a creep like *you*."

Betsy clung tighter to Mel's leg. Walking to the table resembled walking with a cast. Mel sat next to Ryan. "Yes," she told him. "It's always like this."

Lulu by then had made it through the kitchen and onto the back porch, where she ripped the ribbons from Claus's collar. She brought them inside, wailing. "Mom, they're ruined. *Ruined!* And I don't have any more pink ones, and I need pink ones for ballet…"

"No, you don't," Cassie said. "Betsy, time out."

"Mo-om…" Betsy whined, but Cassie pointed a finger toward the front of the house.

"Go."

"But Aunt Mel's here…"

"Go."

Betsy slunk off, head down. Mel could almost see thought bubbles above her head, vowing revenge. She fervently hoped they'd be gone before the revenge happened.

"How've you been?" she asked her sister.

"How do you think?" Cassie shot back.

195

Ryan was uncomfortable. "Is this not a good time? We could always call in…"

"No, it's fine." Cassie laid a hand on his arm, as if to prevent him from bolting. "You walked in on a little drama. Only happens ten times a day or so. The theory is, they'll grow up and laugh about it."

"You have to get through teen years first, Sis."

"I may be long gone by then."

"You're tough. You'll survive."

Ryan's eyes went back and forth between the sisters, following their banter.

Lulu flounced around the kitchen with her ribbons, finally placing herself firmly in front of her mother. "Betsy doesn't deserve this family," she announced. "I bet she was adopted. You ought to send her back."

"Can't do it," Cassie said. "Bought and paid for, no warranty."

"Well, you got a bad deal then," Lulu huffed, and disappeared in the same direction Betsy had gone.

"Dangerous?" Mel asked Cassie.

"Probably. But at least they're not in here for the moment."

"Drink your tea," Mel said to Ryan with a nudge. "This isn't even a day of high drama. Just normal proceedings."

By the time they'd spent a couple of hours with Cassie, punctuated by appearances of one or both of Mel's nieces, Mel could tell that Ryan was at the end of his tether. He'd said little, although he had been scrupulously polite whenever his contribution was called for. But chaos wasn't his natural milieu, and finally she took pity on him.

At the door she hugged Cassie and they arranged to get together soon, one day when Steve was home to maintain peace between the nieces.

On the way back to his place she said, "Not comfortable?"

Ryan's eyes were on the road. "They aren't very well disciplined, are they?"

"Cassie intended them to be, but the effort's proved to be more than she bargained for. It's sort of a crapshoot, what kind of kids you'll get. Steve isn't much help. Believe me, she didn't plan this. Cassie's as organized as I am, maybe more."

They were approaching her apartment before he spoke again. "Surely if you start right from the beginning and train them…"

"Still no guarantee. You could give them the best upbringing in the world and end up with a juvenile delinquent or an ax murderer. Or chaos like Betsy and Lulu." Mel shuddered. "Not my preference either. It gives you pause."

He parked. "One child may be sufficient."

"After I spend much time with Cassie I sort of agree with you. But I've always wanted a big family. Come up for a few minutes?"

"Not if it means creating our own version of your nieces." Ryan's tone was final.

"Don't despair of them. They are growing up, and they are two girls. Mom says Cassie and I drove each other nuts when we were little. I wasn't ever as out of control as Betsy is, though."

In her living room he said, "I'd assumed… I guess I haven't been around kids very much. You want them, but…" Ryan shrugged helplessly.

"Once you've got them, you've got them. Let's have a snack, then I have to head for SI."

"I don't like this. You worked yesterday."

"Every weekend since I took on this position. I'm not happy, but I do need to fit in a few hours."

"But you've found someone to take over from you?"

"A guy. I hope that didn't color my decision." She gave him a nudge and grinned. "He's youngish, keen, personable. His skill set's a near match. My instinct is he'll work out. Hiring's an art, not a science, isn't it? Want a cookie?" At Cassie's, simple things like offering food got lost in the shuffle.

Over cookies and juice he said, "Hiring can be a science. You have to specify exactly what your requirements are, of

197

course. In great detail. I could have worked through your interview questionnaire with you."

"I developed it with our head of personnel, then ran it by Amanda. Our instincts pointed the same direction. He'll have things to learn, but he'll be fine."

"Perhaps." Ryan's voice suggested that he didn't have faith in this female-intuition way of hiring. "I'm always happy to provide another set of eyes, Melanie."

"I appreciate it."

"So now you'll be training this guy?"

"He starts Monday. I'll get his feet under him, then it's over to Amanda to let him know what she expects."

"And you can stop spending your weekends with work. I'd hoped we might go to the pool this afternoon."

"I'd love to, but I have to finish this. Hopefully, once I'm fully anchored in the search team there won't be so much." Mel rose. "Let's go."

"Tonight?"

Mel's eyes crinkled. "I'm having devilish imaginings. Come over around eight?"

"It's not too damn hot, right?"

"Not yet. But it will be." She gave him another quick kiss and hustled them both out the door. The sooner she got through the work, the sooner she could dream about what she wanted to do with Ryan tonight.

Turning up the heat.

Yeah. True. They had a satisfactory sex life. But she had to find a way to tweak it, ramp it up. She was on a quest for that missing spark.

She went downstairs with him, then picked up her car in the parking lot and headed for her small, lonely office at SI.

Mel sighed. It was only Wednesday, and this week threatened to swamp her.

Sunday had been… fun, she supposed. Not the three hours getting caught up on her work, but she always enjoyed seeing Cassie and her nieces, even if they were pretty much out of control that day. And she and Ryan had made... very pleasant... love that evening. She wondered when the zing would make an appearance, the magical extra destined to set her tingling. But in the meantime, no complaints.

No real *complaints.*

Monday she'd lost half a day showing Michael, her replacement, the basics of how to be a good executive assistant to Amanda. The nuances, he'd have to pick up for himself, or follow Amanda's lead. The comfortable relationship she had with her boss hadn't happened overnight. Michael wouldn't dare tell Amanda she was wrong, or fight with her, not yet. She couldn't teach him any of that.

Then there was the golf lesson Tuesday evening. Five lessons down, one to go. She'd tried, but she didn't much enjoy golf. And her aptitude was doubtful at best. How the one influenced the other, she wasn't sure. It was what it was. The mere suggestion of playing nine holes with Ryan filled her with something like dread.

Still, after the lesson they'd spent half an hour on the practice green and that was okay. In her heart Mel wondered if she was basically a mini-golf gal who was happier putting through a windmill or a gaping cartoon mouth than trying to swing a four iron—or, heaven help her, any kind of wood at all—at a ball.

Down market. That's you, all the way.

The trick was to have fun. So far, golf wasn't giving her that.

Restless, Mel lined up her morning's work, then wandered down the corridor to the break room. It was empty, no one to chat with. So she poured a cup of coffee and returned to her desk.

Which was fine, honest. She was getting into the rhythm of the new position. Once Michael was settled, she'd be able to focus, she'd have more time.

The job didn't worry her. The team had welcomed her into her new role, at least as far as she could tell online. They worked independently, and Amanda had recommended a light hand. The rest of it was not so different from what she'd done for Amanda. Different focus, that was all. She picked up the phone and arranged to meet Robert, their expert on import law, to sort out customs on a shipment from Bangladesh, then dove into the first task on her list.

Abruptly she shoved it all aside and stared out her window. Just sat and stared.

And wondered, not for the first time, what she was doing.

Wondered if she would ever love her work again. Or get on top of it, and not haul folders and binders home with her. Wondered how it fit with the pattern that was Ryan, his career, the Club. Golf, heaven help her. Her friends. Even Adrian and the bookstore, now Annie's.

She'd taken on too much. The whole Ryan thing was so new that adding the search team promotion challenged her, all right—challenged her sanity. Done was done, she'd get through it, but in self-defense she'd already notified Amanda she wouldn't be taking the night course. That had cheered her up, since it was one of the few times lately that she'd honored her own instincts and made the decision that was totally right for her.

Her life was a madhouse tunnel. She wished she had a clearer picture of what the future would be like, when she emerged from the turmoil.

With all that going on, it shouldn't have surprised her that Saturday morning Mel more or less forgot to wake up. Normally she was up with the birds on Saturdays, looking forward to breakfast and bookstore time. This day, however, her body rebelled.

Or maybe she was subconsciously reluctant to go to the bookstore, because she had to talk to Adrian. She couldn't maintain the pace of her life any longer.

As soon as she woke up at nine thirty, she phoned. "I'm so sorry. I didn't surface."

"Are you all right?" Adrian asked her.

"Groggy from sleep. I guess I missed breakfast."

"Pancakes remain an option."

"Will they keep? It'll be a while before I could get there."

"Give me an ETA."

"An hour and a half? I need to sort out some SI stuff, or I'll forget what I'm doing."

"A pancake brunch awaits you."

She spent another blissful fifteen seconds in bed being grateful that Adrian was so flexible, then stretched and rolled out.

The SI work had involved a shipment gone awry, paperwork, meetings with Robert in their legal department, and a flurry of messages back and forth among her team member, the company providing the shipped goods, the shipping company, the federal customs agency, and heaven alone knew who else. Plus keeping Inventory Control and Accounting in the loop. Things had moved quickly on Friday, so before she got her pancakes she had to put her notes and documents into a semblance of order. It was important that she have the information at her fingertips when she needed it.

The snafu had taken up most of Friday, even forcing her to cut short her time with Ryan. And her day-to-day tasks were now a day late.

Shower, dress, *very* light breakfast—she knew what to expect when Adrian made pancakes—and dig into work.

It was in fact close to eleven thirty when she got to Annie's. Banana pecan pancake aromas filled the second floor— the first four were already on the griddle. On the table Adrian had placed maple syrup and bowls of raspberries and blueberries.

"Sit. Let me feed you," he commanded from the counter. He turned and looked at her, then studied her more closely. "God, Mel, you don't look so good."

"I'm tired." She sank into her chair at his kitchen table.

"Far too tired. Let's vary the routine. A walk, perhaps? We have a lot to discuss, but you're pale. More than usual."

"I'm hoping it's just growing pains."

Adrian poured boiling water into the coffee press and set it on the table. "Here you go. Artificial renewal. Caffeine's at least more innocuous than some stimulants." He returned to the counter and flipped the pancakes. "Lots going wrong, or just volume?"

"Both. Major crisis with a shipment, plus training my replacement. That part's done with, thank heaven. He and Amanda are getting along like a house afire... sorry. Unfortunate choice of words."

"I don't mind. It sort of turns the experience on its head."

"There was nothing good about that night."

"I don't agree with you. Here, eat." He put a plate of pancakes in front of her, and pulled a can of whipped cream out of the fridge. "Might as well be decadent."

"Adrian, I'll weigh a ton." Nevertheless, after she'd done butter and berries and syrup she seized the whipped cream and added a dollop.

"Once in a blue moon, no, you won't. You know about blue moons? It's the extra moon when the year has thirteen instead of twelve full moons. From old England, betraying the system God made by throwing in that evil extra moon. They aren't as unusual as you might think, every three years or so."

Mel's mouth was full of pancake, and for the first time in a few days she felt calm, as if she could handle it all. Could the secret be gourmet pancakes? She swallowed and said, "So what on earth was good about the fire?"

"Nothing concrete, I suppose. But waking up in the morning glad to be alive, grateful for fresh air. Smoke inhalation does terrible things. Cyanide, carbon monoxide…"

"Definitely nothing I want to hear right now. Is there anything you don't know something about?"

"Plenty." He'd poured more batter on the griddle and sat across from her with his own plate. "The bananas are healthy, as are the nuts and berries, so we can afford a little decadence."

Mel was pleased to see he used butter, syrup, and whipped cream as freely as she did. She'd watched Ryan with desserts; he was much less exuberant.

Silence reigned while they indulged in the pancakes.

"Blue moon. There was a song," she said.

He hummed a couple of bars. "A play on the word 'blue'. He, or she, is alone, and then he finds his true love, and the moon isn't blue anymore. Doesn't always turn out that way in real life, alas."

There was something in the way he said it. As if he spoke from experience. Mel looked at Adrian, returning the scrutiny he'd given her a few minutes ago.

It sank in that he had lived a life, before Annie's. Lovers, maybe one great love. He might even have been married. They'd never discussed it, it had never come up. Part of the romance of the bookstore was its stubborn existence on staying in the present.

But she'd caught a change in his face, gone in a flash. Tension… or pain?

She wasn't going to pretend she hadn't seen it. "Do you want to talk about it?"

Adrian smiled at her a little sadly. Or maybe she imagined it. Mel wasn't sure of her ability to read his signals today. "Not really. I've always wanted to see a blue moon, I mean the kind that actually appears blue. But that's rare. You need dust in the air or a good volcanic eruption."

"I was right. You do know something about everything."

Adrian grinned, and equilibrium was restored. "You're the one who remembered the song."

"I like those old songs. My grandparents had a stack of 78s left over from their parents."

"Don't suppose you still have them? They're getting more and more valuable."

"Long since gone."

"You're looking better. Not so pinched."

"Must be the bananas. It couldn't possibly be the whipped cream."

Adrian made a fresh pot of tea, Mel pushed the plunger on her coffee, and they went out on his deck, where they flipped through catalogs of restaurant furnishings. They marked pages, debated wood finishes and pictures, and made notes.

And talked. Mel thanked her lucky stars she'd found a friend like Adrian. She could tell him anything, almost, and listen to him for hours.

He handed her a pamphlet. "This is me breaking the rules for decorating commercial establishments again, but have you ever seen this woman's wall hangings? They're a variation of batik on silk. I want to go to her studio and have a look. Care to come?"

"When?" Mel flipped open the brochure, then murmured, "Gorgeous."

"Now?"

She glanced at her watch. "I have an hour. Work this afternoon, worse luck."

"It's fifteen minutes out of town. I could bring you back here, or we could take two cars."

"Two cars." She ran a finger across the pictures in the brochure. The hangings appealed to every iota of her love of color. And this could be the last decision she and Adrian made together. Time, and pressures from outside, and her own limitations... things were winding down for her, where Annie's was concerned.

She met Adrian at the woman's studio, Fairy Glen Designs, which was pure earth magic. In the showroom they found an enchanted realm of jewel colors and shimmering silk. She noticed a rack of women's tops she'd return to look at, another day.

Simultaneously they spotted a pair of wall hangings, each three by five feet, one depicting a forest, the other an ocean.

"Over the checkout counter," Adrian said.

"They're perfect." They were, in fact, ethereal. The bookstore proper would be nothing like the coffee shop. The hangings fit perfectly with Mel's sense of the ground floor, open, blond woods, bright and sensuous.

Recognizing their time constraints, he arranged to have the two hangings held for him. As they walked out, he said, "I might commission a long length of silk, in the same colors but without a definite pattern. I was picturing a swag against the brick on the side wall across from the checkout. Opinion?"

"I'd never be able to leave. You're a magician."

"Inspired by a redheaded witch of my acquaintance."

They stood together in the gravel parking lot. Leaving was the last thing Mel wanted to do. There was magic going on. It resembled the bookstore in that it was not quite real, with its trees, flower gardens, and a fountain playing over river rocks.

"I could stay here forever." She stretched out her arms and twirled. When she returned to ground, by unspoken consent they set off along a path that circled the studio. "I hardly ever see you outside of Annie's."

"I regret that. We're sharing an almost make-believe existence."

Mel sighed. There was SI work to do and she was meeting Ryan for a swim and supper at the snack bar at the Club. "The real world's intruding. I hate this, but I may not be around very much for a while."

"Oh." He'd squatted to study the herbs in the bed along the walkway. At her words he went still, then straightened and looked at her, his head cocked.

"I've run out of steam, still getting myself settled in the new job. Something has to give, or I'm heading for a nervous breakdown. I'm really sorry, but..."

He walked a few steps along the path before turning back to her. "I understand. It won't be the same, but it kills me to see you as tired and tense as you were earlier. You're always welcome, whenever you can get there."

"I'd never disappear completely. You're my best friend ever. You snuck in and surprised me."

He was serious. "Surprised me, too, because it's the same for me. Any time, Mel, I mean that. It doesn't have to be Saturday mornings. Even if it's just a few minutes."

She put her hand on his and squeezed. "Thanks. I don't want to lose what we have."

"Me, either." He caught her in a quick hug.

Driving home in the afternoon heat, her mind turned to the new aspect of Adrian she'd intuited. He'd become less mythical, more real. With their friendship contained by the bookstore, and despite the fire, The Bindery, and Aggie's wedding, for her he hadn't had an existence apart from the old building in downtown Calter Creek.

A man with a history and a heart. With friends and activities she didn't share.

She thought back to his dream, the crowded-room, touch-of-her-hand dream, and wondered when he'd experienced it. She hoped he'd find it again.

The next morning, back at her apartment after a dreamy night with Ryan both out of bed and in, she made herself a cup of coffee and flipped open her laptop. Seeing Adrian away from Annie's yesterday had shaken up her fairy tale view of the bookstore. She'd been forced to see him as a whole person, and she knew next to nothing about him.

Mel and her laptop weren't friends, so other than sporadically checking her email she mostly ignored it. Now she did what it hadn't occurred to her to do before then. She looked up Adrian Forsythe on the Internet.

He wasn't hard to find. She paused at a photo of a younger Adrian, with short hair and a business suit, early in his days running The Bindery. He looked serious, careworn. From the photo his resemblance to his more conventional brother was obvious.

There were other pictures, at a banquet, playing doubles tennis with Huff. She found society snaps from Aggie's wedding. A couple of very old shots from before his hair turned gray. She laughed; it was hard to believe this brown-haired devil was the same Adrian she knew.

In one photograph, at a society event years before, he held a good-looking woman in a close-fitted cocktail dress close against him. Brunette, sleek. Mel hated her on sight. Then laughed again, this time at herself.

There were articles. When he'd assumed control of The Bindery, and when he had his breakdown—although the news reports didn't call it that, there was plenty of speculation—after he'd authorized closing the stores. Business articles, the occasional society report.

It had seemed as if Adrian came into her life out of nowhere, but that was pure misconception. They'd inhabited different worlds, which hadn't overlapped.

She closed the laptop, letting her hand stroke its case as it rested on her table. She had this new information, and she wasn't sure what to do with it. It changed things, lessening her sense of unreality. The many faces of Adrian Forsythe.

Having Labor Day off had given Mel a chance to catch up on sleep, as well as errands and housework. There had been a casual buffet on the terrace at the Club, which she'd enjoyed. It had been more relaxed than the usual activities, and that let her relax, too.

It didn't get her out of her last Tuesday golf lesson, though. She met Ryan at the practice green afterward. "Done," she announced. "And thank heaven."

He hugged her and handed her a putter. "I'd like to buy you a set of clubs, as a graduation present."

"That's sweet." She pecked his cheek. "But don't rush into it. I'm not so sure about golf." She dropped a ball onto the green and squinted as she lined it up with a cup.

He took hold of her putter. Not in the romantic, wrap-his-arms-around-her way but from the front, preventing her from making her putt. "Why not? Come on, Melanie, you can see how valuable it is. And enjoyable."

"Yeah, all that fresh air," she muttered. She reclaimed her putter. "You know I haven't enjoyed the lessons very much. Not hated, just not into it. I can't picture spending hours every weekend on the course."

Now he did do the arms-around-the-woman thing, helping her line up the putt. Mel felt a flash of annoyance. Putting was the only aspect of the game she didn't mind, and even had some aptitude for.

"You haven't played a full round yet."

The putt went wide.

"I'll play nine holes with you. Once," she emphasized. "I'll give it a fair trial, but I'm sure I could get involved other ways, like decorating for dances."

"There's a social committee." He lined up and sank his own putt.

"I'm usually up for a challenge, and the class was very well done. But I found myself watching the clock for the lesson to be over."

Ryan rimmed the cup with his next putt. She sank hers, but it was an easy shot. She walked across the green to try a longer distance.

He joined her, the skin around his eyes wrinkled with concern. "Perhaps it's been too much for you at once. You and me, and your new position at Sinclair Imports." She had noted that he almost never called it SI, as everyone working there did. "Then getting burned out of your apartment. It's been quite a summer."

"That might be it. I'll give the golf thing a fair shot, but I'm not ready for a set of clubs of my own. That would be a kind of pressure, too. I'm fine with the loaners."

They both missed the long putt, and both tapped in. After a few more minutes on the green, they dropped the equipment off in the pro shop and wandered over to the terrace, where they found the Davies.

"Please, have a seat." Maureen reached out a hand to Mel. Squeezing, she said, "I've been hoping we'd run into you two. I enjoyed getting to know you, Melanie."

Where the Club was concerned, she was doomed to be Melanie. "Thanks, I enjoyed it, too."

Ryan was happy to join the older couple, so she settled in an empty chair.

Robert Davies had the air of a man who was king of his castle. Ryan had told her he was on the Board here, so she supposed it was true. "You're enjoying yourself?" he asked her.

The ever-attentive waiter hovered, so she asked for a wine cooler. Ryan ordered a G-and-T. "Yes, I am. I've just finished golf lessons. I'm not optimistic."

"It's not my favorite pastime." Maureen winked at her. She sent the other woman a silent blessing. "It wouldn't mean anything to you men, but most of the summer it's a recipe for too much sun and getting far too hot—you understand, I expect," She said to Mel.

Mel gave her a conspiratorial grin. "Yeah, I do, especially given how easily I burn. I hadn't thought of it in terms of the sun, but I should have."

"And then you're faced with showering and re-doing your hair and your makeup. Hours out of your day, dear. What else have you been doing? You mentioned that old bookstore downtown. How's it going?"

"We need investment like that to revitalize the downtown core," Robert added.

Mel responded, but not effusively, leaving room for Ryan to add his opinion. But he was silent, listening to the other three. The drinks arrived and the four of them chatted about Calter Creek, the Landmark development north of town, and the subdivisions springing up everywhere. Ryan opened up once the conversation moved from the bookstore and became more general. He was in an excellent mood driving home.

At her door she didn't invite him in. "I'm beat. These are long days. I need to make notes for a meeting tomorrow, and I have research to do."

"Melanie, I've offered to help you. I don't want this position to be too much for you."

"It's a learning curve, I'll get through it. Thanks, though." This insistence on helping her exasperated her, but she stroked the hand he had placed on her arm. It was his way, and she was grateful for his support. "Friday night? SI could collapse around my ears, but I'm not working Friday night. We could try that Italian place out the Columbus road."

"There's the dance at the Club Saturday, don't forget."

She had forgotten. That's how muddled she'd become. "Guess that takes care of Saturday morning. I'll have to go shopping. I don't own anything formal enough."

"We should stay in Friday. Save money. We'll make our own spaghetti."

"Call me?"

"You know I will."

They shared a brief but satisfying clench and kiss.

Mel considered the evening as she organized her work. The Davies were shaping up to be an okay couple, better than her initial impression of them. Their conversation gave her plenty of food for thought, and perspectives about Calter Creek's retail landscape she wanted to pass on to Adrian.

But damn. Thanks to the Club, she had to go buy a cocktail dress. Mel glumly pictured a closet full of formal dresses, to be pulled out as needed.

Stop that, dope, she commanded herself. There'd never be a row of them. She couldn't afford it, and Ryan would consider it a waste of money.

Her mind had wandered far from where she needed it to be. She snapped it back to attention and settled at her table, grateful that she could do this work from home and didn't have to make the trek into SI. She'd almost caught up after the previous Friday's shipping snarl-up. But she wished she'd been able to clear her desk during working hours. She opened the first binder and got to work.

Heads down.

But darn. She'd hoped to grab an hour or two for Annie's on Saturday. That wasn't going to happen, because she'd be at the mall, shopping for a dress.

Adrian had been understanding when she phoned him, and interested in the talk she'd had with the Davies. Nevertheless, it came as a jolt, to be in the food court in Creekside Mall instead of on Adrian's deck, stuffing herself with whatever he'd planned for their breakfast.

She watched Julie and Bryony, who had joined her for the great cocktail dress search. Her friends' morning selections left a lot to be desired. But hey, to each her own. She bit into her cherry Danish and sighed with content. She did enjoy breakfast, in all its various permutations.

Except, perhaps, pizza. Or tacos.

"So what's the problem with your rust crepe dress?" Julie took a bite from her wedge of pizza.

"Have you ever considered how the smell of pepperoni affects my Danish?" Mel replied.

"Don't be snarky. You like pepperoni."

"At ten o'clock in the morning?"

"You're just jealous." Julie downed another mouthful.

"Not every woman on the planet has an occasion to shop for." Bryony emphasized the word 'occasion'.

"You're right. Sorry."

"And be thinking about the dark circles," Julie said. "Not a good look on you." She rammed the rest of the pizza wedge into her mouth and washed it down with coffee.

"Pardon me if I shudder," Mel said.

"This is a taste combination made in heaven. You're missing out." Julie dabbed her mouth with her napkin. "Now, selection's bound to be limited, so in case we don't find anything, tell me what's wrong with the rust one."

211

"The way it's cut down the back? It's barely decent. This is a conservative place, Jules. I can't wear a foxy dress."

Bryony flipped her hair. "Not exactly letting out your inner vamp, are you?"

"I think she died," Julie said. "This is the new, conservative Mel. No more wild and crazy."

She ignored that. Of course she was still wild and crazy. If she chose to be. "Let's get this over with."

"Dark circles?"

"Nap this afternoon. Cucumber slices? And there's always concealer. At least I don't have to work this weekend."

"And thank goodness for that." They made their way along the corridor. Because they knew Creekside well, there wasn't any need to discuss which shops to browse. "You disappeared this summer, between your two mystery men. And since you changed jobs..." Julie shrugged. "Not so many recent sightings. We see more of Adrian than we do of you."

"I'm glad he met you all."

"He fits right in. Can't see *him* digging out a fancy suit for a dance at your Club," Bryony added.

"Bet he could. You know his family owns The Bindery?" Mel stopped short and put a hand over her mouth.

The other two stared. "You're kidding me," Julie said.

"I shouldn't have mentioned it, but it's on the web, so it isn't really a secret. He's not very involved these days."

"I'm astonished," Bryony said. "I like him. He's a wonky variation on ordinary folks, know what I mean?"

Mel appreciated Bryony's description. "He's got more business smarts than he lets people see. This Club thing's important for Ryan's career, so I'm okay with it, but it's sort of a nuisance right this minute."

"The Bindery, huh? And he's cute, and single," Bryony mused.

Mel was on the verge of warning Bryony to keep her hands off when it hit her that she had no right to do any such thing. In fact, she should encourage her friend. She didn't want Adrian to be alone, and she did want him to have roots in Calter Creek.

The first shop had a dress that might do, in a conservative black. Mel tried it on and reserved judgment. It was possible she wasn't in the mood for shopping.

The second shop yielded nothing. The third—and last— offered a dark green number that covered her back and showed only a hint of décolletage. Enough to catch the eye, not enough to tempt.

"And the green's good with your coloring," Julie confirmed. "Shoes?"

"I've got those black stilettos."

"Jewelry?" Bryony asked.

They visited more stores in search of the perfect necklace, with no luck. "Plain gold chain," Mel said. "It'll do. Let's get lunch."

"Not very hungry," Julie said.

"Not surprising after pizza for breakfast."

They hit the food court again, this time for Chinese. Mel noted that despite Julie's protest, she and Bryony both put away a three-option meal. Nothing wrong with their appetites.

Something was wrong with hers, though. She picked at her lunch.

"Mel," Bryony said around the straw stuck in her soda, "has it occurred to you that you aren't exactly bubbly with excitement?"

"Oh, I am. I'm tired, that's all. Work's killing me."

Julie shook her head. "It's more than that. Look, we're the best friends you have in the world, right? We're your support network."

"It's going fine."

"I did warn you that he's a stick-in-the-mud," Julie said.

"You're wrong, Jules. He's a great guy and he's totally into me and he does have fun. He had fun at the Larsens'," she added a bit defensively.

Bryony shot her a look that said, *Do you hear yourself?* "Okay, ignore us. We just want you to be happy."

Mel pointed a plastic fork at Bryony, then shifted it around to aim at Julie. "He's great. He's planning a future…"

"And you're planning alongside him?" Julie asked.

She nodded, her gaze going misty for a moment. "Yeah, I am. Don't fuss at me, guys. I'm struggling with work these days, but that's easing up. Life's good." She nibbled at her sweet-and-sour pork and ignored Julie's sigh.

15

The shopping that morning had been worth it. Ryan's eyes had popped when he saw her in the new dress, and Mel herself thought she looked darn good. The green of the dress accentuated her eyes, and the heels did equally good things to her legs, and Ryan was enjoying the full benefit.

Mel had stood agog at the doorway when they walked into the clubhouse. From the over-the-top scrumptious buffet in the bar, to the swing band and subtle lighting in the ballroom, to the fairy lights strung around the terraces and in the trees, the closing dance of the season was something to weave dreams from. It more than justified the cost of the dress, the discomfort of the stilettos.

"You're exquisite," Ryan had murmured into her hair as they danced. She believed him. On this one night, she felt as if she belonged in this setting, with these people.

They'd even been cut in on, which had never happened to her before. A scrupulously polite older gentleman had gently and respectfully danced her around the room, making small talk about Calter Creek, the Club, the evening. She'd introduced him to Ryan when the music ended. With Ryan's hand on her waist, staking claim, the two men had chatted and exchanged business cards.

Nearing midnight, during a break before the final set from the band, Mel caught her breath and sipped champagne. Ryan sat next to her, running a thumb over her thigh under their table. Was there any way she could be happier?

"Let's get some fresh air," he said. The band had returned, and the terrace was emptying as people came in for the last dances.

"Let's. I've probably shrunk an inch, I've danced so much."

"I'm the envy of every man in the room." Ryan stood and helped her to her feet. His hand on her back made little rubbing motions as he escorted her through the French doors opening onto the terrace. The lights twinkled in the trees, and the band's music drifted through the mild, late summer night.

"I'm glad it's not too cold yet. Growing up, Labor Day marked the end of the good weather. But this is perfect."

Ryan's arms circled her from behind, pulling her against him. In her heels they were almost the same height. He put his chin on her shoulder, his cheek grazing hers. "Beautiful, isn't it?"

"Do guys even notice things like that? It's heaven, Ryan. I'm in heaven."

"Everyone's gone in. Let's take advantage, shall we?" He turned her in his arms and let her go long enough to put their two champagne flutes on a nearby table. Then they began moving to the music, swaying more than actually dancing on the deserted terrace. She loved the picture they made, he dignified in his gray suit, she elegant in her green cocktail dress. Ryan kept her against him. She gave a contented sigh and snuggled closer.

When the slow song ended and the band switched to a swing number, he drew her over to the stone balustrade that lined the terrace. "This is what I've dreamed of, Melanie. Just this."

"It's like being in an enchanted kingdom. I can't imagine things being better."

"I can. I hope you'll agree." Ryan turned to look at her, catching her hands in his.

Mel's mind, at saturation from the sheer romance of the evening, nevertheless noted that he was nervous. She looked at him, sending him a question with her eyes.

Ryan took a breath. "You know what you are to me, Melanie. I hope… we haven't been together that long, but this seems like the perfect time…"

Mel extracted a hand to place it on his cheek. She didn't speak, just made a stroking movement with her thumb at the corner of his mouth.

He claimed her hand and kissed her fingers. He spoke slowly and deliberately. "Melanie, will you be my wife?"

Time stopped. The others at the dance, the couples who had drifted out onto the terrace, didn't exist. It was only Ryan and Mel. The future, together.

He couldn't have planned it more perfectly.

Wordlessly — but surely he read her answer on her face — he freed his other hand and produced the classic square box. His grin was a little crooked. "I couldn't very well dance with this in my pocket, so I had the concierge hold it for me. Will you accept it, honey?" he opened the box.

She gasped. It was a diamond solitaire in a wide gold band. It sparkled like the stars overhead.

"Melanie?"

She looked up at him, standing there in the starlight and for once not completely sure of himself. Their eyes met, then she threw her arms around him and let him draw her in close. "Yes," she whispered, since her power of speech had deserted her. "Oh, yes."

After a minute he released his hold. "I hope it fits." Mel watched as Ryan took the ring from its box and slid it onto her finger. It was half a size too large, but that could be fixed. They admired the ring as it rested against her hand.

"It looks like it belongs there," she said, wonderment in her voice.

The ring that locked in their future. But she was more interested in his face at that moment than she was in the ring. He looked more open, more vulnerable, than she'd ever seen him.

Then he held out his hand to her. "Shall we finish our champagne? I want to have the last dance with you." He leaned in closer. "Then I want to take you home," he murmured. His hand caressed lower than it had. Her thoughts turned from the romantic ambience surrounding her to the hard body she'd have to herself... soon.

That was enough to overwhelm her brain. "I can't put a coherent thought together. Hang on to me, I'm likely to float away."

"I'll never let you float away, baby. I'll keep you well anchored."

He would, too. But that didn't prevent Mel from floating through the champagne, the last dance, the night that followed.

Waking up in Ryan's bed in the morning, she thought, *The rest of my life next to this man.*

Word swept through SI with its usual lightning speed. Congratulations poured over Mel like water onto parched ground. She got hugs and enthusiastic cheering for the new directions her life had taken over the summer, but especially this most recent one. Even Amanda gave her the biggest hug a seven-months-pregnant woman could manage. The diamond twinkled and positively begged her to wave it under everyone's nose. So she did. She soaked it up. She'd long been the head cheerleader for the positive changes in her colleagues' lives, and it was heartwarming to be on the receiving end.

The enthusiasm didn't affect the workload, though. By Wednesday Mel had a new stack of folders to take home, and the prospect of a couple of hours of work ahead of her. And Ryan coming over for supper.

A complicated evening.

No, it isn't, she corrected herself. *A typical evening.* They'd both have to get used to the occasional time spent working at home. It was in the nature of their jobs.

Ryan wasn't pleased. "I'd hoped to have you to myself. We haven't seen each other since Sunday." They were standing in the door to her apartment, hip-to-hip and nose-to-nose, his arms around her waist and his hands on her fanny. Not the best lead-in to an evening with folders.

"Don't be pouty. I've got lasagna."

"You made it?" He looked skeptical.

"You know me better than that. From the catering and deli company out on Seventh."

He let her go and made for the kitchen, where he rummaged. "No wine?"

"There might be a bottle in there. I haven't made it to the grocery lately." With an elbow she indicated her pantry cupboard, then turned to the microwave, where the lasagna emitted a promising aroma.

"We need a wine cellar. Better yet, we need one residence between us, not two." Ryan came up empty after poking through her minimal stockpile of food. "Any other options?"

"Water? Iced tea?"

"Water."

Over supper he took her left hand and fingered the ring. "When shall we get this resized? I don't want you to lose it."

"It won't fall off, it's just a little swively. But we should. Is it from the jewelers downtown?"

"I looked there, but no, it's from the one in Creekside Mall. We could go out there tonight. It'll take a few days."

Mel swallowed a bite of lasagna. "Let's leave it. It's late and I'm tired, and there is that." She nodded at the folders, which had been relegated to the kitchen counter. "Besides, I'm not tired of looking at it yet."

After supper Ryan sat on her sofa and read through a banking journal he'd had in his car while she waded into the world of shipping. The banking journal had less staying power, though, because after half an hour or so he was hovering. "This looks like international banking."

"My end of our business originates overseas, so yeah, banking's a part of it. There's rarely a glitch, but something's gone wrong this time. This isn't the broker we usually deal with, and the reports don't exactly line up, so I'm making sure I understand it."

"I could help."

"Thanks, but I learn best when I figure it out on my own."

"For instance…" Before she knew it he was studying the numbers on her laptop and perusing the report she had in front of her.

"Ryan…"

"Hmm? I'd query this, for instance." His finger tapped a number on the report. "It doesn't seem reasonable to me."

"That one is, actually. I checked it out this afternoon through our bankers." She named a major bank.

"I don't know, Melanie."

"Ryan…" she tried again.

He took her report over to the sofa and sat down to study it. Mel swallowed, sensing her comfortable evening slipping away from her. But this was SI business. She had to intervene.

She stood beside him and said, "Ryan, I need that report. It's confidential."

"Well, sure, I understand that. But you need help, and you know you can trust me not to divulge—"

"I'll ask if I have questions, I promise, but this is my work to do. And I can do it." She took the paper from him and started back to the table.

Ryan grabbed her wrist. "Wait. Are you saying you don't trust me with this?"

"It's not about me. I can't make SI trust you, and I have to play by their rules. Everyone else does. I honestly am competent to figure out this mix-up, I just need space to work through it."

"Right." Ryan stood. "I'll head home." He put a definite I-know-when-I'm-not-wanted spin on the words.

Mel gave up. She mentally shelved the SI reports and planned for a long night. Changing the subject was the first step in deflecting potential catastrophe. "Don't go. What you said a minute ago… we are almost married, aren't we? But how are we going to get that way? Big wedding with a gazillion people? Courthouse?"

Ryan's face showed her his thoughts. Half of him still itched to storm out, insulted. The other half was tempted to stay. She cupped his cheeks. He must have come to her straight from work, because he'd gone bristly; with his fair hair it hadn't been evident. She gave a shiver at a memory of his stubble on her skin, and brushed his face with her fingers. "Let's talk."

Two hours later Mel was still curled up on the sofa next to him, and they had a rough idea about the wedding.

And the aftereffects of a very nice horizontal interlude to keep them warm. It had loosened him up considerably; he'd lost the hurt look. He idly stroked her, hair, shoulders...

"Spring," he said doubtfully. "It'll really take that long to pull it together?"

"Yes, to make it perfect. This isn't going to be a simple backyard thing. We'd better talk budget."

"Good girl." He squeezed. "But it's your day. We can splurge a little, but I'm glad you're reasonable. And... one more question. Sweetie, how would you like to come back from our honeymoon to our own home?"

How romantic was that? "Straight into our house?"

Ryan grinned. "I called in at Brandon Caine Realty the other day. He has a new subdivision south of town, besides other homes for sale."

"I'm interested. I'd really want to use Julie, though. She's already shown me a few places, and she is a friend."

"I'm willing to see what she has to offer. Brandon Caine's new subdivision... she can't help there. It's exclusive."

"Do you have floor plans?"

"In the brochure. We could have a look this weekend."

"Good idea. I'm tired, Ryan. We'd better call it a night."

He scooped her up and kissed her. "Do you want me to stay over?"

She shook her head and returned his kiss. "Not unless you're okay with falling asleep alone. I still have an hour's work to get through."

"Not this late, surely, Melanie."

"It's my job. I guess we both have to learn to live with it."

It took another few minutes to get Ryan out the door. Mel missed him immediately. And was glad he was gone. She could handle SI's shipping woes much more easily without his energy in her space.

Mel hadn't been to Annie's in a couple of weeks. Adrian didn't expect her, but Ryan was off at an extraordinary meeting at the bank, and she found herself at loose ends on Saturday morning. She missed her bookstore mornings, talking to Adrian, sorting crumbling books, chatting about life, eating his amazing breakfasts.

The bookstore itself had changed in her mind. It felt even more personal since it had become Annie's. Naming it, and giving it a woman's name, made the store feel alive to her, like a friend.

So at nine o'clock Saturday morning she unlocked the door to Annie's and shouted, "I'm here."

"Wonderful."

Adrian had been in the downstairs workroom; he came out, dusting his hands on his grubby slacks. Mel launched herself at him. "Oh, I'm so glad to see you. I'm so happy."

He caught her and held her at arm's length. "I'm filthy, and you need to elaborate. Something tells me effusion is more than your turning up on the doorstep this morning."

"Look." Her left hand came out. "He asked me, Adrian. I'm getting married." She did her own version of a happy dance, which involved twirling.

After a pause, as if he had to adjust to the idea, he gathered her into a hug. "Congratulations, Mel. And blessings. I hope it'll be everything you dream of." She felt him kiss the top of her head.

"It will." She pulled free to look at him. "You know how I've dreamed of this. I'm floating on air."

"Could I offer you a celebratory breakfast? Anything, as long as I have the ingredients."

"Bacon and eggs?"

"It'll take longer, but how about Eggs Benedict?" He headed them up the stairs. "I hope you're going to give me the details?"

"I doubt you'll be able to shut me up." She settled at the table and watched him assembling ingredients.

Ending with a small bottle of Prosecco. "A special day, a special woman. Requires a special beverage." He popped the cork. A minute later he set a mimosa before her and clicked her glass with his. "Now, I cook and you talk."

So she talked. She talked all the way through their breakfast of Eggs Bennie and fruit salad. She talked while they washed dishes together. He didn't say much, but he listened, intently. No one had ever listened to her the way Adrian did. He was the best friend imaginable.

When she ran out of steam at last, he laughed. "Enough? Want to change the topic? Probably not, but I have to ask."

"Like what?"

"The final decisions on the furnishings for the coffee shop. We have tons of notes and no firm resolution. Care to tackle it?"

"Love to."

He'd piled the catalogs on the table under the picture of the ladies. The picture had reappeared sometime over the last two weeks and looked benignly down on them. "That," she said, "is the most perfect thing we could have here. Honest, Adrian, you chose a winner."

"I'm delighted, myself. Now. Furniture first? We need to bring logic into the selection process, or we risk wandering in the maze of furniture marketing."

"We need a list of criteria."

"We have one, but it's not necessarily complete. Style, color, size, the usual. I've been doing research on how many tables of what size. Then things like durability." His gaze traveled across the second floor. A good two-thirds of it was now designated coffee shop.

"What are you putting in there?" He'd walled in an el shape along the back wall and behind the stairwell, with a pair of picture windows looking out over the coffee shop.

"Rare books. It's increasingly evident to me that our fortune will be made through coffee and dusty tomes. It makes sense to keep the new and second-hand departments downstairs, so rare books has a home up here."

"Do we have enough rare books to justify that much space?"

"Not yet. It's a hobby of mine, so I expect it'll grow. It'll be climate controlled, white gloves."

"Oh, boy."

"As in, Wow? Holy Moly?"

"No, as in, Reality. It's real. Are you nervous?"

"Sure, some. The thing is, I love it here. We could have done the work and renovations in half the time, but that would have denied the specialness of the process. Do you know what I mean?"

Mel nodded.

"It can stand or fall, and that'll be okay on some level. I'm pretty sure I could make a go of it with just the rare books, and I said before that we've got a first rate dance studio here. We have options."

She drew her eyebrows together as she studied him. "You do, don't you? Love this place, I mean. I don't think you've ever said it."

"Interesting point." His eyes focused somewhere else. He repeated, with a wistfulness in his voice, "I do love it. I love what we've made it. It's a place of dreams. It's apart from the stuff that makes life so complicated. In my mind it'll be like that for anyone who comes in. A place outside of time."

"That's so poetic, but I wonder. Maybe it's just the two of us who sense that."

"Maybe. Mel…"

"Hmm?"

"Before we debate tables, I wonder if I could… hang on a minute." He left her and fiddled with the sound system behind the counter. Lush music poured from the speakers.

Adrian came to her and offered her his hand. "The last opportunity, while the magic's ours alone." He pulled her to her feet and led her into the middle of the empty space, where he bowed. She caught on immediately. Her eyes dancing, she executed what she hoped was a curtsy, and then he launched them into a waltz like she'd never danced before. In fact, Mel wasn't sure she'd ever waltzed in her life before. This wasn't a dance-lesson waltz, but the kind that covered the whole spacious room. Adrian held her formally, at a distance from himself, and was absolutely sure in the moves. Their eyes met, his equal to hers in sheer delight.

The dance would have seemed silly with anyone but Adrian as they spun around the room in their casual slacks and sneakers. He'd taken her out of the bookstore and conjured a formal ballroom, maybe in Vienna, a hundred or more years ago when people still danced to music like the Blue Danube. She could so easily imagine candlelight, swirling couples, long dresses, carriages waiting outside.

When the waltz ended he returned her to her chair. He bent over her and lightly kissed the back of her hand, then turned off the music. "My gosh," she said when he settled across from her. "Is this what they do in Philadelphia?"

"I doubt it happens anywhere anymore. A moment's madness. This room has that sort of effect on me. It won't be the same with tables."

"No. I'm glad we had the chance. I'll never ever get to do anything like that again."

"Me, either."

"It'll be good here. This space has the kind of energy that lets you imagine a dance. Or whatever you need to imagine."

"Back to practicalities?"

"I'm thinking tablecloths."

"Laundry. Keeping up with them all day long."

"Oilcloth printed to look like lace?"

"Let's talk."

"Right."

They huddled over the catalogs, breaking for tea after a while, pacing the room, always talking. She'd missed these mornings. She wished she could continue to be a part of this dream of Adrian's, but she wasn't sure how. She certainly couldn't work here once it was open for business.

And the time... these days everything came down to time. If she weren't used to keeping her life organized, she'd stand no chance, with the competing demands on her.

225

Well, she'd see how it went. It could be that Annie's was a fantasy. At least she'd always see Adrian when their mutual friends got together. It wasn't as if she was moving away. They'd stay friends. Friends who had shared a magic summer.

While they were disagreeing over cutlery Mel glanced at her watch. "Uh oh…"

He raised his eyebrows. "Forgot something? And that reminds me. I envision a clock on the wall. Classy and elaborate, somewhere between baroque and art deco. What do you think?"

What she thought was that she was late. She'd arranged to meet Ryan at the Club for nine holes of golf, and she'd forgotten. "Yes to the clock, but I'm out of here. I'm sorry but…" Mel flapped her hand helplessly and grabbed her bag.

"Go on then." Adrian got it, as always. "And drive carefully, even if you're late. I don't want to worry."

"It'll be close, but I'll make it."

At least she'd dressed for golf before she left home. Mel bolted, hoping that if she didn't dawdle, she'd get to the Club before their tee time.

Interlude

"What are you doing here?"

Huff had fully expected Adrian to take this Sunday morning from grim to godawful, but he'd hoped to at least get his feet in the door first. "Nice to see you, too, bro. Bad night? You look like hell."

His brother was unshaven and had on clothes that should have been thrown into the trash years ago. He pushed his way past Adrian and into the bookstore. He knew better than to expect him to be gracious, but he was prepared to meet rudeness with their own form of brotherly love. "Make coffee, would you?"

Adrian closed the door and leaned on it. "You flew in?"

"Crack of dawn."

"I don't much feel like being your serving boy today."

"Master of the warm welcome, aren't you?" Huff turned away and headed up the stairs.

Over—thank God—a decent cup of coffee a few minutes later, he said, "Official reason's Bindery business. I sent you the spreadsheets."

"Haven't looked at them yet." Adrian was moving from table to stove to sink, seemingly aimlessly.

"Not to delicately change the subject, but do you think I'm not aware when you're hurting?"

Adrian glared at him. Then went back to pacing the room.

"For heaven's sake, if you can't sit down, at least feed us."

227

Adrian wordlessly pulled out a container of granola and a carton of almond milk. A spoon and a bowl. Huff let the silence grow and put together a minimal breakfast. "I note you're not eating."

"Not hungry."

Huff ate, and then wrestled his brother into an hour-long dialogue about Bindery business, both their laptops open on the table in front of them. Huff respected his brother's competence, but the conversation wasn't fun for either of them. Mainly, he thought grimly, because Adrian was determined it wouldn't be.

Sometimes being a twin was hell.

But it was better to get the official reason for his visit out of the way first. Business done, Huff eyeballed his brother and said, "So what happened?"

Adrian was on his feet again, filling the kettle. "She's marrying him."

"Ring, the whole bit?"

"You got it."

"And she doesn't have a clue."

Adrian shook his head. "She says I'm her best friend."

Huff put his face in his hands. "Of course you are. That's how it starts. I bet this other guy hasn't ever been her best friend."

"My reading on it is, no."

He dropped his hands and scowled. "You're an idiot, brother. You can't let this happen."

"I can't stop it. You should see her."

"I've seen her. I told you, she's one of us. She's marrying the wrong guy."

"No, I guess she's not."

Huff watched and assessed.

"She's... whatever. It's too late." Adrian did all the tea-making things he used to deflect attention from whatever was on his mind.

"And you are the biggest damn fool. I can't believe you're chickening out. Not when it matters this much."

"You know why." Adrian's voice was soft, spoken more to the kettle than to him.

"Deanna was not your fault."

Adrian turned on him, fury in his eyes. "The hell she wasn't. She wouldn't have driven off like that if I... Do you think I'm willing to go through that again? Do you think I even could?"

"You've been living like a damn monk for fifteen years. She's at least had the sense to move on. Grow up and throw away your hair shirt."

Adrian pointedly turned away. Huff could see the muscles quivering under his T-shirt.

Matching his brother's rage, Huff got to his feet and swung Adrian around to face him. "Just once, try to hear what I'm telling you. You were not responsible for Deanna's accident. She made her own choices. This is your *life*, brother. And Mel's, for that matter. You can't let her go."

"You don't even know him."

"The other guy? I don't need to. You're right for her. She's right for you. Dammit all, *do something*."

He might as well have saved his breath. Adrian ignored him. In fact, Adrian had been on his own plane of existence ever since he'd arrived. Huff worried and chose not to show it. Adrian would sense his concern, but at least he'd give the appearance of a calm, stable voice of reason.

He felt tempted to pound on his brother until he saw sense. But he knew Adrian as well as he knew himself. Shifting Adrian from his conviction that he couldn't interfere in this misguided engagement of Mel's was almost certainly impossible.

Besides, Adrian was the superior wrestler.

"So let me get this straight. You move in the same social circles as her. You're hopelessly in love with her and you've got this whole soul mate thing happening, and you're going to go on living in Calter Creek as if you're happy as a lark. This, I can hardly wait to see."

"Then stay away." Adrian wheeled abruptly and stormed through the apartment door. By the time Huff caught up, he was standing in front of the coffee bar, running his hands over the surface. He didn't turn around. "The espresso machine will be here this week, or maybe next," he said conversationally. "It's coming from Italy. Did you know that once you've made it into an Americano or cappuccino, espresso has less caffeine than drip? I read that it's because the water—"

"Shut up, Adrian," Huff said without force. Adrian had always used his capacity to store random facts to divert attention from things he didn't want to talk about, and Huff didn't have the energy to push back. "I'm not going to fight with you. But I'm not going to stay away, either. Last time you told me to get lost, we left you alone and no one saw you for months. Not going to happen again. Are you depressed? Talk to me."

Adrian finally faced him, and grimaced. "Of course I'm depressed. But not clinically. Stop being Mother."

"Good." The silence festered. "You're an idiot."

"So you keep saying."

"Want to grab some lunch?"

"No, but we should. I'm heading for the shower."

Getting away from me, Huff thought.

"If you want the numbers, check on my laptop." Adrian left him in the big room without any further comment and disappeared into the apartment.

Huff sighed and returned to the table, spinning Adrian's computer around so both machines faced him. Adrian was better at running the numbers than he was, so he valued Adrian's output from their morning conversation. He pulled a thumb drive from his pocket.

But as he was browsing the computer for the data he needed, his eye caught on another folder. One that assuredly had nothing to do with The Bindery, and that he'd bet anything his brother didn't want him, or anyone else, to see. He listened. Shower still running, so he had time. He opened the folder.

The faint white noise from the shower was the only break in the silence as he studied what he'd found. Then, with a resolve that was scary, even to him, he hastily copied that folder, too, onto the thumb drive.

Huff left mid-afternoon, literally a flying visit. On his way out he grabbed his brother into a hug, which, to his relief, Adrian reciprocated. The last time Adrian had cut him out of his life, after they'd closed the stores, had been hell.

"I'm with you," Huff said.

"I know. Sometimes I wish you weren't quite so much with me."

"I may be five minutes younger, and I may not have a whole damn encyclopedia in my skull, but I'm smarter than you are. You're making a mistake."

His brother's mouth had drawn into a grim line, and the skin around his eyes was pinched. Huff knew pain when he saw it, especially on his brother's face.

"It's not fixable."

Huff rolled his eyes. "Call me."

"I will."

The closest thing to a declaration of love the two of them ever managed. Huff left, if not satisfied, at least with a plan. He couldn't fix Adrian, but he had an idea who could.

16

Mel was grouchy at work Wednesday. The week hadn't started well and hadn't improved, but it was her own attitude that had brought on her bad mood. It was niggly little things, like how hopeless she'd been when she and Ryan had played golf Saturday. She'd wanted to make him proud, but it had been as if her lessons had drained right out through her toes. She was now an expert at replacing divots and once hit the ground with enough force that it hurt her wrist. The wrist was still sore; she flexed it and frowned.

But the worst of the golf had been when Ryan had undertaken to explain, and demonstrate, what she was doing wrong. That had made her even more tense. She was beyond grateful to see the end of the ninth hole.

What was wrong with her that she couldn't accept his coaching in the spirit he offered it? He was only trying to help. They were a team, and it was like she was fighting it all the way.

Then Sunday he hadn't approved of the top she'd chosen to wear to an impromptu gathering at the Grants'. She'd bought it at Fairy Glen Designs. It was modest in cut but gloriously flamboyant in print, a swirling pattern of orange, blue, and purple. Mel thought it was wonderful. In fact, so did Jenna Grant. But on the way home Ryan had treated her to a discourse on her position as a banker's fiancée, and pulling as a team, and how what she did affected them both. He didn't mention the top, but she'd seen his face when he first laid eyes on it. It was a mini-lecture, and she recognized it for what it was.

So she wasn't happy with Ryan.

But she wasn't happy with herself, either. She felt as if she was missing signals that any dunce could pick up on. Yes, they had to adjust to each other and there'd be growing pains and so forth, but shouldn't they at least *start* pulling in the same direction? With any luck there'd be a get-together with her own group of friends soon. A dose of their casual style might counteract her frustration.

She hadn't seen Ryan since Sunday evening. He'd warned her he'd be tied up with bank stuff most of the week, but their phone conversations were brief and unsatisfying.

Her sunflower had finished blooming, so even her office wasn't as cheerful as it had been. Perhaps she could find a sunflower print. The ocean scene on her wall didn't thrill her.

Well, get thrilled. She was driving herself crazy with her attitude.

She grabbed her mug and headed for the break room, where she schmoozed with Michael, Amanda's new assistant, and Robert from the warehouse for a few minutes. They both told her she was looking like dynamite these days.

Walking back to her office, she ran a hand over the lapel of her emerald green suit, worn today with a rust top and her favorite jungle print scarf. Ryan would cringe. Yes, she'd let him influence her into the haircut. She was glad she'd done it, now that she was used to it. But her work wardrobe was out of bounds.

Becoming half of a couple took a lot of adjusting. But Mel feared losing her independence in the process.

And then there was work.

She turned from her keyboard and stared out the window, idly playing with the ring on her finger.

Bottom line, she was doing the job. But she wasn't enjoying it that much.

Mel met Julie after work at a small wine bar that had recently opened on the outskirts of downtown. She collapsed into her chair with a sigh. "Even the traffic coming into town was the pits. Calter Creek's getting too big."

"That's my livelihood you're talking about. Don't complain."

233

The waiter turned up and Mel ordered a glass of Malbec. "Bad week."

"Good week for me so far. Sold a house in one of Brandon Caine's older developments yesterday."

"Jules, do you ever get sick of your job?"

"Sure." Julie shrugged. "Doesn't everyone? It's a little late for me to train to do something else, though. Can't afford to go back to school, then start at the bottom of the totem pole again. This new position getting to you?"

"It's more responsibility, more authority, less fun. It isn't the same."

Their wine arrived. Mel got through her first few swallows faster than she should.

"Learning curve. Or knowing you, you're obsessing and trying too hard."

"Do I do that? Try too hard?"

Julie snickered and sipped her wine.

"Fair enough, I do. But shouldn't I be getting satisfaction from it by now?"

"How's the rest of your life?"

Julie had heard about Proposal Night, she'd admired the glory that was the ring. She wasn't any more prepared than Mel was for Mel's collapsing spirits. "I'm drowning. He doesn't leave me alone."

"Arguably, that's a bonus."

That drew a chuckle from her. "Not that way. That way's fine. It's the other stuff..." She broke off. "No. It's just me. He wants me to be more conservative, but I expected that. No one's complaining, but... he's learning to adjust, same as I am."

She might have convinced herself, but so far she hadn't convinced Julie. "You're dead certain, right? He's absolutely, positively the one?"

"When we're together all's right with the world. Most of the time he acts as if I'm an angel blessing his life."

"You're not married yet, Mel. Be damn sure."

"I'm doing my best. He makes it hard to be objective." Casting her mind back to that amazing Saturday, eleven whole days ago, was enough to restore her good mood. "It'll settle down. I'm just PMSing."

"How does Ryan handle that?"

Mel flashed a wicked grin. "He's inclined to run for the hills. He's modest about physical stuff, oddly enough. It's kinda sweet."

"TMI."

"Can't help it. Who else can I babble to?"

"Speaking of work, did you know Adrian's house hunting? He dropped in last week."

Mel sat up. "No, really? He mentioned not staying in the apartment forever, but I didn't know he was looking."

"Mm hmm. There's a cottage a few blocks out from downtown that's come on the market recently. Small two-story, big yard, trees. Needs work inside. We're seeing it Friday."

"Do you have the address? I'm curious."

"It's on Palmer, near Third. I haven't been inside this one yet. Definitely a fixer-upper, they say."

"Sounds like his kind of thing. What he's doing with Annie's... wait till you see."

"According to him, it's a shared endeavor. He gives you a lot of the credit."

"I've enjoyed it."

These days Julie seemed to know as much about the goings-on at Annie's as she did. Okay, Adrian hung out with her crowd of friends. But the idea of him doing out-of-bookstore things with Julie left her unsettled, as if she were missing some vital clause in a contract.

Mel was content to nurse her single glass of red wine, ignoring those first hasty swallows. They lingered in the bar until after seven o'clock. The wine and talk had eased her negative mood, so on her way out she phoned Ryan and suggested that he meet her for steaks.

His alacrity restored balance to the world.

A girl can't stay snarky forever.

Saturday, stretched out next to Ryan, Mel had that dreamy vibe going. They'd had the most wonderful day, starting with lunch on his patio. After a walk along Calter Creek, they'd made love in the late afternoon, with the autumn sunlight filtering through the curtains. They had reservations at the Italian place on the Old Columbus Road, but that was a couple of hours away. In the meantime she'd lie there next to him, enjoying his lean body... yes, today had been all she'd dreamed of.

High time, her evil angel nattered at her.

Shut up, she growled back. Ryan would be convinced she was crazy if he knew about the internal dialogues kicking around in her head.

She kissed his shoulder.

"Mmm? I was dozing off." His eyes were closed, and he had a little smile on his face.

"You can doze." She snuggled into him, her head under his chin. "You smell so good."

"So do you." Ryan shifted to run his thumb over her cheek. "I've sensed we haven't been communicating very well lately. I'm glad we've had today."

"So am I. I don't want tension between us. I want to keep the romance alive."

"I'm not romantic." His other hand stroked her back; she wiggled and got an appreciative groan from him. "I'm too practical. It's how I am, Melanie. I hope you understand."

"You underestimate yourself. The night you proposed... that was as romantic as it gets."

Ryan's eyes opened and he heaved up, dumping her back onto the bed. He took her left hand and fingered the ring. "We still have to get this resized."

"I could take it in on Monday over lunch, or after work."

He nodded. "It worries me."

"I told you it won't fall off." She demonstrated, pulling the ring toward her knuckle.

"By seeing to things before the worst happens, you avoid trouble."

"A stitch in time." But Mel deflated, just a little.

At least he was here with her now, and not itching to go read a banking journal.

He swung his legs off the bed. "I'm going to grab a shower."

"I'll join you." She wanted to carry the afternoon beyond the... perfunctory?... lovemaking.

Ryan hovered over her and kissed her. "It's a small shower stall. I'll save you some hot water."

Yeah. But the things you can do in a shower...

Alone in his bed Mel reflected on differences. They'd talked wedding plans while they walked. Dates, venues, costs. Practical things. But she'd gone shopping in Columbus with Julie and Bryony the previous Sunday, and the talk was dresses and dances and romantic interludes. She supposed guys were more interested in practicalities. So, okay, that was Ryan.

And she... well, she conceded that her romance novels must have given her exalted ideas where love and sex were concerned. She wasn't inexperienced, but nothing like what her books described had ever happened to her. Making love with Ryan was fine. It was a matter of taking it in slow stages, respecting his comfort zone.

Her man was conservative. She had to learn to live within that framework.

Still, she kept looking for that electric charge, that cellular connection.

The shower shut off. Mel was warm and sleepy and in no hurry to be anywhere else, but she got herself out of bed, chose a towel from his linen closet, and propped herself in the open door to the bathroom. He'd wrapped a towel around his waist, but his chest was still wet. Mel ran a hand up his back. "What's next? We have an hour and a half before our reservations."

"Why don't we go out to Creekside Mall? We can take the ring in, and I need socks."

"It's a plan." Not the most romantic plan, but certainly practical. That's how marriage would be, mixing the starry-eyed and the everyday. "Out of the way, pal. My turn." She scooted around Ryan and dug into the drawer where she now kept a supply of what he called her 'girl stuff'. Shower gel and conditioner in hand, she disappeared into the shower.

Time enough to seduce her man again over supper. Italian restaurant, candles, Chianti... Mel hummed as she got herself ready for an expedition to the mall.

With Ryan. That's what mattered.

Things were falling into place, Mel thought. Work was smoothing out, despite the presence of her eternal file folders and binders on her dining table at least once a week. She'd had time to hang out with Amanda, which she'd missed, although Amanda at almost eight months had her own set of obsessions. Her hard-headed, all-business boss had gone gooey over a photo of an animal mural for a child's room and gushed at a pattern for baby booties. "Do you even know how to crochet?" Mel had asked. Receiving the expected negative, she'd filed the online location of the pattern in her mind, thinking she'd crochet up a surprise or two.

Ryan... Ryan. The Italian dinner, with all that had preceded it, had gone a long way toward getting them back on a comfortable footing. It had provided the right level of sophistication, and had set the stage for a quiet, domestic Sunday. They'd browsed open houses Sunday afternoon, which had been less stressful than she had predicted. Ryan hadn't even quibbled over one or two painted accent walls.

So Mel got home from work Tuesday tired but no longer snarky. She was puzzled when she found a shipment from an online bookseller in her mailbox.

She hadn't ordered anything. Had she? She wasn't *that* muddled in love.

Had someone sent her a present? She went upstairs to her apartment and dropped the package on the sofa. She was curious, but she'd keep the mystery alive for another few minutes. Had Ryan chosen a book for her? Had her mother ordered a book on wedding planning? Maybe Julie had sent her the kind of book you put in a brown cover, like the *Kama Sutra*.

In comfortable jeans and turtleneck, the kettle on for tea, Mel opened the package.

The book was slender, and unfamiliar. It took a moment for her brain to register what she was seeing.

The picture hanging in Annie's, on the brick wall above the coffee counter, graced the cover, but taken from an angle and not crisply in focus.

It was entitled *Poems for My One and Only*.

It was by Adrian Forsythe.

Mel dropped onto the sofa and stared at the book in her hands.

Then she got up, turned off the kettle, and opened a bottle of wine.

She curled up with the wine and the book. Everything felt off kilter, not quite spinning, but not stable either. She'd called him poetic, but he'd told her he wouldn't let her see his poetry. Love poems, from the title. Why had he sent it to her? Surely he didn't expect her to share it with Ryan.

Nothing made sense.

He had given her Emily Dickenson's poems months ago. She'd enjoyed them well enough, but she certainly wasn't seeking out other poets. So why this? Why now? She opened the book and read, slowly.

When she came to one particular poem, she read it twice. It didn't require much introspection to understand it. It was there, in black and white. She read it a third time, slowly, as Adrian's heart revealed itself to her.

Then she sat and stared across the room, seeing nothing, for a long time.

Saturday, Mel crashed through the door to Annie's. "Adrian," she shouted, then slammed the door behind her and took a few steps into the store.

After the book arrived, Mel had endured a confused, disorienting week. Her focus was shot, along with her appetite. She'd been for a few solitary walks, but they hadn't helped. Her mind was like a jigsaw puzzle when the piece *should* fit right there, but no matter how you turned it, it wouldn't go in.

She'd avoided Ryan. She'd claimed stomach upset, which wasn't true but might have been, the state she was in. Lying to him made her feel worse.

She was clenched up inside, so much so that she'd start shaking if she didn't hold herself in tight control. Coming to Annie's to see Adrian took every bit of grit and determination she could muster.

"I didn't expect you today." His voice came from the storeroom in the back. He appeared and moved toward her, then stopped. "Mel? What's wrong?"

She'd steeled herself, but the dispassionate speech she'd rehearsed flew right out of her mind. "You know what's wrong," she blurted. "How could you? I never expected this from you." Tears were two seconds away. She gulped them back, or tried to. One leaked out and made its way down her cheek.

Adrian started to her, but stopped when she backed away. His smile changed to puzzlement. "I'm sorry, I don't know what you mean."

She swiped at her face with the side of her hand. "This. I'm talking about this." She slapped the volume of his poetry down on the new checkout counter.

The checkout counter whose blond wood shone in the sunlight, catching reflections from the silk hangings on the wall above it.

He didn't move. "What is it?"

"It's yours. But to send it to me, now—"

"Mine? No, it isn't. I've never seen it." Adrian walked over to the counter and picked up the book.

She watched him scan the cover picture, the title.

"What...?" He flipped through it. Mel would swear he paled.

He shut his eyes, then opened them again and gave her a level look. "I don't know anything about this," he said quietly. "I wouldn't do this to you. Or to myself."

"But then..."

"I don't know. I swear, Mel, I don't know."

240

She took the book from him and turned to a page number she'd memorized. "It was this one." She read. "'Her hair, like a copper halo, capturing, holding, merging with the sun....' It's me, isn't it? These are about me."

He closed his eyes again and continued the verse from memory. "'... until, blinded, I am forced to my knees'." He didn't have to say any more. She was right.

Adrian loved her.

"How long?" she said.

He went to the foot of the stairs and gripped the curved end of the banister. He didn't look at her. "When you tried to break the door down? You couldn't see it, but there was a mist trapped on the ends of your hair. It was like jewels, even in the gray day. Of course, by touching it I destroyed it when my hand brushed away the mist. It's a metaphor for my life," he concluded bitterly.

She turned to another page. "'... Secrets are pointless, and if there is mercy in heaven and earth, we will live in this awareness forever, not together, but as one.'"

"You don't have to quote my words back at me. It hurts."

"But this..." She closed the book and stroked its cover.

He turned around and faced her. "I never wanted you to see them."

She wasn't blind to the panicky expression on his face. "I believe you." She put his poems on the counter, then went to the stairs and sat on the second riser at his feet. "What do we do now, Adrian?"

He smiled at her, but it was bleak. "Now, I suppose, you go home and plan your wedding, and I stay here and plan the grand opening. Same as before."

Mel heard what she'd missed all these weeks, the pain in his words. She reached up and took his hand. "Seriously? After this?"

He gripped her hand and looked over the low, blond shelves across from them, awaiting their burden of books. "Yes. Yesterday I could have shown you around, made you lunch, any of a dozen things. Now... any other viable possibility would hurt too much. It's better if you go home."

"I can't marry Ryan."

He wrenched their hands apart and spun away from her. "Because I wrote you a few poems? Mel, he's everything you've dreamed of. Please…" He stopped and swallowed. "Please don't put me in the position of having to convince you to do the one thing I want least in the world."

She spoke slowly, to his back, "Remember once we talked about dreams, and that they were important but they had to be the right ones, the ones that fit in the context of your life."

"Mel, I beg you." He turned to look at her, but actually backed a step away.

She let him keep his distance; it made it easier get the words out. To toss out every certainty she had, with no guarantees for the future.

"I'd been living a dream that wasn't the right one, even if it looked perfect on the surface, because everything lined up. I couldn't see that the magic wasn't there, possibly because I wanted it to be, so much."

She stopped, to see if he'd speak. He didn't.

"When I'm here, it's as if time stands still and the outside world doesn't exist for the hours I'm here."

His voice was choked. "The magic."

"And now… I've had the book since Tuesday. I've had time to think."

They stared at each other. He took off his glasses and put them on top of one of the bookshelves. His face was that of a man not quite daring to hope. She thought he might be close to tears. She'd never known Ryan, or any other man for that matter, with the courage to look so vulnerable.

Adrian came to her, keeping his eyes fixed on her face. She waited, watching him. He reached out his hands, and without thinking, she took them.

He pulled her up, with no hesitation at all, releasing her hands to wrap his arms around her, smoothing his palms over her back. "Grant me just this once," he said into her hair.

She gave a small negative shake of her head against his chest. "I've read the poems."

Then she looked up at him, and he kissed her. It wasn't a first kiss. There was nothing tentative or exploratory about it. It was a kiss between two people who were halves of a whole. The shape of his mouth, the way he used his lips and tongue to explore her, were as familiar as her own dreams.

It was beyond sexual, beyond emotional, although it included both. Her fingers clutched at his back, she moved a hand up into his hair. She delighted in the faint scent of him, composed of soap or shampoo, and Adrian. The one man who completed her.

Somewhere, far, far away, Ryan waited, Sinclair Imports and the Country Club and her family and friends, they were all out there. But not here. Here, there was only this man's body and soul. The rest was lost to her.

Leaving nothing but Adrian.

It had always been Adrian, and she hadn't been able to see it.

His mouth left hers, his fingers tunneled through her short hair, cradling her head as he had the night of the fire. He ran kisses over her cheekbone, down to her jaw, under her ear. With every touch of his lips something exploded and released inside her, like chains snapping.

Later she'd deal with the enormity of the mistake she'd almost made. Now, her world had a new axis.

A spasm ran up his spine under her hands as he turned his face into her hair. She felt him take a shuddering breath, and held on to him with all she had, hoping he'd know that eventually it would all be right.

Later—she wasn't sure how much later because time had stopped the instant he'd taken her into his arms—he released her and took her hand again. "Let me make you a cup of tea," he said, his voice shaky. "I'm untethered from reality right now."

Hand in hand they went up the elegant staircase. The tables and chairs were in place, gleaming against the hardwood floor. The daylight through the stained glass in the windows warmed the walls. He sat her at their table, where they'd spent so much delicious time together.

Mel had hit overload. While she wanted him close, she sensed that it was as much a relief for him as for her when he went behind the bar to prepare the tea.

He brought the tray to the table and placed it in the middle. "Ryan," he said.

"Sit down, Adrian." Overload or not, for the moment she was more in control than he was. Adrian sat.

Mel put her chin on a hand and studied the teapot, which she now knew was Wedgwood. "Ryan meets every point on my checklist."

"So I understand. He's a good man, Mel."

"I know." She watched Adrian pour the tea, not waiting his usual two and a half minutes. He was nervous.

"The thing is…"

"Mel, are you thinking—"

"I meant what I said. I can't marry Ryan. Especially not now."

Adrian's voice was still unsteady, and as hoarse as it had been in the aftermath of the fire. "It's what you want. What happened downstairs, it was just… an understanding, perhaps. Or a gift. Between friends. We are still friends, aren't we?"

"The best. But that wasn't all it was. Please don't say that."

He sighed. "No, you're right. For me, it was everything. I'm sorry to lay that on you, but… that day, when I was so obnoxious about your hair, I was terrified I'd lost you forever. It was a plunge into hell." He gestured meaninglessly at the teapot. "What, then?"

"You know what."

He didn't answer.

"You were going to let me marry Ryan and never say a word, weren't you?"

He nodded. As he'd done their first breakfast together, he put a spoonful of honey into his cup of tea. He stirred but made no move to drink. "Maybe. I'm not sure. Huff gave me hell. But it wasn't my place. I wanted it to be, but I watched you, how excited you'd be when you were seeing Ryan. Your elation after you'd been with him. I couldn't mess that up for you." He paused, took a breath. "Okay, listen. I lied to you once."

She frowned. "That's not like you."

"When I told you I didn't have any secrets from you. I couldn't have told you this, not then. Now I think I have to, so you'll understand."

He stopped talking.

The honey spoon was in her hand. She put it down and waited.

His face was tight, his delivery choppy. "There was... her name's Deanna. We fought, I don't even remember why. She stormed out and drove off. There was an accident."

Mel watched him. She'd never seen this Adrian. Burdened, not wanting to reveal himself. "Did she die?"

"No. Lost an arm and needed facial reconstruction. They did their best, but you can tell. She'd been lovely."

"You blame yourself."

He didn't answer.

"You were how old?"

His mouth twitched. "Twenty-five."

"Twenty-five," Mel repeated, as if to herself. "So that's when your hair..."

He latched onto it. "They say there's no proven link between trauma and loss of pigment in hair, but there's plenty of anecdotal evidence. The pigment's called melanin, there are two different—"

"Adrian." Mel put her hand on his arm. "What happened to her?"

He let the deflection go with a sigh. "Married, two kids. She lives in Virginia now. Our paths cross periodically, if we both happen to be in Philadelphia. She avoids me."

"But that was fifteen years ago. How does this relate to you and me?"

His words were serious. "It doesn't work out so well when I involve myself in other people's lives."

The enormity of his statement left her speechless. She sensed there was no point in arguing, at least not with words.

245

When she caught her breath she said, "Adrian, you got help, didn't you? You haven't been dealing with this on your own all these years?"

He nodded. "Mostly it's okay, but when there's a trigger, like closing the stores..." He closed his eyes, hard. His expression, when he opened them again, was bleak. "I wasn't going to risk messing up your life."

"I guess fate had other plans. Maybe it's predestined."

"I don't believe anything is predestined."

She finally stirred honey into her tea. She couldn't look at him. "That checklist in my head, I forgot to put magic on it. With Ryan... I wanted it to be right, but the color disappeared from my world. I lost who I was."

"Deep inside you didn't."

"It's been insidious." She glanced up.

His smile was tentative, but there. "Stealthy."

She returned his smile, hoping he'd relax. "Underground? But when I really look at where I am now... I've lost the work I loved. I almost never see my friends. The Club's an alien environment. Molding myself into what he..." She shook her head. "No, that's not fair. We all have our preconceptions, but he honestly does want what's best for me. The thing is, I liked myself. I liked my life. Now I'm not sure I do."

Adrian took her left hand, his fingers stroking hers. "I did notice."

Of course he would. Ryan's ring was in her jewelry box at home.

"What happens next?" she asked him.

"I don't know. I never had any faith we'd find ourselves here."

"Then..." She reached across to put her hand over Adrian's and watched as he added his hand to the stack. Their four hands, together. Mel felt a giggle rising and fought it back, sensing it could too easily turn into sobs.

And that was all. No more than that, not now, not yet. Not until she'd reclaimed herself. Not until she'd spoken to Ryan.

"Let's have our tea," he said. "Maybe start sorting the secondhand books. Stick labels everywhere. Like always."

"It'll never be like always again, you know."

"I wanted to call this place Mel's," he told her. "That was my first choice. A dozen good reasons not to, of course."

"Did I ever tell you my middle name's Anne? Melanie Anne."

The smile reached his eyes this time. "So it was always yours."

"Ours. Magic flows both ways."

"There's one other thing. It matters to me that you know."

"Tell me."

Adrian took a breath. "Since Deanna. There hasn't been anyone else."

She was speechless for a moment. "At all?"

"No. I've never been one for casual affairs. And…" His voice trailed off, and he shrugged. "Perhaps I had an intimation you'd be in my future. Nothing about this is casual for me."

"Not for me, either." She used her embedded hand to squeeze his.

He shook off his gravity. "I can guess who published that book and sent it to you."

"Please don't kill him. He's family, after all."

Adrian finally laughed. "I made the mistake of leaving him alone with my computer. I should have known better." He broke up the hand stack, claiming one of her hands in one of his.

They finished the tea in silence, then washed the teapot and cups and went downstairs to sort and dust the remaining second-hand books and plan their arrangement on the shelves.

Business as usual. As usual as it had ever been, anyway. The difference was, now she saw it for what it was. That in touching her life, he hadn't destroyed it as he feared, he'd freed it. She prayed he'd see it too, one day.

Before she left she took his hand again. "You won't hear from me for a while. I'll come when I can."

247

"It's going to be hard for you."

She nodded. "But it's what I have to do. I can't see you again until I do."

"I'll be here."

She stood on tip-toe and kissed him, a barely-there kiss. "I'll come," she repeated, very quietly. He handed her the book, his book. She left, feeling torn in two.

17

Mel needed time, and space, and that meant getting out of Calter Creek.

It had been hard. The hardest thing she'd ever done, because she did love Ryan. But…

She took Friday and Monday off and flew to visit her parents in Florida. It was only for a couple of days, and an extravagance given the airfare, but she needed it. She'd made the biggest decision of her life, and she was sure about it but shaken, too. She needed to be just herself, just Mel, needed to sit on her parents' deck in the Florida warmth and write in her journal and sort out the conflicting feelings that assaulted her, without warning, day and night.

She was, in sum, a mess.

But writing it down helped. The change of scene and climate helped. Even her parents' love, if somewhat ineffectual, helped.

All the assessing in the world couldn't get her away from the simple fact that she loved Ryan. Or the bigger fact that he was not the right man for her, on far too many levels.

She fingered the blank spot on her finger where the ring had been. What she'd done to him… better now than in a year or two, she supposed, but it didn't make her any less wretched.

And Adrian. His kiss had blown her fuses, big time. She cast her mind back over the happy, relaxed Saturday mornings they'd spent together. Annie's was a playground they'd imagined into life. She'd become enmeshed in the store without even realizing it had happened.

The store that was Adrian. He was the core of the magic that was Annie's. But she hadn't grasped what he meant to her. She still wasn't sure.

Best friend? Yes. Mentor? Yes again. She'd learned tons about bookselling, business planning and stocking and a dozen other things they'd worked through. Not to mention the odd bits of information he always had at his fingertips.

Lover? They could already be lovers, if you counted the expression on his face. She could read him like a book, like his poetry, now that the mask was down. He loved her, and had loved her all summer, and she hadn't seen it. Instead she'd told him about Ryan, drowning out his feelings by her obsession with another man. She'd never given him a chance.

Did she love Adrian? Maybe. Probably. It was bigger, deeper than anything in her life before.

His mouth on her neck, his hands in her hair… Sitting in the Florida sun, a happy shiver ran up her back at the memory.

She felt like a wounded animal, going to ground, hiding out while she healed. But healing required time, and she couldn't do it alone. Even if she hadn't sorted out anything else, she knew that her grounding came from the reality of Adrian.

But not yet. She was still too raw.

Mel shook herself out of her reverie and left the deck to pour another glass of iced tea.

It was Saturday, like all the other Saturdays. Sort of. It had been three weeks since she'd last visited Annie's. She knocked, then unlocked the door and called, "Hello?"

A woman's voice answered her. "Hang on a sec, I'll be right down."

Huh?

Mel eased through the door and closed it behind her, half wondering what new calamity was poised to tumble on her head. But the older woman who descended the stairs looked ordinary and friendly in jeans, a t-shirt, and a cardigan. Hair working its way from brown to gray, and calm, happy eyes.

She stopped on the bottom step, studied her a moment, then smiled. "You're Mel."

"Yes. But—"

"I'm Helen, Adrian's mother. I came to visit. Neither of my sons has ever been able to say no to me, so when I announced I wanted to see what he was doing, he was defenseless. Come on in. Isn't this wonderful?" Helen descended the remaining step and made an enthusiastic gesture with her arms. "I can't decide if it feels like a private club or a luxury resort or just the best bookstore imaginable—and believe me, I've seen my share of bookstores. I love what you've created here. It's amazing."

Mel was never speechless for more than a second, but it looked as if she was going for a record. "It's got some magic to it, and it was Adrian mostly," she finally said.

"Not to hear him tell it. But I'm sorry, like most of our family, I can be overwhelming at times. I'm so thrilled to meet you. He needs someone who believes in magic. Shall we have tea?"

She looked around. "Adrian...?"

"In the shower last time I heard. It's early, but I gather the two of you have always gotten an early start. Come on." She nodded her head at the stairs, then started up. Mel followed, meekly.

"I love those instant hot water things," Helen chatted on. "I ought to demand one at home."

This woman's family ran one of the largest bookstore chains in America, and she doesn't have an instant hot water tap? Well, that said something about the nature of the Forsythe family, something that was perfectly in tune with Adrian's old, comfortable kitchen.

Almost before she had seated herself at their usual table, Helen was on her way from behind the serving counter with a tray. Mel surveyed the contents. "Tea bags? He'd kill you."

"I never said my boys weren't opinionated." Helen put the tea bags into mugs of hot water, then rested her elbow on the table, her chin on her hand, and her light blue eyes on Mel. "Anyway, he's been forced to compromise and use high-quality tea bags in the coffee shop. It's the only practical choice. Now. About Adrian."

251

Mel gulped. She was his mother. What was she about to reveal? Given Adrian, anything was possible. "What about him?"

Helen shifted in her chair. Mel got the feeling that this wasn't the easiest conversation she'd ever conducted. "I'm moving quickly because I have a couple of things I want you to understand, and he's going to turn up any minute. Forgive me for being pushy. You know he's had long periods of frail health?"

"Yes. Not recently, though?"

"The last time was when we had to close the stores. That was rough. It was hardest on him since it was his decision. Don't think we're callous, Mel." Helen put a hand over hers. "We knew, or at least it was obvious to me, that he shouldn't assume responsibility for The Bindery. But George—that's my husband—George had prostate cancer, and I was determined that he'd live to see his grandkids grow up, and we wanted that more than anything, and Huff was off doing his own thing, so he wasn't free..." She wound down to take a breath. "And Adrian said he'd do it. He didn't want to, but that's how our family is."

Mel nodded, adding this to her understanding of the Forsythes.

"Anyway, please don't judge us harshly. It was a family situation. We should have ended it sooner, but things seemed to be going well, and..."

"I have a family, too, Mrs. Forsythe," Mel said. "Things happen."

"Thanks, and it's Helen. I knew I'd like you. But since then he's been different. I mean he's always been different, IQ off the charts and the strange way his mind works, I guess the year he spent with the flu intensified it. But that time after the layoffs affected him. When he got the idea to create a bookstore—that's what he called it, 'creating' a bookstore—we figured it was best to just let him do it."

"Not to mention," Mel interrupted, "that he's a grown man. I doubt you could have stopped him."

Helen shrugged. "Family ties run deep. He listened when we threw up the reasons why not. But you're right, the negatives didn't faze him. Now that I've seen the result... drink your tea, Mel."

"Yes, ma'am." She had long since fished out the tea bag. She sipped. "Anything else?"

Helen shook her head. "I wanted you to understand that he's a little strange, and he hasn't always been robust. I worry."

And you're placing him in my keeping. The handover had happened, from this cheerful woman to her.

It occurred to her suddenly that she was looking at a God-given opportunity. "Can I ask you a question?"

"What's that, dear?"

"When Adrian and Huff were little and they skinned a knee or something... did you say to them, 'It's all right, my love'?"

Helen frowned at her. "It's possible, I suppose. I don't remember ever calling either of them 'my love'. I usually said 'sweetie' or something like that, but you say nonsense things sometimes. Why?"

Mel smiled. "Nothing. Nonsense things."

But the barrage wasn't over. Helen regained the floor. "Now, you and Adrian."

Mel set her mug on the table. "Between Adrian and me. End of discussion."

Helen beamed at her. "Oh, I *do* like you. You'll watch out for him."

A familiar and much-missed voice cut over their teatime chat. "Mom? Want me to make blueberry panca... Mel?"

She looked up. Adrian stood in the door to the apartment, holding a frying pan and looking like someone had hit him over the head with it. The room went silent. She got up, walked to him as if it were the most normal thing in the world to do. *Which,* she thought, *was the simple, actual truth.* She took the frying pan from him and set it on a nearby table, then held out her hands.

He took them and wove his fingers into hers. "You're here," he said quietly.

"Yes."

"It's done?"

"Yes."

"And may I—?"

She didn't wait for him. She covered the last step to him and enfolded him.

And he enfolded her.

Helen probably was still there across the room. Blueberry pancakes probably were still on offer. None of that mattered. His hand found her chin, tilted up her face, and then his mouth was on hers, offering her everything he was, claiming from her everything she might ever be.

She broke off the kiss, by about a half an inch. "Your mother," she whispered.

"Awkward timing," he agreed. Instead of kissing her again he pulled her against him. "As I was saying," he spoke over her head, "Mom, does blueberry pancakes sound good? I already know Mel will eat whatever I cook. Including sardines, I might add."

She nodded against his chest, vigorously.

"That would be delightful." Helen's voice couldn't have been coming from across town, but that's how it sounded to her dazzled senses.

He touched the tip of her nose with a finger, then let her go. "Coming up."

Mel turned to Helen with a smile. "I'm crazy about him."

Helen's mouth quirked. "Good," she said.

They ate blueberry pancakes and talked. About the shop, tea bags, the grand opening. About Huff and George and more aunts, uncles, and cousins than Mel had a hope of keeping track of. She concluded that Adrian wasn't that different from the rest of his family. She gave up thinking and just went with it.

They admired the wooden sign, with its non-neon, old-fashioned look. He'd left it plain 'Annie's', no mention of bookstore or coffee shop. He'd never hung the paper back up over the windows, so everyone downtown had been able to see the progress. "They can always come in and explore. Every other option I tried sounded corny."

"We can't have corny," Mel said. "They'll come."

They spent the day in the store, adjourning to the apartment's kitchen when they broke for food. Helen talked, and Adrian talked, and Mel watched the interaction between mother and son and considered how her own future might be tangled up in Adrian's family.

After a soup supper, Helen kissed Adrian, hugged Mel, and grabbed her purse. At Mel's puzzled look she laughed. "I love my son, but we're both too old to share a tiny one-bedroom apartment when we don't have to. I have a room at the Madison Inn."

And Adrian was alone tonight. She hadn't even considered that, not since first meeting Helen that morning.

He went downstairs to see his mother off. When he came back he stood in the door to the apartment, across the kitchen from her, and said with a trace of regret, "I'd always imagined there'd be rose petals. Instead you get my mom."

"I like your mom, and I don't need rose petals. I'm not sure I'm a rose petal type."

"Not needed, but what I wanted for you. Rose petals are said to purify the atmosphere, keep you safe from plague and other nasty things." Their eyes met. "Daisies? Yes, there should be bouquets of daisies."

She gave him a delighted smile. "He loves me, he loves me not?"

"I hope that's not a question. Daisies are happy and innocent, as well as being the home of fairies. I think we'll have fairies, don't you?"

She crossed the room to him and put her hands on his waist. "It's inevitable. We'll make a fairy garden."

"I do have a new toothbrush. Do you suppose there's a symbolic meaning for new toothbrushes?"

"Maybe a modern version of rose petals?"

"Today's been what I've dreamed it could be. You, my family, the store."

"Me, too."

"I don't want to wait for daisies. But if you'd…"

She shook her head.

He took her hand and led her through the old apartment to his bedroom.

When he touched her, not because it was sex but because it was ordained… when they lay skin touching skin, soul locked to soul, Mel knew, with every fiber of her being, that her romance novels hadn't lied after all. And that she'd never leave the side of this incredible man.

Epilogue

They'd added a second sign downstairs and completely rearranged the ground floor to allow access to the stairs and the elevator when the bookstore was closed.

Annie's Upstairs.

Mel sought refuge for a few minutes in the break room. She'd been run off her feet since they'd opened at seven thirty that Saturday morning. No one had expected they'd be so busy that early on a Saturday. Even after three years, they were still learning the ins and outs of running a café in Calter Creek.

Annie's had grown to be much more than coffee. They had contracts with two different bakers in town, and a woman who specialized in gourmet soups and sandwiches. They did a brisk business not only in pastries and muffins, but also in lunch and, increasingly, breakfast.

Mel didn't work on the floor very often these days. She was usually holed up with the bookkeeping or managing deliveries, personnel, everything it took to make Annie's run seamlessly. Sinclair Imports had proved to be an invaluable training ground. But an early flu season had taken its toll, and whenever they were shorthanded, she or Adrian or both of them were out there bussing tables or staffing the counter.

There was a rap on the open door. Once upon a time that door had led to an enchanted kitchen, where a magical man created mind-blowing breakfasts. Now he created them in a much nicer kitchen, looking out on the back yard of their cottage. Light poured in the windows there, and she'd painted the walls in yellow and orange to pick up the sun.

Mel broke into a smile. It was Amanda at the door now, for once child-free. "Come in. I'm giving my feet a break."

"Jacob's got the girls. I'm meeting Pat in a few minutes, and I heard rumors about a coffee-muffin special." Amanda dropped into a chair by the old table that still sat in the kitchen. Annie's employees hung out around the table or on the deck, catching their breath, eating lunch, chatting. The former living room and bedroom did duty as offices.

"Did you try it? The muffins are an experiment, a woman south of town who bakes from her home, getting a business going. We're pleased."

"I thought I'd stop here first. You look good, Mel. We miss you, but you look good."

"I miss you, too. I miss everyone at SI."

"But you're loving it."

"Every minute." She took her hand away. "I have news."

"What is it?"

"The Popes. They're moving to Columbus. They've put their house up for sale."

"You're relieved," Amanda said gently.

"I am." Mel fiddled with a salt shaker. She wondered if she'd ever lose the lingering pain from what she'd done to Ryan. "I haven't run into him in a while. It's been better since he left the bank." She shrugged. "But still…"

"This is good news, then."

"Mmm."

Amanda changed the subject. "On a happier note, I hear that you're a customer of ours now."

Mel's grin reappeared. "We've got some coffee and tea oriented things out in a display case. SI's a treasure trove."

Amanda met Mel's eyes and held for a moment, then both women laughed. "Even I have to admit you were wasted at SI. I love it here. I don't know how you ever get anyone to leave."

Adrian wandered through the door. "She uses her broom. Hi, Amanda." He turned to Mel. "Good news. Rare books did better than the café last month. You owe me."

Mel turned the grin on him. "We never agreed on what we were betting."

"Don't worry, I'll think of something. I hate to interrupt, but you've had your two-minute break. Could you take over behind the counter? Terri's going to collapse otherwise."

"You can see what a slave driver he is." Mel winked at Amanda and got up.

Amanda stood also. "Hi, Adrian." She gave Mel a hug. "Talk to me soon. We'll have coffee."

"Bring the girls. Or the four of us could go out. We could dump the kids on Jason." Jason, Amanda's friend Pat's teenager, was their go-to sitter. Amanda's girls and their son all loved him.

"He'd like that, he's saving for a car. Next weekend?"

Mel and Adrian shook their heads in unison. "Annual closure," she explained.

"One day you'll clear up the mystery behind this closure of yours. Talk to you soon."

Amanda left. Adrian took Mel's hand, kissed it. "You good to go?"

"Yep. You?"

He nodded.

She'd put her other hand on the back of his head when the overworked Terri appeared at the door. The near-clench that Terri interrupted didn't faze her; she was used to it. "Guys? I'm dropping here."

"On our way." The kiss transmuted into a peck. She headed for the counter while he disappeared down the stairs.

She never told Amanda or anyone else the real reason they closed Annie's for a weekend, once a year in October. Of course, it was practical. On Saturday morning a crew gave the place an in-depth cleaning. When they finished they left the furniture stacked against walls, except for one table and two chairs, placed under the picture of two women sharing coffee.

From then on, Annie's was theirs.

She'd go home, change, and give instructions to the sitter. When she came back, they'd climb the magnificent staircase together, hand in hand. Candlelight softened the old room, with

259

a spill of light from the kitchen. There would be music, and a slender book beside her place setting. He'd never stopped writing poetry to her.

A gourmet dinner followed — because Adrian's kitchen skills extended beyond breakfasts — at their table under the picture. Free of decisions and day-to-day tasks that made Annie's so successful, for this one night they would linger for hours, talking, remembering.

Later, when everything had been said, he'd change the music and offer her his hand, and they would dance, her many-hued silk dress swirling around her ankles. She would waltz in Adrian's arms, just the two of them in their vast, empty room.

Sunday morning they'd share breakfast in the old kitchen, planning for the coming year. Talking, touching, laughing together.

The weekend was a return to the way it had been, when they were building Annie's. *Renewing the magic,* Mel thought. *Keeping it alive.*

Back in the present, she took her place at the espresso machine and began the next latte order.

Selections from Poems for My One and Only

The Memory of Her Hands

A crowded room, a hot night,
meaningless laughter, sounds that give nothing,
someone speaks to me and I reply,
words lost as soon as they are spoken.
Background music, clinking of glasses,
and you, lost to sight,
somewhere across the room.

And the memory of your hands
on me, learning the feel of my skin,
the samba rhythm of my heart
as I draw your touch
into me, safe with the sacred things.

You Fill Me

You fill me, until
the time without you becomes bearable.
You awaken my senses, until
I come alive to the artistry in a dusty room,
        the fugue of a shared meal.
You show me the way forward, a heart-taxing climb, until
I arrive at the summit, my reward the view
        that was hidden before,
and I see the far distance.
You teach me the wonder of dreams,
however hopeless those dreams may be, until
even alone, I know I can fly.

Union

Time is meaningless.
A single dimensionless moment,
your touch, your eyes saying all
that sustains my heart.
Our souls unite in the deep communion
of all we've become. Secrets are pointless,
and if there is mercy in heaven and earth,
we will live in this awareness forever,
not together, but as one.

Halo

Dense sunlight fights its way
through dust-laden air
toward the bookshelves,
only to become entangled
In her hair.

Her hair, like a copper halo,
capturing, holding,
merging with the sun,
until, blinded,
I am forced to my knees.

Testing Unreality

Surreal, that I am with friends,
who mention your name.

That they know you, apart from the way
that I know you,
that your life transcends the narrow realm
we share.

Friends of friends, shared friends
in a shared world;
I've resigned myself to a lifetime of hearing your name,
drawing you constantly to my awareness.

Surreal that you are in the world,
and not with me.

Aftermath

The pain, in your eyes and voice,
and the word you chose:
Deflate.
Words spoken are ephemeral,
but never dissipate.
Their harm follows us
through dark tunnels of regret,
bind us, so we cannot attain
the light, far in the distance.
My love, what I would give
to have seen *you* in that moment.
What I would give
to shatter this pain, yours and mine,
into nothingness,
to never see a guarded mask
when you look at me.

Proposal

I can see it, the starlight,
the fairy lights dancing in her eyes,
the fairies, unseen, blessing the night.
I can see it, because I've seen it,
in the way her face reveals her joy.
Her love.
Tonight I will imagine that I was the one
to cause this radiance.
And I will ask this blessing of the universe:
guard her, wrap her heart
in gossamer threads of forever.
All I have left
is to let her go.

Jealousy

I want for you
the best, your heart's desire.

It kills me to admit
that he might be good enough.

It burns me raw.

I see the way he fills you
as you offer me a window
into your happiness.

If only I were less aware
of my own flaws.
If only I could find the thing
I could give you
that he cannot.

Lament for What Is Not

It's knowing I can never say
those overworked and unpoetic words,
or ever hear them said to me –
though you will say them,
morning and night, in laughter and whispers.

Sometimes, when the planets and moon align,
a soul calls out into the void
of empty arms and silence.

On those nights, the cosmos hears,
and that has to be enough.

The Creation of Magic

Recipe for magic: begin with a large, empty room.
Add a sprite, and a dream, and towering windows
to capture the ribbons of daylight.

Provide a picture on a wall, a benign presence
gracing and blessing the space.

Throw in a desire for one, just one
impossible moment, in which she and he
forget, for that moment, the world's reality.

Then, dance.
As if the centuries have rolled away
and all the elegance of a bygone time
has sprung to life, and the bare walls
are not bare, but gilded, and floors
are a platform for whirling couples,
and candles light their faces.

The dancers cover the floor with three-part rhythm,
the two together,
as if they might dance forever
in each other's arms.

Magic happens.

And magic ends. But its tendrils linger,
soothing the heart that remains behind.

My One and Only

There's a terrifying full stop
to the words One and Only,
implying as they do
a sacrifice of free will on the altar of longed-for union.

But One and Only is the only phrase that works.

I think it is a form of blindness, because surely,
somewhere down the road,
there will be an intersection, a means to turn away
from this one-directional path.

But right now I don't believe this.

The structure is too solid, composed as it is
of silken bindings, jewel colors in the breeze,
a flight of stairs rising to heaven, with no way down,
memories of breakfasts shared.

This much has been given me. Dare I be selfish enough
to ask more?
I rail against my chains, then acquiesce
because I have no defenses.

My One and Only.

To My Readers

Hello, and thanks for choosing Mel. I hope you'll be inspired to check out what else is happening in Calter Creek, where Amanda and Pat both have their own stories of romance and discovery.

If you enjoyed this book, well, I don't need to tell you how much reviews mean to writers.

To keep up with upcoming romances, visit my website, http://lizanncarson.com. There you'll find notices about book events and my musings about life as both a writer and an inhabitant of the real world.

Happy reading,

LizAnn

About LizAnn Carson

It's interesting, trying to condense who you are into a paragraph or two. For openers, there are the basics: husband, three kids, and three kids-in-law, with a shifting grandkid count. I live in Victoria, British Columbia, a smallish city that's large enough to have all modern conveniences, but not so large as to have hours-long traffic jams or heavy duty pollution. I can follow a trail to my local supermarket, or I can be downtown in twenty minutes.

Yes, I spend most of my time writing (and editing, formatting, critiquing for other writers, battling computer problems, and occasionally tearing my hair out). But beyond that, I enjoy a variety of crafts. I love the new craze of coloring books for adults—in fact, almost every woman I know loves to color. I walk a lot and enjoy weight training and yoga. Once, a long time ago, I owned a yarn shop, and for a while I taught English as a Second Language. My career, on the other hand, was in the world of computer systems development.

You can follow some of my explorations on my website/blog, http://lizanncarson.com.